ROCKS AND STARS

Visit us at www.boldstrokesbooks.com

Rocks and Stars

by

Sam Ledel

2018

ROCKS AND STARS

© 2018 By Sam Ledel. All Rights Reserved.

ISBN 13: 978-1-63555-156-3

This Trade Paperback Original Is Published By
Bold Strokes Books, Inc.
P.O. Box 249
Valley Falls, NY 12185

First Edition: April 2018

THIS IS A WORK OF FICTION. NAMES, CHARACTERS, PLACES, AND INCIDENTS ARE THE PRODUCT OF THE AUTHOR'S IMAGINATION OR ARE USED FICTITIOUSLY. ANY RESEMBLANCE TO ACTUAL PERSONS, LIVING OR DEAD, BUSINESS ESTABLISHMENTS, EVENTS, OR LOCALES IS ENTIRELY COINCIDENTAL.

THIS BOOK, OR PARTS THEREOF, MAY NOT BE REPRODUCED IN ANY FORM WITHOUT PERMISSION.

Credits
Editors: Katia Noyes and Barbara Ann Wright
Production Design: Stacia Seaman
Cover Design by Tammy Seidick

Acknowledgments

A special thank you to Bold Strokes Books and to my editor, Katia Noyes, who guided me on this journey and helped mold this story into what it was meant to be. Thank you to Kirsten Watters for taking on the task of reading the early drafts. To my family, who has always supported me in this dream of being a writer. And thank you to Alyssa, for everything.

Part One

PROLOGUE

Fresh air. I need fresh air.

Not like I don't get enough of it six days a week between club practices, school practices, and weekend games. Still, I think I need it. Fresh air has to do me good. Help me clear my head or something. Because clearly, I'm not thinking straight.

Straight. Has anyone actually thought about that phrasing before? The irony is staggering. And quickly becoming too much for my seventeen-year-old brain to handle.

I grab a water bottle from the fridge, my ball, and my phone and head to Kade Park. When I step outside at ten in the morning, it's already hinting at the blistering central Texas summer heat that looms just hours away. From my parents' house, the park is a half-mile walk, which I hope is enough time to get in some practice and ideally, figure out just what in the world is going on with me.

Let me try to explain: I've been having thoughts. Lots of thoughts…about one of my club teammates. You know, *those* kinds of thoughts.

Her name is Beth. We've known each other for years. We've had at least one class together since the fifth grade. She's one of those girls who is unbelievably sweet to everybody. I'm pretty sure she has no mean bone in her body. She's the girl whose mom bakes brownies on obscure holidays like International Save the Whales Day and has Beth hand said brownies out to every student in class with a sticker that reads, "What will you do to help?" She's the girl who always has five extra pencils on hand when yours breaks during a test. And currently, she's the girl I can't get out of my head.

Though, if I'm being honest, Beth isn't the only one I've noticed lately. Actresses on TV soaps have started to catch my eye in a way they haven't before. Then, one time, there was that girl—maybe college-aged with a gorgeous sleeve of tattoos—who smiled at me in the local smoothie shop on a Saturday afternoon. I nearly fainted when she handed me my drink. Heck, even the meteorologist on Channel Five has me pausing to watch the next day's forecast every other night.

So, sure, a few more people are on my radar these days. Still, most can't hold a candle to Beth. She's just amazing. She has this beautiful smile that makes even the sprints at practice feel like an easy jog. Her hair is often done up in an elegant ponytail (probably courtesy of her mom), or in the case of our soccer practices, is set in a professional-looking braid. A few adorable freckles dot her nose and cheeks.

Actually, when it comes to Beth, I am painfully aware of a lot of things now. I notice every time she grins, which sends my stomach into a crazy gymnastics routine. I notice the way our hips bump when we both go for the ball in a one-on-one. I feel the tug on my jersey each time we battle for a spot in the goalie box before a corner kick. And lately, I find myself relishing those tugs, wishing she would lift my jersey just a little bit higher.

Beep!

Oops.

I'm apparently loitering on the corner of a crosswalk, unfazed by the blinking WALK flashing at me on the other side. I wave apologetically at the driver and hurry across the street. The park is about fifty yards away, so I drop the soccer ball and kick it ahead of me. I pass a playground with a few kids enjoying their summer vacation, scrambling along the brightly painted metal stairs.

I walk over to the side of the elementary school located on the other end of the park. A large oak tree provides some shade as I set my water bottle down and put my earbuds in.

"Let's see." I hold the ball in place under my foot and scroll through the song list on my phone. Eventually, I decide on a singer-songwriter and hit play.

After juggling the ball twice, I kick it over to the wall. I adjust my feet, and it bounces back against the instep of my foot. Then I chip it back to the wall before falling into my usual routine with my brick partner.

Instantly, I start to feel better. Soccer has a way of doing that. It's therapeutic. I don't have to think when I'm playing. Soccer is the one time I can forget about everything else and just enjoy the game. I take a deep breath and juggle the ball between my feet, letting the lyrics float around me.

The ball skids off my foot. Huh. I never really noticed how ambiguous these lyrics are. What do they even mean, "the secrets we keep" and "people like us"? I press skip and drop down onto my hands and knees. So, maybe soccer isn't always completely therapeutic. Push-ups. Push-ups could help.

The opening notes of a Demi Lovato song starts, and I smile. She can always put me in a good mood.

I exhale and ignore the burn in my arms. Then I turn over, clicking next again.

Melissa Etheridge's guitar strums its opening chords…

"Oh, you have got to be kidding me!" I turn off my phone, tossing it away from me. It lands with a thud in the grass and I roll over onto my back, resting my hands behind my head. Closing my eyes, I exhale.

The squeals of the little kids from the playground ride the breeze over to me as I try to organize my thoughts.

"Okay, Kyle," I tell myself. "You got this." I grab the ball and toss it up toward the sky. "So I think Beth is pretty. That's totally normal. Lots of girls think other girls are pretty. Emily, my best friend since forever, commented on how I looked at last semester's soccer banquet. That wasn't weird at all."

I toss the ball higher, and it lands in my hands a foot over my chest.

"And well, surely it's natural to want to kiss other girls. Girls kiss each other all the time in movies. And they talk about it all the time in magazines. I mean, who wouldn't want to do that?"

The image of Beth at last night's practice pops into my head. She's running past me as the ball sails over us. Sweat glistens on her forehead.

I close my eyes. She has this freckle on the corner of her lips. I'd noticed it a few weeks ago when she came up to high-five me after assisting on my goal. The way she smiled at me afterward nearly made me swoon. Or there was that one time after algebra class when I explained the homework assignment to her in the hallway, and she leaned into me, listening; she smelled like tulips. Oh, then there's the way her lips shine after she takes a drink of water…

Once again, I see myself alone with her out on the field. We're standing against the goalpost. She presses me up against it. Her body is flush with mine. Her breasts press against me. Her hands grab my hips. My lips touch hers…

The ball I had thrown high overhead lands with a smack on my nose.

"Shit," I cry out and grab my face while the ball rolls away. After a painful few seconds, I turn over onto my stomach. My nose still stings as I grab the ball and rest it under my chin, watching the kids running back up the slide over on the playground. A dark-haired boy with copper skin sits among the wood chips, his only concern the monarch butterfly flapping over his head. Behind him, a girl, about six with strawberry-blond hair, scampers up the shiny red slide, giggling while she chases her friends.

I try to remember what being that little was even like. I try to recall a time before things were so complicated. Like when my mom would pick me up from school. Or when my brother Kevin and I played spies with Emily on long summer days until we had to run home for dinner. Or when Jacob Sparks sloppily kissed me in the hallway outside the girl's bathroom in second grade. Or when I lay next to my dad on the overstuffed leather sofa watching basketball and sharing a bowl of popcorn.

What was it like before I realized I was gay?

Chapter One

Emily closes the patio door of my parents' house behind her, the blinds shimmying before slowing to a halt once she's sitting opposite me in one of our wicker patio chairs. The humid June breeze floats over us while strands of clouds grasp at the sun, painting the sky a light blue, scattered with strokes of pink.

"Fun party," Emily says, adjusting her floral-patterned skirt and touching the rim of her red glasses.

"Thanks," I reply, glancing back into the house through the brightly lit living room windows. Uncle Will is demonstrating a new trick that his Yorkies have learned to my dad, who laughs loudly, his eyes sparkling after a few beers. He manages to look both impeccable and casual thanks to his finely pressed suit and tousled brown hair. My dad runs his free hand through it while the other holds a half-full glass. Several of my parents' colleagues sit among the plush furniture. The drinks placed neatly on metal coasters make the whole scene look like the cover of *Austin Weekly* instead of my high school graduation party. My brother Kevin stands near the back table, pretzels in one hand, his attention parked on one of our neighbors, an elderly man with thick gray hair who is telling an animated story. My mom, meanwhile, is a mere flash, a well-dressed, effervescent shadow as she flutters between everyone, making sure they are happy, satisfied, and smiling.

"You're lucky, getting all this," Emily says, gesturing to the crowd inside. "When I graduated last year, my dad handed me a gift certificate for Two Bucks Sushi. And then my mom spent the whole night crying over my first communion photos, accompanied by her sobbing about how 'I'll always be her *niña preciosa*.'" Emily's dark brown eyes rove over our backyard as she speaks, eventually landing on our old swing set. "Remember playing spies on there when we were kids?"

"Yeah. And we always made Kevin be the double-crossing mole and would tie him to the tree when my parents weren't home."

Emily laughs and we both look out over the backyard. Now the paint on the swing set is faded, and chips of white paint litter the manicured lawn around its base.

I lean back in my chair, the brown wicker creaking. "At least your mom was proud of you when you graduated. At my college signing the other week, all my parents could talk about was how excited they were to show my pictures to their coworkers. I had accomplished another milestone on the 'perfect little family' checklist."

"I'm sure they are proud of you, Kyle," she says. "You got a full ride to Meadowbrook. You're going to be a Division I athlete. Pretty impressive if you ask me."

I sigh. Part of me is thrilled, then I think about Beth. I wonder where she will be next year. I try to imagine a team where she isn't there, and an unease settles in me. I blink a few times, sitting up in the chair and forcing myself back into the conversation with Emily. "Well, you helped," I finally say. "You got Coach to come out and see me."

"True." Emily shakes back her dark, shoulder-length curls. "But it wasn't that difficult. She does know our school has a history of talented soccer players." She smirks, and I nudge her lightly with my bare foot, having kicked off my heels the second I sat down.

"Humble as ever," I reply.

After a playful nod, Emily sits back. We watch the branches sway and listen to the cicadas begin their summer song. After a few minutes, Emily crunches a fallen leaf with her red ballet flat.

"Have you told them?"

I don't have to ask to know what she's talking about. Slowly, I shake my head.

"It's not that easy, Em."

She nods, and I wait for the rest of what she has to say.

"This is your last season with the Tornadoes."

I bite the inside of my cheek and clear my throat. "I know."

"Did you…are you going to say anything?"

I look at Emily. Immediately, I flash back to almost two years ago. I had spent so long crushing on Beth, not understanding the reason why I needed to rush to practice, or why I felt elated each time she looked my way. Or why leaving the practice field each night left me feeling like a deflated ball kicked into the garage. Then, one day, I had gotten the courage to open up the book *Desert of the Heart*. I'd spotted it in the local bookshop when I'd gone to buy *Othello's Spark Notes* to help with my Lit final. When my eyes landed on the cover, and I hurriedly read the back, it was all I could do to not sprint out then and there to devour the book in the parking lot. That night, I stayed up until three a.m. reading. And as soon as I turned the last page, I called Emily.

"I understand now," I had cried through ragged breaths. I held my sheets close, trying to muffle my voice while my parents slept down the hallway. "I like her, Em. I really like her." I cried into my phone for half an hour while Emily sat on the other end of the line, letting me know it was okay. Everything would be okay.

Sitting on the back patio now, my eyes drift away from my best friend and toward the old swing set. The feeling that had hit me that night, that epiphany, had overwhelmed me and threatened to swallow me and rip me open at the same time. I could feel myself coming apart as something deep within clawed and pushed against my lungs, shouting to be free. It was the same feeling that left me dizzy each time Beth flashed me a smile on the field. It was the feeling I had noticed even before Beth, like with that girl in the smoothie shop, but had forced deep into a drawer, locked away with a key buried under years of denial and efforts to be the perfect daughter. But just like that, after reading that book and seeing myself in those pages, there it was, desperately yelling for me to recognize it.

As the warm blanket of summer air begins to lift with the setting sun, Emily doesn't push me to answer. I hold her gaze as mosquitoes buzz overhead. Eventually, she smiles and turns to watch the light disappear over the trees.

"College will be different," she says. "Just wait and see."

CHAPTER TWO

"Are you excited for the school year to start, sweetheart?"

I bite down into my slice of pepperoni pizza and glance up at my mom sitting across from me at the kitchen table. An oversized bowl of fake fruit takes up the space between us, always playing host to whatever is in season.

"Umghhmm," I reply through my mouthful. "Sure."

"Nice, Kyle," my brother says. "You're sure to win over plenty of new friends like that."

I toss my used napkin at Kevin, and we earn a look from our mom before she sighs, "I'm sure Kyle will make plenty of friends. Are you looking forward to Meadowbrook, sweetie?"

"I still have a few weeks before move-in day."

"I know," my mom muses, dabbing at the edges of her mouth with a napkin. Her manicured nails look like they should be handling a polished knife and fork, not a thickly sauced pizza from the local Italian restaurant. She takes another delicate bite, then sets it down to smooth her sweater before adding, "Emily's mom says she can't wait for you to join the team. You must be so excited to play with her again."

I nod. "It'll be nice." I take another bite of my pizza, the sauce dribbling onto my chin. I swipe at it with the back of my hand and can feel my mom's eyes willing the disregarded napkin into my grasp.

"Though I am surprised they make you move in so early. School doesn't begin for almost two months." She says this like she just remembered an item on her shopping list, mildly interested but still preoccupied with a dozen other things on her mind.

"Soccer requires I move in early. We begin preseason in August."

"So I get the house to myself even sooner," Kevin grins over his slice. His technology club T-shirt, which looks two sizes too big on his lanky frame, looms dangerously close to the pool of garlic butter creeping across his patterned plate.

I scrunch up my face at him, and he mimics me before brushing strands of light brown hair from his eyes.

Our conversation, I guess, has come to an end when my mom sighs. "We may have to order a moving truck. What do you think, sweetie?"

Kevin kicks out his long legs and nudges my shins beneath the table in continued retaliation.

I shrug. "I don't know. You should ask Dad."

Then Kevin glances at me over his can of soda when he says, "Where is Dad tonight, anyway?"

"Working late, honey."

"Again?"

My brother stops kicking, and my mom's eyes move to me.

"Kyle, you know that your father and I both work very hard to let you kids live the way we have."

Kevin shoves his pizza crust into his mouth as I reply, "I know, Mom." I take a breath before willing myself to continue. "It's just that I feel like Dad's been gone more and more lately." The words feel loaded as they stumble out of my mouth. But maybe that was my intention.

"You are as aware as I am that your father's business is expanding. He's got that new office opened up in Austin."

"Isn't he trying to get one out in New Mexico, too?" Kevin asks, to which my mom nods.

"Great," I mumble.

"Kyle."

My mom's staring at me now. Her eyes have grown cloudy. She looks like she wants to say something. I *know* she wants to say something. Maybe even yell at me. But that's not how we work. We can push buttons. But that's as far as it goes. We don't scream. We don't get yelled at. Or grounded. What we get is worse. What we get is years and years of unspoken truths piled up around us in our

Pottery Barn home; mountains of words that we are all too scared to speak. Words that have the potential to shatter our picturesque little family life if someone finally decides to utter them aloud.

I stare back into my mom's honey-colored eyes and I know it kills her as much as it kills me. It would be so much easier if we could actually talk and not fill all the space around us with empty chatter and shallow commentary. I wish I could shake her and tell her to just admit it. Tell her to admit what I've suspected has been going on between her and my dad for a while. And I wish I could just tell her my truth. Then maybe she could tell me hers. But I can't. And neither can she. Not yet.

The garage door grumbles open from the other side of the house. My mom gets up from the table and sets her plastic plate in the trash. "That'll be your father," she says.

"Mom," I start.

"Let me know if you need anything from Griffin's for your school supplies. I'm making a trip tomorrow."

My shoulders fall, and I pick a pepperoni off my next slice. "I will," I mutter before she excuses herself from the room. I reach for my napkin to clean the sauce from my hands.

It's quiet in the kitchen, the only faint sound coming from the large wall clock ticking above us.

Kevin finally breaks the silence. "Smooth, sis. Smooth."

Chapter Three

"You're sure you have everything, honey?"

"Mom," I groan, dragging out the vowel like only a tired teenager can. "That's, like, the twenty-seventh time you've asked me that."

My mother, her trim figure clad in a light green sweater over the only pair of jeans she owns, fluffs the two pillows on my dorm bed once more before looking back at me. "I know, sweetie, I just want to make sure that you're going to be okay. And that we aren't missing anything."

"Karen, sweetheart, we live two hours from here. If Kyle needs anything, we're just a short drive away."

I mouth a thank-you to my dad as he stands up from behind my television where he'd bravely attempted to untangle the cables. His slender frame is accentuated by the salmon-colored polo shirt tucked into his khakis, and the belt around his slim waist sits a little too high, something that always reminded me of the scholastic types from TV who tried too hard to look cool. I sometimes imagine him, the successful technology consultant, as a young man. A gawky teenager who looked up to suave executive types and who—having grown up and achieved a well-paying job—dresses the way he pictured a man in his position should, even if it didn't quite match up with his goofy personality.

"Jason," my mom starts, and Kevin, who is splayed out in my chair with his feet up on my desk, shoots me a look. We both know Mom's about to go into one of her rants she has on reserve. "Our *only* daughter," she begins, adding extra effort to each word, "is about to start the next big chapter of her life. I'm just trying to be useful. Shouldn't we help her get off on the right foot?" She turns around to face me. I want to roll my eyes at her words: a string of phrases you can hear the parent recite on any teenage drama airing every Thursday night on TV. Then I'm a little surprised when she reaches out to grab my hand. "I'm just going to miss you, sweetie, that's all." Then she pulls me into a hug. The snarky retort I had ready falls flat in my throat. It takes me a second, but I finally pull my arms around her. I'm trying to recall the last time we hugged when Kevin laughs from my chair.

He tosses the garnet rock paperweight on my desk between his hands as he says, "Is this what it takes to get some love around this family? Leave for four years?"

My mom releases me, then wipes quickly at her eyes. She pulls a hand mirror from her bag and adjusts her freshly cut bangs, and I feel a pang. I'm not sure if it's because I'm suddenly anxious, standing here on my first day of college, or if I'm actually going to miss my mother. But I don't have time to decide before she gives my brother a wave of her hand. "Oh, Kevin. You just wait for your turn."

My brother gives a fist pump. "Two more years to go!"

I walk over to put a six-pack of Gatorade into my mini-fridge and give Kevin a punch to the shoulder on my way there.

"Yeah, maybe by then you'll be ready for the big, scary world of books and babes," I joke.

"Kyle," our mom sighs.

"Speak for yourself, sis."

His comment hits me like a soccer ball to the gut. I'm thankful my face is hidden behind the door of the mini-fridge as I wonder if my parents were paying attention. At the same time, I kick myself for teasing him; after all, he once walked in on me scanning the *Lesbian Love* section on Netflix. We talked about it, and he was surprisingly amazing about everything. But he's still my little brother…a certain amount of taunting is part of the game. I can't forget that.

"Oh, Kyle," my mom says, pushing the conversation along. "Maybe you'll meet a nice young man. Perhaps a member of the boys' team."

Just then there's a knock on my open dorm door. A tall redheaded girl with translucent blue eyes is standing in the doorway.

She sounds breathless when she says, "Hey, sorry to interrupt, but you guys haven't seen a ferret anywhere, have you?"

I glance around and we all look at each other, a little bemused. "I didn't think pets were allowed in the dorms," my mother says in her polite but guarded tone. Meanwhile, I take in the girl's tall, lean stature.

"Technically, they're not," the girl replies. "Hence the sense of urgency to find him."

"Well," says my dad, clapping his hands together. "I can give you this guy." He moves to stand behind Kevin and tousles his hair. "He's close enough, right?"

"Dad," my brother mumbles.

I laugh and so does the girl still standing in the doorframe. I notice her smile: wide and bright. I continue to watch her when she steps forward into the room.

"I'm sorry," she says, "I'm being rude. I'm Joey. Joey Carver."

She shakes my dad's hand.

He glances at me. "See what would have happened if you'd eaten your Wheaties, honey?" We all chuckle at his comment while Joey moves to shake my mom's, then my brother's hand. Then she's standing in front of me.

"Hi," she says.

I smile and stick out my hand, hoping to God it's not too sweaty. Pretty girls talking to me has, lately, had that effect on me. It's even made me forget my own name. And this girl is pretty. Her nose, featuring the most adorable bump just below the brow, sits between the clearest blue eyes I've ever seen. Her fair skin is the color of my mom's pearl necklace. And her hands are soft but feel strong when her long fingers grip mine. And those arms she's sporting under a purple cotton tee: wow.

We shake hands and she nods over to the soccer ball at the foot of the bed. "Full ride, right?" I nod. "Looks like we'll be seeing each other around, then. I'm one of the goalies." She pauses. "I'm, um, just down the hall, too, if you ever want to get together to practice before preseason starts."

I realize then that her hand is still in mine. Joey seems to just notice this as well, and we drop them back down to our sides. She steps backward, back into the doorway.

"Well, it was great meeting you folks," she says, nodding at my parents, who had both been busying themselves with adjusting a shelf over my bed. "Kevin," Joey adds with a nod in his direction. "And hopefully I'll be seeing you…"

"Kyle! Kyle Lyndsay," I spurt out, mentally kicking myself for forgetting my own name again.

But Joey just smiles. "Kyle. I'll see you." Then she disappears out into the bustling hallway.

"She seems nice," my dad says.

I nod.

Then my mom chimes in. "Looks like you made your first friend, honey."

"Yeah," I say, my eyes lingering where Joey had been just moments before. "Looks like I did."

CHAPTER FOUR

"Ah yes, the party duo is here," says Emily.

Two girls wearing our practice jerseys are strolling up to the field from the parking lot. One is brunette with olive-toned skin, the other a slightly taller blonde who is laughing loudly. Her laugh is one of those that I imagine always turns heads, making you want to know what could be so funny. Like you're missing out. Her ponytail is set high, and her stride exudes confidence.

I finally tear my gaze away from her to concentrate on pulling on my socks. "Party duo?" I ask, hoping I sound only vaguely interested.

"Yeah. The brunette is 'T.' Theresa, that is." She makes the "re" sound like "ray" as she pronounces it. "She's a junior. The blonde with the legs and wrist tape is Jackie. Or Jax. She's a sophomore." Emily takes a swig from her water bottle.

"Apparently, I need to shorten my name to be on this team. Instead of Kyle, from now on, you may call me K. Or maybe just *kuh*."

Emily gives me her "All right, smart-ass" glare as she tugs on her cleats. Jax and T. have made their way over to us and drop their stuff on the bleachers below Emily and me. While pulling my socks over my shin guards, I pretend to take in the rolling hills behind our soccer fields and not Jax's midriff, which peeks out below her top as she stretches.

"Who's this?" T. asks.

Emily nudges me. "Kyle. Fresh meat on her first day at practice. Be gentle," she adds with a wink.

"Not too gentle, I hope."

The grin on Jax's face following her comment makes the heat rush to my own. I bow my head and stare hard at my suddenly very interesting shoelaces.

"Geez Jax, don't scare all the newbies away. I hear this one's good, too," T. says.

"That so?" Jax asks. I quickly look up. Her ice-blue eyes are set on mine. Finally, I recall the fact that I do actually have the ability to speak.

"All-State captain for two years in a row," I add with a shrug and hope this helps me look cool and collected.

The eyebrow she raises says she's impressed but also makes my stomach shoot into my chest.

"See," T. starts, "we need this one. So, play nice, will you?" Then she takes off for the group of girls already standing in the center of the soccer field. Emily quickly follows after giving me a brief *calm down* knee pat.

I make sure that my laces are secure, then stand up from the bleacher. Jax reaches out her hand, her polished black nails glistening in the afternoon sun. "Hey, just messing with you. Welcome to the team."

I take her hand, and she helps me down.

❖

Once we huddle around the top of the goalie box, Coach blows her whistle to get our attention. I'd met Coach Gandy several times during my high school recruitment games the year before. Of the handful of coaches who had come to scout me during my senior year, she was the one who actually treated me as if I had a say in my future. Most of the coaches from the Division I schools had all but ignored me during postgame chats with my high school coach and conference calls with my parents, but Coach Gandy had actually scheduled one-on-one time with me. Over a lunch in a café a few blocks from my house, she had asked me about my history, why I wanted to pursue collegiate sports, and really wanted to get to the *why* behind my reasons for playing the game. And even though I was pretty intimidated by her at first—she'd been a member of the

National U-18 team ten years ago, and her tall, fit stature alone will make a girl do a double take—she won me over, and I signed on for the next four years as a Meadowbrook University Mockingbird.

Now Coach Gandy lifts her sunglasses up onto her head, and her dark eyes peer around the huddle. A hint of a smile graces her lips, but her square jaw is set firmly. One hand holds a brown clipboard, while the other sits on her sweatpants-clad hip.

"Welcome, ladies," she says. "Today we begin the new season. I want to welcome those of you who are new to the team this year. We have five fresh recruits, including a new keeper." At this, she nods toward Joey, and most of the circle turns to face her. I follow suit, and Joey gives the crowd a small wave. She catches my gaze and throws me a smile as everyone turns back to Coach.

"Now, we did well last year, ladies. We had a solid record and even made a run in the playoffs. Semifinals were good. I could taste that division trophy. And it tasted sweet. But Greenhill snatched it off our plates before we could get our hands on it. So, let's stay focused. Let's work hard. And let's get ready to see them again in a few weeks in our first road game and—eventually—in the Division I finals. What do you say?" We give a cheer, and the whistle blows again. "All right then. Let's get started." The group shifts, and I can feel the energy in the air as everyone is eager to move. Coach shifts the clipboard to read off it. "I almost forgot. Before we get going, a quick update. Since Masters is out for another month with her knee, Carver will be with us in goal to start off."

Joey gets a congratulatory pat on the back from a few players. Jax, who had been standing with her arms crossed next to T., speaks up.

"Coach, Haley's been our starting goalie since I got here." One of my teammates—Haley, I assume, who has a knee brace snaking down her tan left leg—grimaces a little at the comment but doesn't say anything.

"I am aware of that," Coach replies. "But she also tore her ACL over the summer. And until I get a clear bill of health from her doctor and the trainer, she'll be here as a leader on this team and a model of solid goalkeeping. From the sideline."

Haley nods like she already accepted this news before we

stepped on the field. But Jax doesn't seem to be on the same page. "I understand that, Coach, but shouldn't seniority have a little bit of say in this?"

Emily looks like she's about to say something, but Coach beats her to it. "Jax, let's not start the first week off like last year, all right? You, T., and Madeline are still the defensive line on this team. The three of you will work together just like you have before. I suggest you meet with Joey and talk with Haley to work through any adjustments. We will see how things progress. But in the meantime, Haley rests, and Joey's in the box. Got it?"

After a moment, Jax finally speaks. "Sure, Coach."

The whistle sounds again. "Okay. Warm up, ladies. Get to it."

An hour later, we're about to start a four-versus-four drill. The tension from earlier has quelled, thankfully. I was anxious to join a new team for the next four years of my career, after growing up and playing with the Tornadoes since I was ten. Team chemistry is important, and I'd been spoiled with my select team; we could practically read each other's minds on the field once we reached high school. But Emily had spoken highly of her Meadowbrook team since before I signed on, making me optimistic and hopeful that the transition won't be too rough. It does help that I have Emily here with me, who is a *Who's Who* of my new teammates.

"Remember that Katie is a lefty, so feed her from the opposite side you would normally," she tells me quickly while I tug on a blue pinnie. Coach hands out three more to Katie, a senior named Allie, and Mary, a fellow freshman.

"I see why they gave you captain this year," I reply with a grin.

She shrugs. "I can't help it if I'm good with people. Blame it on having to keep up with my seven *tías* and *tíos*. Plus their kids."

I nod. "Having twenty cousins has finally come in handy."

Emily swats at me, and I laugh. "Okay, got it, got it." I glance behind me at Jax and T., who are huddled with Madeline and Sarah a few feet away. "And the defense duo? Any suggestions on getting around them?"

Emily stands with her hands on her hips on the outside of the box Coach has made with four orange cones just inside the goalie box. Wiping some sweat off her brow, she says, "Madeline is low D, and she's tough. She anticipates well and almost always knows when I'm going to fake. With her you have to be one step ahead. I don't know about Sarah—she's your group—but I hear she's more of a midfielder, so she will probably float higher." Coach blows the whistle then, signaling for the four of us with pennies to get ready to start on attack. "As for Jax and T.: together they're hard to beat. Try to split them up. T. is a wall, but you can get by her. She's slower on her left side. And Jax is handsy. She's a notorious jersey puller. Watch for fouls. And she's fast. Use your teammates to get around them, and you'll be fine."

I nod, suddenly nervous when I jog over to join my teammates at the top of the box. I was a low midfielder for four years in high school but was asked to move to attacking midfield when I joined this team. Standing at the top of the box, I look ahead to where Jax and T. stand five feet apart, with Madeline and Sarah stacked behind them. Joey hops on the balls of her feet just outside of the net. I wonder if she's as nervous as I am.

Another whistle, and we begin. I try to hold on to what Emily just told me. I dribble through the designated area, Coach's mini-field, zigging and zagging through the defense as best I can. I manage to escape a slide tackle from T. and take off to the right sideline. Madeline leaves her mark and makes a beeline for me. I glance to my left and see Katie raise her arm on the other side of the box, about twenty yards away. Jax is in front of her, but there's room.

The ball sails off my foot when I cross it. Katie leans back and receives it off her chest. The ball bounces off her foot a little wildly. I run forward, anticipating that Jax will snatch it and take off. But instead, she lunges in the wrong direction. Once she does, Katie is free to move to her left, and she lets a shot fly.

Joey leaps from her line and is stretched out entirely once she's in the air. The ball flies toward the top right corner of the net, and just as I think it's past her, Joey's fingers tap it enough so that it sails inches to the right of the goalpost.

"Holy crap," Madeline mutters behind me. "That girl's got a wingspan on her."

Joey falls with a thud onto the grass but stands up quickly. She's grinning when Coach blows her whistle.

"Nice one, Carver," Coach Gandy calls from the top of the box while Emily and a few others cheer.

Joey grabs an extra ball from the back of the net and tosses it out to Katie. "Nice shot," she says. Katie nods and jogs back up top. "Jax," Joey adds, and I slow my jog to listen. "Watch her left side next time, yeah?"

I can't read Jax's face when she turns and mumbles something to T., who snickers and shakes her head.

"Nice pass, Kyle," Emily tells me once I'm reset at the top of the box and waiting for Coach's whistle.

I exhale. "Thanks. Your intel helped."

Emily shrugs. "Just doing my part. Unlike some people," she adds with a nod toward Jax.

"Yeah, you saw that, too?"

She nods. "I bet she's sore about Haley still. I mean, I get it; Haley's a junior and walked on as a freshman. Bit of a big deal. And she's Jax's hero or something. Which I've never really understood since Haley is, like, the sweetest person ever, and Jax is, well…Jax. But I guess she's planning to make things a little difficult for our new goalie."

Turning back, I watch Joey in her box. She crosses and re-crosses her arms over her chest, staying loose. Her eyes are on Jax, but she must feel my gaze because they quickly shift and meet mine. The smile is on my face before I can stop it. Joey grins back, then moves to crouch when the whistle blows.

"You know, a picture will last longer."

I turn to Emily as Katie passes me the ball. Her comment makes me fumble the pass when I receive it, but Mary recovers it as it rolls away from me. Emily looks way too entertained as she shakes her head, and I take off down the field, blushing.

Chapter Five

I switch my cell to my right ear, maneuvering around a group of people on my way to the foreign language building. The university flag waves eagerly in the breeze from its pole anchored between stalwart oak trees. Even it seems joyful to stretch out on such a beautiful day. The sun shines on the manicured lawns and carefully maintained flower beds lining the many sidewalks cutting between the white stone campus buildings.

"Kyle, great news!"

I turn my face to soak up some of the sunshine. "Let me guess. They've decided to put in a Four Brothers Burgers on campus?"

Emily's incredulous sigh makes me laugh. "Oh my God, do you think of anything other than food and soccer?"

I step onto a curb that leads to a pebble laden pathway I take each Wednesday to class. "Not really."

"Well, anyway, we now have the perfect plans for next weekend. Alex is throwing a house party with some of his friends. The ones whom I've already met are very cool. Super chill. And he said anyone I want to invite is welcome. So clear your calendar, Kyle. We've got a party to go to."

"Party?" I ask warily, glancing at my watch and stopping to sit on a bench outside of the foreign language building. "Isn't it a little early in the school year for parties?"

"Come on, Miss Tightly Wound," Emily pleads. "It's time to get you out there to meet people. People who aren't on the soccer team, that is."

As Emily says this, I notice several of my teammates walking through the science building doors and out into bright afternoon

Texan light. Among the crowd, I spot Haley, her leg brace tight against a pair of leggings. T. is next to her, laughing loudly as they walk my direction. Behind her, Jax strolls languidly, looking like she is in no hurry to get to wherever the group is going.

"Kyle? Are you still there?"

I adjust the backpack on my shoulders and nod, my eyes still on Jax. "Yeah, sorry, Em. I just realized what time it is. I should probably get going to class."

I hang up just as the group strolls past. Haley sees me first.

"Hi, Kyle," she calls from a few feet away. Her long blond hair is braided on one side as she waves. They pause when they're next to my bench. "What're you up to?"

I gesture to the building behind me where herds of students are streaming in, the next class period beginning in a few minutes. "Spanish class," I say. Then I brush a few hairs from my face when I notice Jax eyeing me from where she stands. This is the first time I've seen her off the soccer field. Despite the warm weather, she's in black jeans paired with a deep red tank top. Her blue eyes are nestled into coves of dark eyeliner and her blond hair is down, falling to her shoulders. Several rings line her fingers, which she has hooked into the belt loops of her jeans. I realize I'm staring when T. speaks.

"Who do you have for Spanish?"

I clear my throat, tearing my gaze away from Jax. "Professor Jimenez," I say, fumbling to stand.

"Oh, I hear he's tough," T. says. "Abby had him last year." She sticks her chin up a little. "That's why I switched to German."

"Yeah, because *so* many people speak German." Haley rolls her eyes. T. playfully shoves her.

"Whatever, man. My family is from Germany. And I'll visit one day."

Haley laughs. "T., we're in Texas. Half the population speaks Spanish."

While they continue to banter over the relevance of foreign languages, Jax watches me from behind them. Meanwhile, I try not to panic at the fact that my incredibly hot teammate is looking at me like a cat who hasn't eaten in days and has just cornered a mouse. I start to wander backward, toward the doors.

"Well, it was really good seeing you guys," I say. "But class starts any minute, so I should probably get going."

Jax nods slowly. "Okay. See you later, Kyle."

I give a short wave that I'm pretty sure looks more dorky than cool, then duck into the building as fast as I can.

❖

Another scholastic day done, and I've got three hundred pages to read by Friday on top of online practice sessions for Spanish and a lab to prep for geology. I figure I can get a jump start on the reading in the locker room before practice begins at four. On my way to the bus stop, I'm about to pull out my phone to call Emily, when I notice somebody leaning against a tree, emerging from the shade beneath it. I squint and realize that it's Jax walking over, one hand in her pocket. I glance over my shoulder, figuring T. or Haley must have just gotten out of class somewhere nearby, and she's probably waiting for them. But I can't find either girl anywhere. Eventually, I turn to walk toward Jax, and she gives me a half-smile when I reach her.

Her eyes are slanted from the sunlight when she speaks. "Hey, I thought you'd never get done in there."

I stare in disbelief. "Me? You were…were you waiting for me?"

"What does it look like?" she replies, her gravelly voice slinking from her lips, each word in no rush to pass between them.

"Oh," I say, rubbing my toe into the sidewalk.

Eyeing me from where she stands, she asks, "Can I interest you in something sweet?"

My stomach leaps into my throat when she throws a nod to the other end of campus and starts walking that direction. She steps back a few feet, her smile growing with each moment I stand awestruck. Finally, she turns but calls over her shoulder. "Well, are you coming?"

My mouth has fallen open a little as my gaze briefly lowers to her swaying hips. Jax, the Queen of Cool, wants me to go with her. Where? Why? Before I can think too much about it, I shove my phone into my back pocket and scurry to catch up. I'll see Emily at practice, anyway. Just wait till I tell her about this. She'll understand.

❖

"Two cones, please. Cookies and cream for me." Jax turns to face me. She's standing so close I can smell her perfume—like roses and honey—when she asks, "What about you, Kyle? Pick anything. My treat." She finishes this with a quick brush of my forearm. I swallow and blush before I manage to order a scoop of plain chocolate, the only flavor I manage to remember with Jax so close to me.

After she pays and grabs our cones, she leads me over to a corner table away from the front of the little ice cream parlor we've ventured into. We had crossed the street from our campus, to the other side of a road lined with stores bedazzled in blue and gold university regalia. Most of the shops are school supply stores, but a few cute restaurants and snack shops sit nestled between them, like the one we're in now. It's ten degrees cooler in here than it is outside, and the AC blows gently around us, making two ceiling fans turn slowly over the patrons settled among gleaming tables on the checkered tile floor. Jax takes us past everybody and over to a corner table that I have seen occupied by fawning couples each of the times I've been here with Emily.

Once we sit catacorner with each other, Jax crosses her legs and hands me my cone.

"Thanks." I take it and sit back, and she does the same. I allow myself a few seconds to really look at her. Seeing Jax outside of soccer is like seeing your middle school science teacher at the drugstore on a Saturday: completely bizarre and curiosity inspiring. Her toes and fingernails are painted a deep blue today, and she loosely bounces her foot while she starts into her ice cream. The jeans she wears look worn, but fit her like a glove. Several tears in them expose light skin along her knee and upper thigh. Her tank top lands just over the top of her jeans, and my eyes rove over her freckled arms. Her hair has a slight wave to it and looks blonder than it does when she has it up. After another bite into her scoop, she licks her lips.

"So," she says, and I sit up, hoping she hasn't noticed my wandering gaze, "you're looking good at practice so far."

I take a napkin from the holder on the table and dab at my mouth, then set it down beside me.

"Thanks. I'm really excited to be a part of this team. I hope I can contribute to a successful season with you guys."

Jax raises her brow and takes another bite into her cone. I immediately cringe after sounding like a complete robot who's sat down for an interview instead of a college girl out to ice cream with a teammate. God. Whatever effect Jax has cast over me seems to be amplifying the longer I'm with her.

"It should be a good year," Jax goes on, unfazed by my comment. "Emily talked you up a lot last semester. Says you're a rock star in the midfield."

I carefully start on my own cone before answering. "Emily is always a little extravagant in her opinions of people."

"Well, I see what she means so far. It's hard to keep my eyes off you out there." At that, she tosses the last bit of cone into her mouth and chews through a grin.

My stomach flutters. *Is she flirting?*

"Well, um, you guys are really good down on defense," I manage to say, glancing quickly up at her between licks of my ice cream. "I read that you allowed the fewest shots on goal in the whole division last season."

Jax nods like this is old news. "Well, we also had the best goalie." She frowns, frustration shadowing her face. "I told Haley not to play summer league. But she had to go and do it, and look where it got her."

I bite my lip, instinctively wanting to voice my optimism regarding Joey. But I know Jax isn't a huge fan, which I understand. One of her best friends lost her starting position. But Joey has shone in the box so far. She deserves a chance. Finally, I can't help myself. "Haley's been really great for Joey, though. I bet she learns a lot from her."

Jax sighs. "Maybe." Then the clouds vanish, and she is smiling again, her eyes narrowed at me. "I guess we shouldn't be worried, now that we have you."

I blush and go for another bite into my cone, except when I do I suddenly feel the ice cream racing down one side of my chin. I cringe and turn my face away. "Oh crap."

"No, let me."

Before I can snatch my napkin from the table, Jax leans forward and reaches out. My body freezes. A stunning girl has never reached out to touch me, let alone on my face. My brain simultaneously shuts down and races a thousand miles per second when her index finger starts at the bottom of my chin, then traces the river of chocolate up to the base of my lip. It lingers there for a moment, and Jax, who is now only a few inches from my face, watches me with her blue eyes. My face grows hot. Finally, after an agonizing amount of time under her gaze, she leans back.

"Um, thanks," I mutter. Then my eyes widen as she places her now ice cream covered finger into her mouth. Jax's eyes don't waver from mine as she makes short work of the chocolate. I swallow and bite loudly into my cone to keep myself from passing out.

Meanwhile, Jax smirks, the smile lines etched deep in her cheeks, and I just wriggle in the dim corner of the ice cream parlor, imagining Emily's face when I tell her about this, and hoping to God I make it out of here alive.

CHAPTER SIX

Mile two. One more to go!" Emily says from the treadmill next to me. I glance down at the bright green numbers on my machine and groan.

"This has to be illegal. Coach Gandy can't make us run until we puke." I tilt my head; a trickle of sweat runs down the back of my neck and into my already soaked T-shirt. "Can she?"

Emily just laughs through her heavy breathing while we continue our run. The steady whirring from the treadmill intermingles with the *clomp clomp* of our feet. For the first twenty minutes of our run, the sound consumed my mind, which helped ease the burning in my legs. *Whir, clomp. Whir, clomp.* Something was calming about the beat, and it allowed me to drown out the too-loud rock music blaring over the gym's speakers. Not to mention it let me focus on my steps, and *not* on the room filled with spandex shorts and revealing tank tops.

"How's the book for your English class?" Emily asks, grabbing the white towel from the edge of her machine and lifting her glasses to swipe it across her brow.

My eyes drift over the rest of our team working out in the crowded room before I respond. "You know, fine."

When I glance at Emily, her face is incredulous. "You haven't read it, have you?"

"All right, you got me," I respond between breaths. Then I shrug. "It's hard to get into. It's an old book."

"*Rebecca* is not that old. And it's such a good read!"

I grab the water bottle from its holder and take a swig. Emily does the same with her own. "The Spark Notes are kind of boring."

A cold splash hits my arm and the left side of my neck.

"Hey!" I cry, stumbling a little as Emily looks satisfied and takes another drink. When I lift up the bottom of my shirt to wipe my neck clean, I notice Joey on the rowing machine several feet to my right. We lock eyes for a second, and when her gaze falls to my abdomen, I swallow and focus back on Emily.

"Spark Notes, Kyle?" she says. "I swear you've kept them in business since we were in middle school."

My arms pumping, I glance back over at Joey, but she's staring straight ahead as her arms pull back on a metal bar, making the chain connected to it pick up sixty pounds' worth of block weights. Her back ripples under the white tank top she wears, and I momentarily feel light-headed.

"Earth to Kyle."

I shake my head. "Sorry." My stride quickens, and I'm not sure if it's because our third mile is almost over or if the feeling that surged through me watching Joey has given me an extra jolt.

"I guess we can't all be stellar student-athletes," Emily says, which warrants a water bottle squirt from me. She puts up her hands when I hit her right hip with a spray of water. After a little while, our treadmills beep, indicating we've hit our mile marker, and we both slow to a jog and eventually a walk.

"You know," I say, "I would read *Rebecca* if I had any semblance of free time. Between classes, practices, and workouts like this one, I barely even have time to sleep."

Emily nods, wiping the back of her neck after snatching the towel off her treadmill. "I suppose the first few weeks can be a bit of an adjustment period." She sighs dramatically. "I remember it like it was yesterday."

I give her a shove before we step off our machines. Callie throws us a thumbs-up from her treadmill nearby, and I spot T. next to Jax along the left wall. They're alternating on the calf-raise machine. Jax lifts herself up onto her toes, and the distinguished line running down her leg dries my throat. Suddenly, a thought occurs to me.

"How exactly was last year for you?" I ask, throwing back another swig of water.

Emily shrugs. "Fine."

We move over to a section of mats on the floor and sit down. "There was nothing," I pause, "eventful?" I ask, hoping she doesn't pick up on where I'm trying to go with this.

"No," she replies, reaching out to her toes in a stretch. "Well, I guess when it came to the team there was all of that drama with Jax. God, I haven't thought about that since last semester. I think I blocked it out."

I ignore the flip my stomach does at the mention of Jax's name. Ever since that day in the ice cream shop, the image of her licking the ice cream off her fingers kept popping up in my head. It was distracting, to say the least.

Emily, taking my silence as an opening, divulges further in a low voice. "Jax had this on-again, off-again boyfriend. They had—have, I don't know—the strangest relationship. We would literally have to peel her off him sometimes just to get her out of the parking lot before practice. He'd even hang around during scrimmages, hollering like a caveman whenever she did anything of notice. Then there were those screaming matches." Emily swishes some water and swallows. "Those things always ended terribly. Especially at parties. The two of them can hold their liquor, but man, do those claws come out."

I nod.

"Then, of course, an hour later there was the chance you'd stumble upon them going at it in somebody's spare bedroom."

My latest drink of water gets caught in the back of my throat. I cough and sit up, pounding on my chest.

"Whoa, are you okay?" Emily pats me on my back.

Finally, I clear my throat. I didn't realize the image of Jax on top of some faceless guy could make me gag. "I'm all right."

"Well, good," Emily says. "Speaking of couples going at it..." She grins. "Has anybody struck your fancy since the school year's started?" She pokes at me.

As if reacting to her comment, the fluorescent lights seem to brighten, ricocheting off the metal throughout the room and hitting me like a spotlight. I begin a set of crunches, hoping to hide the flush in my face. "Come on, Emily. I don't know."

She moves next to me, her hands behind her head. "Nobody

can hear us, worrywart. I can barely hear myself think over that noise they call music. Plus," she adds, gesturing to the room, "nearly everyone has earbuds in."

Looking around, she seems to be right. Haley, with her bright blue headphones on while doing the elliptical across the room, sings a Beyoncé song as her head bobs along.

Emily sits up and rearranges herself to face me. "Come on, Kyle. We haven't really talked about this since before school started. Don't you remember how excited you were to begin college? This was going to be your fresh start. New places. New people. Away from your family." She pauses. "This is a new place where—"

"Where nobody knows I have a thing for the same sex?"

Emily eyes me over her glasses. "Well, yes, there's that, too." She pulls back her shoulders. "But, Kyle, seriously! Nobody cares. Here is your chance to be open about it. Maybe you could even meet someone."

My body squirms at the idea, and my legs stick unpleasantly to the mat beneath us when I sit up. Emily has a point. And I really thought that by now it would be easier to talk about it. It's not like I just realized I'm gay. I've known for a while. But it was so easy back in high school to just shrug and say: Oh, just wait. Soon I'll have this all figured out. Soon it won't be a big deal.

But here I am, in my first semester of college, and all I have managed in terms of progress is a steady collection of LGBT literature, which is still hidden away in a special shoe box beneath my dorm bed.

"I don't know, Em. You're still the only one on the team who knows. I haven't even told my parents yet." She nods. "I know I said this would be a new start for me. But how can I even imagine dating somebody when you're the only one I can be honest with?"

Emily gives my knee a squeeze. "Hey, we don't have to think long term here. Just…relax a little." I take a deep breath. "I'm sorry if this upset you. I was just curious. Besides," she adds with a quirk of her eyebrow, "I am your wing woman. Maybe if I know who's left an impression, I can help to make an introduction."

I blush when I look over at Jax, who has begun a set of push-ups next to the leg-press machine. Her shirt hangs down while she lifts herself up, then lowers herself slowly down.

"Okay," Emily says. "I see that face. Let's see."

"Emily—"

"No, let me guess," she says and I sigh, forcing my eyes away from Jax. "Since we're all here, let's start with the team. Mary?" she asks, starting her way through the roster. "No, not Mary. Kris? She has a nice body." I follow her gaze to the mirrored wall, where Kris passes a medicine ball with Sarah. Her arms are chiseled, and I wonder if she's always been that cut.

I smirk. "You noticed, did you?"

Emily slaps my arm. "Oh, I know. What about Joey? Maybe your type is the tall Amazon girl." She looks pleased at her description and raises an inquisitive brow. And admittedly, the image of Joey on that first day I met her in my dorm room does rush back to me. I smile, recalling the touch of her hand in mine. When I turn and catch Joey in a low leg stretch, something stirs inside me. But before I can dwell too long on the feeling, Emily has pushed on with her inquiry. "Am I in the ballpark thinking it's someone on the team?" she asks.

My eyebrows shoot up, which makes Emily smile.

"All right, wait." Her hands go up dramatically. "I thought this day might come."

"This day? Tuesday?"

"No, Kyle," she says, her voice now an octave lower, as if we've suddenly breached the topic of some national security scandal. "You know that I love you. I do. But I'm sorry. I just, I *love* men. Well, I mean, I kind of hate men. But you know what I mean."

My mouth hangs open while she flips herself over and gets into a plank.

"Please," she continues, her head tilted toward me. "Let me know if you need some time apart to get over me. I'll understand."

Before she can fully situate her feet, I've slapped her across her backside with my towel.

"Oh my God, Em."

She collapses into a fit of laughter on the mat as I swing again, delivering a solid *thwack* to her hip.

"Fine! Fine! I couldn't resist." She adjusts her glasses while we recover our breath and sit up again. "Just, for all that is good in the world, at least tell me that it's not Jax. I know she took you out for ice cream that one day, but it was just a getting to know you thing, right?”

A wave rushes over me and takes my laughter with it as it recedes, and I watch as it hits Emily, full force.

“Oh,” she says quietly. “Well, this ought to be an interesting year.”

CHAPTER SEVEN

I'm not gonna, like, end up trashed out of my mind with my head in the toilet by the end of the night, am I?"

"Come on," Emily says, lacing her arm through mine as I round the passenger side of the car. "When have I ever led you astray?"

"Well, there was that one time at the Sara Bareilles concert."

Emily bumps me with her shoulder. "Really, Kyle? We were, like, ten."

"Hey, I'm just saying. As the older one between the two of us, I feel like it only makes sense to say that you were the one responsible for losing me."

"And apparently, you're still not over missing 'Love Song.'"

I shake my head, mock disappointment on my face. "My little heart was broken."

"Oh my God." Emily laughs as we stroll up the sidewalk to her friend Alex's house. The weekend had finally arrived, and the house party she was so excited about last week is here. She spent the car ride talking about how good meeting new people would be for me. I have a feeling, though, that my confession to her the other day about Jax left her feeling like she has to help me realize I have other options. So, here we are now, knocking on the door that has a steady bass thumping on the other side of it. I toss a small sandstone rock I'd picked up outside of Emily's apartment into the bushes when the door swings open.

"Hey!" A guy who I assume is Alex greets us, raising his red Solo cup enthusiastically. "You ladies made it, awesome."

Emily talks about Alex a lot. I'm pretty sure she has a crush on him. This theory is quickly given further proof by Emily's dorky cheer, which makes her freshly coiffed curls bounce. Then she gives our equally enthused party host a hug that lingers just a little too long.

"Alex, this is Kyle," she says once they've pulled apart. "My partner in crime and freshman rookie for our team this year. Brought her out to pop that college party cherry," she finishes with a little shimmy of her shoulders.

I wince at Emily's choice of wording. "Hey."

"Come on in!" he says with so much energy I briefly wonder if he's always at an eleven or if he saves his enthusiasm solely for Friday nights.

It's about what I had expected to see from a college guy's house, based on every TV show and movie I've ever watched. Our school's banner hangs next to a small mirror. Shoes litter the tile floor. I glance into a dark side room and find gym equipment set up. We move down the entryway and eventually end up in the kitchen. It's modest in size but feels small since it's full of guys who look like Alex: tall, bearded, and the majority of them clad in untucked plaid button-downs over a white T-shirt.

"Would you ladies like a drink?" Alex is next to us and gesturing grandly to the makeshift mini bar lining the counter. None of the liquor looks appealing—granted, I wouldn't know whiskey from tequila—so I just look at Emily.

"Got any beer?" she asks. Alex nods and in one move, slides over to the fridge. He pulls out two and pops off the tops. "M'lady," he says with a smile when he hands Emily her drink. Her brown cheeks gain a tint of pink, and I snort as he hands me mine. She nudges me, giving me one of her looks that says I better shut up before I say anything.

We spend the next half hour in the living room, which, props to Alex, is pretty nicely decorated. I learn that he's a junior, studying art history (explains the décor) and works part-time for the city's local museum. Emily's eyes practically fall out of their sockets she's so in awe of everything Alex says. I give Emily a nudge with my knee, my worn jeans bumping against her bare skin since she opted for a skirt this evening. The reasons for which are now more obvious to me.

Emily and I exchange glances when the voices turn quiet.

Everyone watches a couple guys play *Grand Theft Auto* while somebody who sounds like a mixture of Justin Timberlake and Ed Sheeran fills the air around us to an odd techno beat. I finish the last of my beer and stand up. Stretching my legs seems like a better alternative to watching my best friend get her flirt on.

"I'm going to get some air," I tell Emily and nod toward the back door, where a few people are hanging around outside on the patio.

"Want me to come?" Emily asks, but she doesn't stand.

I smile and glance at Alex. "No, I think I'll be fine."

"Okay. Come find me if you need anything."

I nod bye to Alex and step over an enamored couple making out on a pair of beanbags at the end of the couch. Sliding open the smudged glass door, I step out into the cool night air. Then I zip my black jacket and shut the door behind me.

There's a small circle of people to my right in a mixture of metal patio and kitchen chairs. One girl gives me a wave while a guy smoking a cigarette says, "Hey." I nod at the group and move to join them when I hear a loud roar of cheers coming from around the side of the house.

The cigarette guy mutters, "Beer pong tournament," with a hitch of his thumb over his shoulder.

"Right," I say, like it's the most obvious answer there could be. At least he didn't immediately assume I was an oblivious freshman. A beer pong tournament has to be more interesting than video games.

"Boom! What did I tell you guys?"

These are the exuberant first words I hear as soon as I'm on the other side of the house. In the sparsely grassed lawn stands a tall redhead, triumphantly posed with her hands on her hips on the opposite side of a Ping-Pong table, facing her opponents and now me.

"Whatever, dude," one of the guys with his back to me grumbles before lifting a red cup off the table and to his mouth.

I take in the scene: a group of people leaning against the brick wall of the house, a makeshift scoreboard hanging in the middle of them from a precarious nail, and the name "Joey" is written in bold letters on the left-hand side of the board, with three W's underneath.

"Hey, Kyle!"

Joey waves and starts toward me. I wave back meekly and my right foot fumbles over a rock. My face heats up. I haven't seen Joey outside of practice yet. Despite the fact we live in the same hall, she must keep busy off the field. And seeing her now is kind of making my head spin. She looks taller outside of the goal. She's wearing a pair of red skinny jeans and a blue V-neck. Her eyes are lit up, and I really can't look at anything else but her.

"Hey there," she says, now in front of me. "I didn't know you'd be here."

I stare for a second, swallowing and fighting my nerves.

"Yeah, uh," I mumble, motioning toward the house, "Emily thought…I mean…I came with…" Joey watches me, amused.

"I mean, I'm here with Emily," I finally say, cursing my inability to speak to girls.

Joey nods. "Cool." She steps back and motions to the table. "You up for it?" I look over her shoulder at the two guys setting up the red cups into a triangle shape on their side of the table.

"I've never played," I say, hoping that doesn't sound as lame as I think.

Joey shrugs. "Neither had I."

One of the guys behind her groans. "Don't rub it in."

She grabs my hand then gently pulls me over to the other side of the table. "Come on, you and me. Just one game. If you don't like it, you don't have to stay."

"All right." I smile. "One game."

❖

Before I know it, one game turned into three. Turns out I'm actually pretty good at beer pong, which as it happens, is not great news for the teams of guys we keep beating. I drop the Ping-Pong ball into the cup of water next to me to clean it off. Beer pong is actually pretty darn fun.

"Okay," Joey says, her hands out in front, and like a coach talking to her players, her voice is low and serious. "No pressure or anything. But if you make this shot, we win."

I shake the water off the ball and try to hide my smile. I thought

I was competitive. But Joey? Joey is in a whole other league. I practically had to restrain her in our second game when one of the guys watching—not even playing—started heckling us that our win streak was simply beginner's luck. It took me and two other guys to keep her from throwing an empty beer can in his direction.

It's hard not to smile now as she bounces nervously next to me on the grass.

I look first at the lone red cup across from me, then at the two guys we're playing. One has completely lost interest and chats with a girl in a lawn chair nearby. The other watches me warily.

Lining up the ball with the cup on the other side of the table, I take a breath and let it fly.

Plop.

"Aw, come on!" the guy who had been watching moans and picks up the cup to chug the beer it holds. A faint mix of cheers and boos follow from the crowd. Thrilled, I pump my fist and turn to Joey. As soon as I do, she wraps her arms around my waist and, with unbelievable ease, picks me up off the ground and spins me. The crowd around us transforms into a whirl of colors, and the stars spin overhead. Their light seems to glow brighter as I tuck my face into her neck.

"Yes! You are amazing!" she cries.

Seconds later, I'm back on the ground. My head feels light, and butterflies have taken up residence where my stomach used to be. My face grows warm when I glance up at her.

"Well, you did most of the work," I say, gesturing to the table as the crowd starts to disperse from the wall.

"No way," she says, joy radiating from her megawatt smile. I shrug and she adds, "We make a pretty good team." Then her hand is up, and I take the cue to high-five her, getting up on my toes to do so.

I mutter, "Short girl problems."

"You got that right, short stack."

Our hands have fallen back down, but mine is still in hers. She looks down at our fingers holding on to one another, and I do the same.

"Ladies and gentlemen!"

Our hands quickly fall back to ours sides, and we look toward the other side of the house. Joey gestures for me to follow her around to where we find the patio door ajar and Alex clearing his throat under the moth-covered patio light. Emily stands next to him, her arms crossed and her eyebrows raised in my direction.

"If you would please make your way to the living room, the weekly round of King's Cup is about to commence!" Alex steps back inside after his declaration. Then, after giving me the "You better spill later" look, Emily follows suit.

I clear my throat and turn to Joey.

She shrugs and says, "After you," with a flourish of her arm.

No wonder Emily wanted me to play here, I think as we head inside.

I remind myself to give her a hard time about pushing me to sign on at Meadowbrook. Only my best friend would know I can't resist a pretty face in soccer shorts.

Chapter Eight

Aside from the fact that King's Cup has about two thousand different versions and an ungodly number of rules to try to remember, it's actually pretty entertaining. About ten of us are seated around Alex's coffee table on the couch, love seat, and floor. Alex got us started by explaining what each card number stands for—some rule or action we have to do after each card is turned over. The goal, of course, is to ensure that we drink as much as possible.

Emily reaches out from her spot across from me and flips over a card. An eight.

"Eight is date," one of the girls to her right says. "You have to pick somebody to drink with you each time that you do."

Emily looks from her to me. I shake my head, so she looks to her left.

"Alex," she declares and nudges his shoulder.

"Cheers," he says. They raise their beer cans to each other before taking a drink. Then Alex reaches out for the next card. As he does, I am very aware, as I have been all game, of Joey's leg resting against mine. We're seated on the loveseat (which, by the way, looked a lot bigger before we sat down) and her left leg has been bumping against my right since we started playing. I keep telling myself it's because her legs are twice as long as mine, and she's probably feeling crowded. However, five minutes ago, I also couldn't help but notice the way her hand landed, and then lingered, on my thigh when she had turned over a two and said, "That means you, short stack."

"Five," Alex says, pulling me from my thoughts by the excitement in his voice. "Never have I ever."

"Oh, gosh, I love this game," Emily says, prompting inquisitive looks from both me and Alex.

"How does it work?" asks Joey.

"Everybody puts up five fingers," explains Alex, and we all do as he says. "Then we go around, and when it's your turn, you have to say something you've never done before. And if you have done whatever it is the person says, you put a finger down and take a drink."

"It's a great way to get to know people," Emily adds, giving me what I swear is a knowing smirk.

"For example," Alex says, "never have I ever gone skinny-dipping."

A few people put a finger down, and I do a double take at Emily as her thumb goes down. She notices and mouths "soccer camp" at me like that's supposed to explain everything.

The guy next to Alex takes a second to think, then says, "Never have I ever smoked pot." A few more fingers are down around the circle, and I try not to think about the fact that I've apparently done very little in my life.

"Never have I ever kissed a girl," the girl on the other side of Joey says next with a curious grin.

All of the guys put a finger down, along with two girls. One of which is Joey. I look at her as she takes a drink from her beer. When she notices me, I glance away and ignore the flush in my face.

Eventually, the game within a game ends with Alex and the "never have I kissed a girl" girl running out of fingers. They toast one another as the guy next to Alex flips over a new card.

"Six is chicks," he says.

"Cheers, ladies," says Emily, raising her beer up. It takes me a second, but I toast with the rest of the group and end up finishing my beer in the process. And either the alcohol goes straight to my head or all that I've learned about everyone in the last hour makes the room start to spin.

"I need another beer," I say before standing up. But what I really need is out of the circle of overshared information.

"You want us to wait for you?" Alex asks as the girl next to him flips another card.

"No," I reply, giving what I hope doesn't look like a forced smile. "Don't wait for me. I'll be back in just a minute."

I move through some people lingering around the kitchen entryway. The couple who had been making out on the beanbag chairs has now moved to the kitchen counter, oblivious to the stack of beer cans being formed into a pyramid right next to them by a loud and eager group of guys.

I'm about to open the fridge when I realize I have to pee. I head down the dimly lit hallway that's off one side of the kitchen. I try the doorknob but hear a girl's voice say, "Just a minute!" from the other side.

I lean back against the wall, my eyes flickering over several photo collages Alex has hung up. Most seem to be from his years at Meadowbrook. I'm looking at a particularly funny one of him in a mockingbird costume doing a beer bong when a tall figure from the kitchen moves my way.

"Hey, you." Joey's hair falls over one shoulder like a ruby waterfall.

"Hey," I say, shoving my thumbs into my jean belt loops, trying to act and look as casual as possible.

She leans against the wall next to me so that she too has a direct view of the photo collages. "I was wondering what was taking you so long."

I gesture to the bathroom. "Ocupado."

"Gotcha."

It's quiet for a minute, just us standing in the hallway while the music from the living room drifts toward us. Suddenly, there's a crash like a hair dryer falling from inside the bathroom. The girl's voice from before giggles, followed by somebody else shushing her. Joey and I exchange looks.

"Doesn't seem like the bathroom will be available anytime soon," she says.

I shake my head and, with a deep breath, decide to take advantage of the dim lighting to regard her tall, lean figure. She could be a model, I think as I take in her long legs and clearly taut stomach beneath her shirt.

"So," she says, turning so that she's leaning with one arm flush against the wall and facing me. She crosses her arms. "You've never kissed a girl, huh?"

Heat rushes into my face and I run a hand through my hair, looking down. My mind runs a banner exclaiming *"Holy shit!"* over and over while I try to think of something to say.

I glance anywhere but at her. "Um."

Joey uncrosses her arms. Her fingers touch my elbow. "Hey," she says, her voice matching the softness in her eyes. "Sorry. I didn't mean to offend you or anything. I was just messing around." She pauses. "I guess I'm feeling a little overconfident after all that beer."

"It's okay." Then I gather myself and turn so that we're face to face. "You were just curious," I add with a shrug. "And, um, no. I haven't kissed a girl before."

I have to remember to *never* play Never Have I Ever again.

A door across from us opens suddenly. We watch a couple stumble out from inside the room. They see us and grin goofily before wandering out into the kitchen.

"Cute," Joey mumbles before she quickly lunges forward into the now open doorway and says, "No way!"

I glance at the bathroom door, which shows no signs of opening anytime soon. So I follow Joey into the room.

It must be Alex's room. There are a few photos of him and people who I assume are his parents on one of the walls near his bed. There are also tons of art supplies scattered on every available surface. And the bedspread has Van Gogh's *Starry Night* stretching out across it. Definitely Alex.

Joey, however, is paying no attention to any of those things. Instead, she's in the far corner of the room, nose to glass with a lava lamp.

"Um…Joey?"

She doesn't move, and I find it hard not to laugh the longer her towering figure stands bent at the waist to take in all that is Alex's lava lamp. I lean against the doorjamb, smiling while I watch her clearly joyous discovery.

"I love these things," she finally says, her voice a whisper, as if she might disturb the floating goo if she's too loud. "Kyle, can you get the light?"

Standing upright, I swallow. "What?"

"The light," she says, throwing me a look over her shoulder. "These things are so much cooler in the dark."

My palms begin to sweat, and I flick off the light switch.

"And the door," she adds.

I close the door. The small square of hallway light disappears, so that now I'm standing in a dark room alone with Joey, watching her watch globs of blue goo float around a tube of water.

"Isn't this great?" she asks.

I have to admit, once I tear my eyes away from her, the effect is pretty impressive. Crossing the room, I take in the almost ethereal blue light surrounding us. I feel like I'm underwater, walking at the bottom of a pool.

Once I'm next to Joey, she straightens up so that she's once again a good head taller than me. Her eyes are still on the lamp when she says, "Can't you feel that?"

I raise an eyebrow, then look at the lamp. Part of me wonders if she took some sort of hallucinogen when I wasn't looking. But when she finally tears herself away from the lamp and looks at me, her eyes are clearer than I've seen them all night. "Yeah," I say, though I'm not exactly sure what I feel. A bit like I'm floating, maybe. The blue hues dance around us and over Joey's face.

Now I know exactly what I feel: exhilaration.

Joey smiles and my eyes won't look anywhere but at hers.

I'm barely aware of her hand reaching out to move some of the hair away from my face. She tucks it behind my ear. I swallow, my body ice cold and on fire all at the same time. Then she leans down, cupping my face with her hand.

When her lips connect with mine, her other hand reaches up, too. Her fingers run slowly through my hair. I stand on my toes just slightly, returning her kiss before I can tell myself that I'm afraid.

All I can think about then are her lips. They're so soft moving against my own. I open my mouth a little and she mirrors me. I move forward, and her hand gently pulls my head closer, pulling me deeper into the kiss. Our hips bump and something rises up inside me that I haven't felt before. And then her tongue parts my lips, finding my own. She kisses me slowly, deeply, like she's pouring whatever that silly lava lamp made her feel right into the core of me.

Kissing Joey is like all of those cheesy romance movies come to life. Everything else disappears until only she and I are left floating in the blue haze. All I feel is her. All I feel is our kiss.

Eventually, our lips part slowly, as if even they don't want this to stop. I open my eyes. Joey still has my face cupped in her hands, and her eyes flutter open to meet mine.

"Are you sure you've never kissed a girl before?" She runs a finger along my brow, then tucks more strands behind my ear.

I nod, my breath coming fast. "I'm sure," I finally say.

But I could definitely get used to it.

Chapter Nine

A week after the party, I drag myself out of bed, throw on a bra, and scamper down the dorm hallway in my PJ's. If I'm quick enough, I can avoid Joey and make it to the cafeteria scot-free. Not that I don't want to see her. It's just…complicated. I've managed to go six days since Alex's party with hardly any Joey encounters outside of soccer. I would run past her in the hallways on my way to class, shouting some excuse over my shoulder about being late or having to meet Emily. Or stand awkwardly in the bathroom while we brush our teeth side by side after dinner, then rush out with a quick good-bye. One week of not talking about what happened. One week since we kissed.

My house shoes scuff along the tile floor when I swing open the cafeteria doors into the large and practically empty room. Considering it's only eight o'clock on a Saturday morning, I'm not surprised that most of the student body is still asleep, probably recovering from their respective parties the night before. Though a few early risers are up. As I grab a tray and start down the buffet line, I notice three soccer guys at a corner table and one couple sitting near the soda fountain machines to my left. Otherwise, the only souls awake at this hour are the apron-clad cashier and two cooks who come in and out the kitchen behind the buffet line.

I grab a tiny box of Frosted Crisps and a carton of milk, placing them on my tray next to a banana. Then I pour myself a plastic cup of orange juice and slowly make my way over to a table in the opposite corner of the room. The table I choose faces floor-to-ceiling windows that look out into our dorm's courtyard. At this hour, it's completely vacant of activity. I plop down and stare tiredly out the window, my back to the rest of the morning's early risers.

Crunching into my cereal, my mind drifts to an assignment I have due in Spanish class. With some encouragement from Emily, I decided to take the language again after a mediocre showing through high school. Emily, though, is minoring in Spanish and can carry a basic conversation with her professors. She claims her parents only taught her slang and enough to bargain at markets when they visit her grandparents in Tijuana, but I have begun to doubt that. And despite her tutoring me at least twice a week since high school, I am still trying to figure out how to properly pronounce "I play soccer and like eggs."

After a few more bites of my cereal and reviewing the past tense verbs Professor Jimenez gave us last week, my mind drifts to the team. Specifically, to Jax. At first, the visual of her jogging along the sideline in warm-ups makes me bite my lip. I realize that despite seeing her at practice all the time, I haven't had an actual conversation with her. Not since the ice cream shop, and that had been mostly me trying to not panic.

Somebody drops a fork on to the tile floor. The *clang* parts my muddled thoughts slowly, like a winter fog lifting. Before I can help it, Joey and everything from last week is at the forefront of my mind. My stomach gives a jolt at the memory of us at Alex's party, and I smile into my OJ.

I run the word *jugo* through my head to practice the pronunciation when everything suddenly goes black. I'm about to panic, wondering if the lunch ladies are revolting and poisoning the cereal but realize it's only a pair of hands that has left me blind. The hands press slightly against my eyelids, and I feel a body against the back of my chair.

"Guess who."

I smile. "The reigning beer pong champ?"

Joey laughs and moves to my right, removing her hands. My eyes flutter, readjusting to the light before they fall on Joey taking a seat next to me at the table.

"Hey," I say, poking at my cereal. My eyes flicker back to the milk floating between the flakes in my bowl. The momentary exaltation at seeing Joey again is replaced by sudden nerves.

"Hey, yourself," she says. "I feel like I haven't seen you much lately. Aside from practice that is."

I shrug, my eyes moving between her and the trees outside. "Yeah, you know how it is. The first couple weeks of school are so busy. Long lectures. Buying overpriced books. An insane amount of reading to do."

Joey nods. "That's true. I used to read for pleasure. But I haven't enjoyed any of my reading since having to push through two hundred pages a night."

"Seriously," I reply. "I had no idea Intro to Geology would require three textbooks."

"Intro to Geology?" asks Joey, her brow raised.

I grimace. "Yeah. I apparently need two science credits for my major."

"So you picked rocks."

"It was rocks or stars."

Joey watches me, her mouth fixed in an amused grin. I resist the urge to let my eyes linger on her lips.

"I'd have gone with stars," she finally says, propping her elbows up on the table to rest her chin on her hand.

"Well," I say, taking a sip from my juice, "I actually know a decent amount about astronomy already. My dad was fascinated by all of that. He would buy me and my brother books on the universe each year for Christmas. I remember being in the car with Kevin in the back seat, our dad driving us out to fields to watch meteor showers at two a.m." I clear my throat, Joey's gaze still on me. "So, I'm familiar with the constellations, how stars are made, how the solar system works, all that. But rocks…I mean, I feel like they get the bum deal, you know? Like, if you see a rock on the sidewalk, what do you do?"

Joey shrugs.

"You probably kick it, right?"

She nods and picks up my banana, beginning to peel it.

Watching her, I continue. "Right. It's an instinct. People kick them. Hundreds, thousands of years ago, rocks were used as punishment against criminals. Creepy things hide under rocks. They're what crooks use to break through glass. But if you think about it, rocks are a lot more than that. I mean, they're essentially where we come from. In a way. We started as a big rock. And gasses and microbes and things, of course. But we're all just hanging around on a big floating rock in a galaxy of other floating rocks. And within our rock are billions of other rocks, all different types and sizes and colors. Everything began with rocks. We used rocks to build a cave door. The first wheel. Castles. And now we carve them, clean them, and wear them on our fingers. Rocks are kind of a big deal. So, I figured I owe it to them to at least learn a year's worth of information."

When I take a breath, Joey's taking another bite out of my banana. I'm not entirely sure what her eyes are saying, but heat rushes up the back of my neck. The air grows thick around us, and I fall once again into the memories of last week.

"Sorry," I mumble, taking a quick bite of my cereal. "I got a little carried away."

"I saw that."

I gulp and take a swig of my juice.

She chuckles. "Now I know what to get you for Christmas. I'll be sure to gift-wrap the next pebble that gets lodged in my cleat at practice." I laugh. The tension that I felt before vanishes. "Well, short stack," she says, stretching, "thanks for that brief but very thorough insight into your take on rocks. It was, um, educational. However, there is actually a reason why I came in here."

"To start your daily hoarding of people's breakfasts?" I ask, eyeing my now half-eaten banana.

She smiles and takes another bite. "No, but good guess. Actually, I was hoping to talk to you."

My cereal is gone now, so I swirl the milk around in my bowl. I don't dare look up at her despite the fact that I can feel her eyes on me.

"Oh?" I say, my gaze still down. "What about?"

She's quiet, and I can practically hear the "Really?" that bounces around the air from her to me.

Okay, I'm playing dumb. But how the hell do you even start a conversation after a night like that? What do you even say?

"Kyle, we kissed."

I guess that's one thing you could say.

When I finally look up, she's folding the empty banana skin

down onto the table in front of her. Her fingers fumble with it, and it gives me the slightest dose of courage to see that she might actually be nervous, too.

"We did," I eventually say.

"Well," she says, shifting in her seat, "I feel like we ought to, I don't know, clear the air about it. I feel like you've been avoiding me since that night at the party. I mean, you ran out the back door of our dorm hall the next morning when I walked out of the bathroom."

I grimace at the memory of me spotting Joey and shoving through the heavy back door next to my room before hiding behind the dumpster with my toothbrush for twenty minutes.

"I may have panicked a bit."

"And we had conditioning three days last week, so there were a few days in there when I didn't really see you at all," Joey adds.

"We've hung out at practice," I offer, knowing this isn't what she's looking for.

"Sure," she says, still watching me. "And while that's been great, I thought that...well, I thought that you and I were friends. Or at least were going to be friends. I love the team and all, but you are, like, the least weird girl out of the rest of our freshman class. Although that tangent you just went on about rocks kind of makes me second-guess that."

We both grin. "Gee, thanks."

She gives my arm that's resting on the table a playful shove. "I'm kidding. But seriously, Kyle. I like you." My eyes flutter back down and I swallow. Joey must sense my unease because she quickly says, "As a friend. I like you...as a friend." The tone in her voice, though, makes me think that other words were trying to make their way out instead.

"I like you, too, Joey."

"And, look, I know you'd never kissed a girl before that night. And that's totally fine. And, well, I'm not going to lie and say that I didn't enjoy it," she pauses, catching my gaze, "but I don't want to start ourselves off on muddled footing." I nod, my ears hot. I briefly wonder if the cooks are listening. Joey looks down, fiddling with the banana peel. She swallows before she says, "I am curious, though. Did...um...did you have fun that night?"

Her uncertainty is kind of adorable, and the anxious feeling in my stomach quells. When I first met Joey, I could tell that she was confident. She has to be, I suppose, to be a goalie. They're the last line; all that's left standing between the opposing team and the ball hitting the back of the net. And that self-confidence was evident from the moment I met her. But this Joey: the stammering, nervous Joey?

She's pretty darn cute.

I smile when her eyes finally flicker up to meet mine. "I did have fun," I tell her, and I swear her whole body relaxes.

"Good," she says. "You, um…maybe want to hang out later? Not like that," she adds at my raised brow. "No lava lamp included."

I laugh. There's something hopeful in the bright smile she gives me. My heart rate picks up as I take in her clear eyes and the curve of her nose. I find myself wondering if she always wakes up this beautiful. Then my mind flashes back to that night. I can feel her hands cupping my face, her lips against mine, and her tongue slick against my mouth…

"Kyle?"

I blink, realizing I'd been staring out the window. My body is hot and my heart pounds. Hold on. This is scary. What am I thinking? There is no way I'm ready for this. Or for what it could be. Joey is amazing. And stunning. But I'm not even out yet. Nobody here aside from Emily knows that part of me. I just started at this school. And here is this ridiculously amazing girl next to me telling me… what is she telling me? That she wants to be friends? Can we just be friends after a night like that? It was…I don't really know what it was. Confusing. Fun. Surreal. Breathtaking.

I look back at Joey, whose right foot bounces slightly against the floor.

What if, at some point, she wants that part of me I'm not ready to give?

"I can't."

"I'm sorry?" asks Joey, her foot stopping.

I shift in my chair to face her. "I can't," I say again. "I mean… yes, I want to be friends and hang out. But that kiss. That whole night…" Her brow raises expectantly. "It was…a lot. And I'm still not sure I've fully processed everything from that night. And you are so amazing. But…"

Her brow furrows, but her face relaxes a second later, her confidence at the forefront. "But I should make sure you and I aren't alone in a room together for a while, huh?"

I stare at her and she winks. Then I exhale. "Yeah. I'm sorry, Joey."

She shrugs.

I reach out and rest my hand on top of hers. "We're friends, though, right?"

Her eyes flicker from our hands to my gaze. "Of course. I mean, we're teammates, dorm mates…of course we're friends."

"Good." I pull my hand back and take one last drink from my OJ. My heart is still pounding and I take a deep breath to calm myself down. I'm grateful for Joey's acceptance at my attempt to explain myself. She really is amazing. I stand up. "Walk with me back to the rooms?"

Joey clears her throat, then stands. She flourishes her arm and smiles. "After you, short stack."

CHAPTER TEN

All right. PK time, ladies. Line up."

I grab the closest ball and jog over to the line forming just outside the goalie box. It's been a few days since the conversation with Joey, and things have settled back into a normal rhythm. I don't run away anymore when I see her in the hallways, so that's progress. We even walked to classes together on Tuesday. And practices, if possible, are even better since we've cleared the air about things. I scan the net, still congratulating myself on handling things pretty maturely, when somebody is suddenly standing very close behind me.

"Nervous?"

The hairs on the back of my neck stand up and the inevitable flush flies to my face. "Should I be?" I stammer.

Jax slides out from where she'd been behind me. Now perpendicular to me, she places her hands on her hips. My eyes fight to stay focused on hers as I swear she pushes her chest forward. "I don't know." She shrugs. "Our first game is next week. Coach is evaluating everybody. Who's gonna start? Who's going to be keeping that bench warm?" she adds in a voice I can only label as "laced with innuendo" while she simultaneously lowers her gaze to my hips.

I shift forward as the line moves. "Are you saying I won't cut it because I'm a freshman?"

"No, not at all," she replies, juggling a ball between her feet. "I'm only saying"—she kicks the ball up and catches it inches from my face—"don't screw up." Then she winks and strolls to the back of the line, leaving me wondering just who this girl is and why she keeps talking to me.

My thoughts quickly shift and panic washes over me. Wait, does she know? How could she know? Did Emily say something to her about me? Did she hear about the party—about what happened between Joey and me? Emily swore she wouldn't say anything. Oh, God, Jax knows.

"Kyle, you're up!"

I'm pulled from my thoughts as Coach blows her whistle. I blink a couple of times. Finally, I regain my focus. Joey stands across from me, bouncing on her toes in the goal box with her arms stretched out.

"Yeah, Kyle!" she calls while I place the ball on the PK spot. "I'm growing old over here."

I back up, but my thoughts still have a hold on me. Jax was definitely flirting. That's not so bad, right? I probably need the practice. But the idea alone makes my stomach flip-flop. I barely register the go-ahead whistle before starting forward. My movements are stiff and automatic, like a windshield wiper sprung to life.

I grimace and watch as the ball sails two feet over the right goalpost. When I look behind me, Jax is grinning. I groan beneath my breath.

Maybe things aren't as worked out as I thought they were.

CHAPTER ELEVEN

I carefully set the chilled armful of energy drinks down on top of my mini-fridge when there's a knock on my door. I skip over and open it a few inches before running back to my computer where the practice sessions from my Spanish class are finishing their download.

"Hey, Em," I call over my shoulder, "sorry, just a sec. I'm finishing up this program installation that Professor Jimenez gave us. It's been downloading for over an hour, but I think it's just about done." I walk over to the plastic Quick-E-Mart bag on my bed and pull out the snacks I'd bought earlier that day. "And I picked up some studying essentials for us. Fruit, granola bars, and a family-sized bag of Doritos for when we're feeling especially depraved." I turn to Emily, proudly holding up the giant bag of chips.

What I expect to see after Emily had agreed to help me study for my first Spanish exam is something more akin to what I am currently wearing: sweatpants, crew socks, an old practice T-shirt, and a messy ponytail. Instead, she is in a knee-length black skirt and a simple white sleeveless blouse. She has on eye makeup behind her red horn-rimmed glasses, and her black curls are set perfectly, falling gently to her shoulders. A trace of red lipstick makes her look almost glamorous, her brown complexion glowing.

"Um, Emily, I did mention that we'd be staying in to study, right?"

She looks both guilty and excited when she says, "I know, Kyle, I know; oh, gosh I'm so sorry." She nervously adjusts the red purse on her shoulder. "I was so ready to study with you tonight. I really was. But around four o'clock, Alex called me."

I raise an eyebrow, and she holds up a hand before I reply. "I know, hear me out. Okay, you know I like him. A lot. And he's always super busy between his work and studying and everything. And I'm busy, too, with soccer, as you know. But he called earlier and invited me to this Art Walk tour the university is hosting tonight. It's over on Conrad Street, where those warehouses have been converted into breweries? Well, he told me he and his friends have a few pieces in the Walk, and he hoped to introduce me to more of his art group and show me his work." As Emily talks, her face lights up the longer she goes on about Alex. Her excitement is contagious. "Would you hate me if I went with him tonight?" she says, her face apologetic. "I can come over first thing tomorrow. We'll go over everything!"

"It's fine, Em. Seriously," I add at her imploring look. Then I laugh. "The puppy eyes are not necessary. Really. I can go over everything on my own. Go, have fun."

She actually jumps and yells, "Yay! Oh, Kyle, thank you so much." Then she runs over and pulls me into a hug before hurrying back to the open doorway. "I'll let you know how it goes."

I prop myself up on my bed, one leg pulled up close to me. "You better."

Just as she's about to go, shouts come from down the hallway. We both turn toward the noise.

"Katie, how many times have I told you that if you're going to do laundry in the bathroom, *please* do not hang your boyfriend's jockstrap where I can see it!"

Through my open doorway, Joey appears near the other end of the hallway, just outside the bathroom. Her hair is a darker red, still wet from a recent shower. She's in athletic shorts and a fitted black T-shirt. I realize I'm biting my lip when Emily suddenly spins around. Her face is something between Christmas morning and a state championship victory before she says, "Wait, doesn't Joey take Spanish?"

"Um, well, yes, but, Em, wait—"

Before I can stop her, Emily sprints off down the hallway.

I stare wide-eyed as she skips toward Joey, and I run a hand through my ponytail, loose strands falling over my eyes as a result. I hadn't told Emily about my cafeteria conversation with Joey yet—something I am now quickly regretting. She knows about the kiss, and she knows I'm being tight-lipped about my feelings, but I hadn't had the guts to share the "let's be friends since we made out but I'm terrified of what it all means" conversation from last weekend.

I watch Emily, whose back is to me as the conversation with Joey continues. Then Joey glances up and meets my gaze, and it seems that, for a moment, she shares my hesitation.

My thoughts are interrupted when Emily is back in the doorway, Joey standing behind her.

"Problem solved!" Emily says, beaming proudly. "Joey is in Spanish II, the one you'll take next semester, and she even has Professor Jimenez on Tuesday/Thursdays! After a little encouragement, I got her to agree to help you study." She says all of this with a huge smile and flourishing hands, like she's just completed a tap number in a musical.

"You really don't have to. It's Saturday night. I'm sure you have better places to be."

Joey shrugs, her clear eyes holding mine. "It's not a problem, short stack. I was just going to marathon some TV while pretending to read for Government. Nothing terribly exciting."

"Perfect then!" Emily says, gleefully nudging Joey farther into the room while she edges herself between the hallway and the door, which she starts to close. Her head is all that pokes through the doorway when she sings, "I'll see you guys later!"

I swear she winks when Joey turns to face me. My mouth falls open a little, and all I can do is wave before Emily closes the door and is gone.

❖

"Personally, I think we've done pretty well so far. And my hands are only a little shaky from the stuff you keep insisting we guzzle down."

"Hey, I'm not forcing you," I say and throw the final drops of my energy drink back, then squeeze the can until it's dented. I toss it into the trash bin near my bed. It may be due to the borderline-dangerous levels of caffeine surging through my veins over the last three hours, but it seems laughable now how worried I was earlier. What was I so concerned about when Emily suggested Joey as my study partner? I reach for another handful of Doritos next to the clock reading 10:37 on my desk. This has actually been enjoyable. And helpful. Joey, I didn't know, has taken Spanish since elementary school; her parents had enrolled her in a quirky little hands-on primary school that immersed kids in foreign languages earlier than most. And while she claims to not know much, I couldn't ignore how much she seems to enjoy speaking it while simultaneously watching me fumble over rolling my *R*'s.

"Besides," I add, bouncing a little on my bed, "the caffeine is keeping us awake. And I feel like it's helping!"

"Just try not to shoot out into the hallway, and I think we'll be fine," she says, one hand patting my bouncing knee. I unsuccessfully try to sit still.

"Okay, moving on. We've gone over family member pronouns, common weekend activities…What else did you say the exam will cover?"

I wipe my hands on a paper towel lying at the edge of my bed. Joey and I have parked it on top of my dark blue comforter since Emily left. She sits with her back against the same wall the length of my bed is flush against, her long legs stretched out in front of her while she shuffles through my textbook. I, meanwhile, am cross-legged next to my pillows. Admittedly, I was a little nervous when she so casually hopped up and made herself comfortable. I had made sure there was sufficient space between us when we started. But as time passed and I was actually remembering things from class thanks to her, I relaxed. Studying with Joey was actually productive.

"Um, let me check my notebook." I frown, scanning the cluttered comforter. "Where *is* my notebook?" We both lift papers and pillows until my eyes raise to the shelf about a foot above our heads. Sitting with one corner dangling off the edge is my yellow Spanish notebook. "Aha." I reach up, leaning forward a little. My right arm strains, but my fingers only manage to brush the edge of it, and I actually push it farther onto the shelf.

"Hold on, let me get it," Joey says. She pushes herself up a little, her long arm reaching up.

"I got it," I insist, still straining my arm, "really."

"Kyle, let the tall people have their moments," she says with a grin. My gaze, which had been concentrated on the shelf, falls down to her. Thanks to our notebook rescue mission, we have both shifted forward. Now Joey is only a few breaths away from my face when our eyes meet. My hand has found the top of the shelf, and my fingers crawl along the edge to grab the journal. At the same time, Joey's hand lands on top of mine. We sit like this for a moment, my breath quickening. Her gaze moves up to the notebook, and my eyes rove over her neck. Some of the hair is still wet and curled gently behind her ear from her shower earlier. The V-neck cut of her shirt leaves her collarbone exposed. I never noticed how smooth her skin is.

"Here we go." Joey lowers the journal back onto the bed.

"Thanks." I'm about to reach out my other hand—I'm not sure to where, but it suddenly aches to touch that collarbone. Just as I'm about to, Joey clears her throat and nudges the journal toward me.

"Is that one of your dad's Christmas gifts?" She nods back up toward the shelf, but her eyes stay fixed on my sheets.

My eyes flutter, and I take a deep breath. I glance up. "Oh, yeah." I point to the thick book on black holes sitting below a picture of me and Kevin. "Birthday present, actually." It's quiet for a moment. Focus, Kyle. Flipping the pages, I scan my notebook with class notes scrawled through it. "I think the last section we covered was body parts."

Joey nods, her gaze still anywhere but on me. "Got it. So, what do you know?"

I sit up and tuck a few stray hairs behind my ear. "I know *cabeza*. Mostly because it rhymes with *cerveza*."

"Really?" She shoots me a look of disbelief, but I shrug.

"Whatever works, right?"

"I guess so," she says. My eyes linger on her for a moment. Since our study session began, I couldn't help but notice that Joey has seemed guarded. She is friendly, as usual, and doesn't hold back on sending sarcastic remarks my way regarding my choice in study music or dorm décor. But ever since we started, it's like she can't bring herself to look at me for more than a second.

"Um," I mumble, "I think I may have drifted off a bit when Jimenez covered that topic." I flash her a page from my notebook that has "Body Parts" in bold title letters and nothing but blank lines beneath it.

Joey's eyebrows raise, but she just nods. "Okay, then. We've got our work cut out for us." I dip my head sheepishly before she adds, "Better open up one more of those drinks."

❖

Thirty minutes later, we're sitting amongst piles of flashcards and granola bar wrappers. Joey stretches her arms as she rearranges herself to face me on the bed. "Okay, Kyle. Crunch time."

I stretch my neck in mock seriousness. "Let's do this."

We're face-to-face now. Joey collects several of the flashcards into a neat pile, clearing her throat before she says, "All right. Are you ready?"

I sit up straight, my face serious. "I'm ready."

She nods, and with a glance down at the first note card, she reads, "Okay, in Spanish, how do you say 'eyes'?"

"Easy. *Ojos*."

"Very good." She places the card behind all the others and continues. "Leg."

"*Pierna*."

Another nod, another card. "Ear."

"Oh, um…*oreja*."

"Almost got you there," she says, smiling but still avoiding my gaze. New card. "Knee." This time, as she says it, she taps my knee with her left hand. Just two quick taps and her hand is back on the cards. But my eyes stare at where her fingers had been, my knee suddenly itching to move closer to her.

"Knee," I say, swallowing. "That would be *rodilla*."

"Very good. How about nose?"

"Oh, that one's easy. *Nariz*."

She scans a few cards. Then she quirks an eyebrow before the next one. "Hands?"

"Hands?" I frown, then stretch my hands out in front of me, running them over the top of the bed as I try to recall the vocabulary word. "Hands…"

As I'm thinking, Joey reaches out one hand and her fingers gently rub along the top of my right hand. "Any guesses?" Her fingers dance over my knuckles, then glide slowly toward my wrist.

For what feels like the first time, she looks up and holds my gaze. My face warms. I force myself to remember what we are doing and finally reply, my voice a little shaky. "I, I can't seem to recall that one."

Joey allows the smile to stretch across her face. Her fingers pull back to hold the cards again. "*Manos*."

I nod, blinking a few times as I'm suddenly dizzy. "Right, *manos*. Thanks."

Joey runs a hand through her hair. We both adjust our sitting positions. I wonder if she's as anxious as I am. Though I'm not sure why. We're friends…right? That's what we decided. Just friends, helping each other out.

"Okay, let's switch it up," she says, but her voice is different now. Did I hear it quiver? "In English, give me *boca*."

My eyes fall immediately to her lips. I lick my own before I can help it. Joey swallows, and the room grows heavy, the air between us thick, like it was that night. And there's something else. Something like a magnet. A force holding us and everything else in free fall. Like we are two stars pulling against one another in the night sky.

"Mouth. That…that's mouth." I finally say, my voice barely registering above a whisper. I flash back to Beth: still on the soccer field, her lips enticing. She stands alongside all of the other girls I've ever dreamed about kissing.

I don't know if Joey's leaning in or if I'm moving closer. Maybe both. She reaches up, places a few strands of hair behind my left ear. My own hand moves to her face. My fingers trace down from her temple to her chin. She tilts her head into my palm.

My thumb traces over her bottom lip.

The phone rings. We both jump back at the sound of my ringtone.

Joey leans against the wall, and she looks like she does after a hard practice, her face flushed and her breathing staggered.

She runs a hand through her hair as I answer. "Hello?"

"Kyle!" Emily squeals on the other end. "Oh my God, I have to tell you about tonight."

I take a deep breath. Joey smiles, then organizes the flashcards into a pile and closes my textbook. She slides off the bed, standing up to face me. Then she mouths, "I'm gonna go," and throws a thumb toward the door.

My mouth is open to respond, but my breathing is uneven and I can't seem to form words. So I nod. Before she leaves, Joey waves to me, which sends my stomach fluttering again.

"Kyle, you still there?"

The door closes after her, and I brush a hand through my ponytail. Finally, I respond. "I'm here, Em. I want to hear all about it. And come over tomorrow," I add with a glance to where Joey had been sitting on the bed. "We have a lot to catch up on."

CHAPTER TWELVE

Our fourth week of practice has me feeling pretty defeated. Between classes, homework, and my confusing social life, soccer has taken a beating. As a team, we're clicking pretty well. Yet I know I can play better than I have been. Coach started me the first two games, but since last week, I've felt off. Like every move I make is a second slower than it should be. Like in our last drill at practice today, when I completely missed a slide tackle and then gave up a shot on goal against Emily.

"Hey, you weren't that bad."

I lift my head up. It's been hanging between my knees like the long-deceased flowers in Emily's apartment, ones she insists are still alive. Joey stands a few feet away, taking off her gloves.

"Yeah?" I say, heaving a huge sigh. "Tell that to Coach. She's had me on second squad all week." I roll my head back, admittedly a bit dramatically. "I sucked. Royally. I might as well call my parents and tell them not to bother coming out for another game this season because I'm never going to see the field again."

Joey drops her gloves into her bag. "Come on now," she says before grabbing her water bottle and moving closer. "It's not that bad, drama queen. Coach is probably just trying to give some other girls a shot at starting. You're good. I think you're just in your head too much." She pauses, then asks, "Are you sure there isn't anything else bothering you?"

For a second, I consider telling her how confused I felt during our study session. Or how Jax seems to be making sure I'm within two feet of her every time she tosses water on herself to stay cool during our breaks. Then I think better of it.

"No. There's nothing wrong. I'm fine." I give a smile—hoping she can't see how forced it is—and then a thumbs-up, for good measure. Even though her eyes have lit up with curiosity, Joey doesn't pressure me to explain any further. I toss my cleats into my bag and hop down off the bleachers next to her. She reaches out and taps the top of my head.

"You really are short, huh." She grins.

I slap her hand away. "Hush. You're just freakishly tall."

"You know it. And I can still block shots from short stacks like you." She reaches toward my head again, but I jump back. We laugh and gather our stuff to head home. As we walk toward the parking lot, we wave to Emily as she chats with Mary and Katie. I notice Jax tossing cones into a car trunk, and it's briefly like stepping outside for the first time all day, when your eyes want to go directly to the source of all of that bright light. My eyes are drawn to her. That burning, blazing force.

Joey's voice is distant in my mind when she says, "Well, speaking of short stacks, they're serving pancakes all day in the dorm cafeteria. Feel like a carb reload?"

Jax disappears behind the other side of T.'s car in the parking lot. Finally, my eyes adjust, and I can focus again. Joey's words replay in my head, and the rest of me is on delay, too, thanks to Jax's pull. My stomach growls at the acknowledgment of her proposal.

"That actually sounds really good."

Joey smiles. "Perfect." She tosses me my keys. "You're driving."

CHAPTER THIRTEEN

"I feel like there's something you want to talk about."

I pick at the syrup-drenched pancakes stacked on the plate in front of me, then glance up at Joey as she continues talking. But as soon as I do, my mind is overcome with the image of Jax on the practice field. I can feel her standing behind me, so close her breath is on the back of my neck.

"Nervous?"

"It's just that, you know, as much as I love your general company, I should probably tell you that I am very well known for my listening skills. Like, top shelf. My superlative in high school was actually *Best Listener for Those in Need*," Joey says, grinning at me from across the table. Finally, I shake myself out of the memory of Jax. "Okay, fine." She sighs and stabs at another bite of her double stacked pancakes. "That's not true. I actually got *Most Likely to Join the WNBA*, which by the way, is super prejudiced against me. I mean, just because I'm tall does not directly mean that I play or even like basketball."

I can't help but smile at her comment, which is returned triumphantly. "Aha. There you are. I'm telling you, I am practically a bona fide therapist." She tosses back a swig of Gatorade.

"Yeah, not bad for a political science major," I say through a mouthful of sugary dough.

Joey shrugs. "Po-tay-to, *po-tah-to*. But really," she pauses, her face serious, "if you do ever want to talk about anything, I'm here if you need me."

My gaze meets hers. Joey has lately had this uncanny way

of peering so far into me. Like she can see the walls I've built up but simply jumps over them like they're molehills and not the mountains that constantly cloud my vision. She seems to see me. The real me.

But I still can't let her in.

"Why don't we talk about you? I feel like I'm always going on about me." I sidestep her question and hope she doesn't notice. "Like, how come I'm the one of us who's always driving to practice? I've seen your car. I would show that thing off if I were you."

Joey has an impressively well kept '87 Mazda RX-7, black as the night sky. I always see it parked near the back of our dorm parking lot but rarely see her behind the wheel.

She tilts her head, then shrugs. "Please, why put miles on that beauty when I have a perfectly willing chauffer so close by?"

"You're just lucky I'm nice. I could start leaving for practice earlier, without you."

"No way, short stack," Joey counters, arranging half a piece of bacon onto her fork. "I've got half a foot on you. I could take you down if you changed your mind."

"You do not have half a foot—"

The piece of bacon from her fork goes flying and hits me square on the nose. My eyes go wide and I fight back a smile, not wanting to give her any satisfaction. Then without missing a beat, Joey turns to look over her shoulder, then back at me.

"Can you believe that? Oh my God, Kyle. Who would even do something like that?" She grins behind her Gatorade bottle while I reach for the small bowl of powdered sugar placed between us. I hold it in my palm, pretending to look it over. Joey shifts in her seat. "You wouldn't dare."

"I don't know," I say, mocking seriousness. "I mean, what's that saying again? 'Do unto others as they have done unto you'?"

"Actually, I think it's—"

She can't finish correcting me before her entire face is white. The powder sticks to her cheeks and coats her eyebrows like freshly fallen snow. I snicker and watch the sugar settle onto her shoulders.

"Okay, Kyle, you asked for it."

But I'm already ahead of her. I've grabbed my bag and am

halfway to the swinging cafeteria doors when I hear her chair scrape against the tile floor.

"Good luck finding me!" I holler over my shoulder.

Who needs talking? I rush past two of my dorm hall mates, grinning. Ignorance is bliss. Isn't it?

Chapter Fourteen

I round another turn and push past the heavy door that leads into the designated boys' side of our dorm building. A few guys from the soccer team poke their heads out their doorways when I rush past.

"Bathroom?" I ask one who's clad only in boxer shorts while he watches me run by, his hair a mess. He points down the hall in the direction I'm heading.

I wave my thanks and continue down the brightly lit hallway. The sound of water running from the showers makes my ears prick when a door to my right swings open, and I slip inside.

"Oh, wow." I cover my nose as the scent of Old Spice and aftershave invades my nostrils, almost knocking me out. Through the haze of body spray, I quickly scan the bathroom, weighing my options. There are seven bathroom stalls to my left, three of which appear to be occupied. One guy watches me over his shoulder from the urinal wall.

I nod casually. "Carry on."

Then I walk over to the opposite wall of showers and find all with their curtains drawn. I bend down in front of the first one. A pair of feet stand over the soapy drain. I move on to the next one, and just as I start to bend down, the curtain flies open to reveal a short guy with a Star Wars towel wrapped around his waist. He looks slightly bewildered to find me standing in front of him.

"Whoa," he says, taking a step back. "I'm still in the guys' bathroom, right?"

"Sure are," I reply, then glance down into the stall next to his to find another pair of feet. The bathroom door opens behind me, but it's not Joey. I turn back to face Star Wars. "I'm actually hiding from a friend of mine. Just having a little fun."

He scratches his back with a light saber inspired back scrub and smiles. "Very cool. A little dorm hide-and-seek. Keeping the classics alive." I glance past him. He reads my thoughts and steps aside, gesturing to his empty stall. "All yours."

"Thanks. And if you happen to see a tall redhead out there—I was never here."

He pulls himself up into a salute, then walks past me to the bathroom door.

Carefully, I step into the first part of the stall, avoiding the soapy puddles splattered over the blue tile floor. In the three-by-three space, there's a small seat used to store towels and toiletries. On this, I drop my bag, then hop onto it, crouched with my knees tucked close to me. Slowly, I pull the curtain shut right as heavy footsteps thunder through the hallway outside. A second later, I hear the bathroom door swing open.

"Dude," a guy cries out near the sinks.

"Oh, please," Joey's voice scoffs. "You're not that special."

I stifle a laugh and pull my knees closer to my chest. I listen to her knocking on all of the bathroom stalls, which is followed by the occasional yelp from whichever poor soul had just been barged in on. Then her footsteps move over to the showers. I hold my breath, but it proves fruitless when the shower curtain flies open.

"Got ya." Joey grins as she stands with one hand on her hip, triumphant.

"Really? How did you know to look for me in here?" I ask.

"Easy." She shrugs. "I thought about the one place I told you I would never want to go."

"And you say you're the good listener." I move my feet down off the seat.

Joey reaches out her hand to help me down. "Yeah, apparently, I need to watch what I say around you from now on."

I take her hand and move to stand. But my sneakers slip on one of the soapy puddles and I fall forward.

"Whoa," Joey says, stepping forward to help me balance. But in doing so, she slips, too. Suddenly, she's turning and lands hard in the seat next to my bag. Her hand still holds mine, which pulls me down after her. I crash into her lap and Joey's arm is cradling my back when I look up at her.

"Sorry." I groan. "Not my most graceful moment."

Joey just laughs. "It's all good. Though, Kyle, if you had wanted to get me alone, I should tell you I usually like dinner first."

We laugh and without thinking I say, "What do you call those pancakes we just ate?"

Joey's smile transforms. It widens and brightens, like a star expanding, stretching its never-ending light. And suddenly the lights around us are blue, and I can hardly breathe and that lava lamp swirls around me. I blink to focus, then remember where I am: in Joey's arms. And she hasn't moved since I landed in her lap. I dare another glance up at her. Those clear blue eyes are locked on mine.

My heart skips a beat, and I swallow hard. But my eyes drift down to her lips, and I wet my own. Joey leans in.

"Ladies."

Like a knife tearing through fabric, the air is sliced between us. We both turn to find a tall, bearded guy standing outside of the shower in front of us. He clears his throat and speaks again. "As this hall's RA, I'm going to have to ask you to please return to your side of the building."

I'm still reeling when Joey shrugs and moves to stand. Slowly, I hop off her, and we step out of the stall. My hand is still in hers when she squeezes it gently. She hands me my bag, then says, "Come on, Kyle. Let's get out of here."

❖

Joey pulls me down the hall, and I run to keep up with her long stride.

"Where are we going?" I ask while trying to ignore the sudden pitter-patter my heart is doing.

"Well, first we are going back to the cafeteria."

"Indulging in seven pancakes wasn't enough for you?"

She glances over her shoulder. "Ha ha," she drawls. "In my rush to go find you, I left my bag with the register. I need to go collect it really quick."

We turn another corner and the cafeteria doors come into view.

"And then?" I ask, unable to hide my smile and my subsequent joy at our little banter.

"You'll see."

We push through the doors and start for the register next to the salad bar.

"There you are."

Joey and I freeze. Jax and T. are sitting at a table in front of us. Joey's bag is at T's feet, along with a smaller purple backpack.

Realizing Joey and I are still holding hands, I release hers and drop mine to my side. Jax eyes us both like we've been caught coming in past curfew. She stands up slowly. "We were afraid the two of you had skipped town for the weekend."

Joey clears her throat. "No. We just…um…"

"Joey was helping me with some research in my room. Helping me grab the books off the top shelf. You know." I shrug and gesture between us. "Short girl problems."

Joey and I exchange grins.

T. stands up. "Well, whatever. You're here now. Let's get going."

I look from T. to Jax, whose dark, ripped jeans hang low on her hips as she hitches a black backpack over her shoulder. Wait a second.

"Is that mine?" I crook my neck to get a better look.

Jax smiles. "Sure is."

"Your things are all packed for the weekend," T. explains, her arms crossed matter-of-factly. The two of them standing across from us suddenly feels very much like some sort of shootout in an old Western film. But instead of guns resting in their holsters, Jax and T. are armed with eyeliner and knowing grins.

"Are we going somewhere?" asks Joey.

T. laughs, then walks over to us with the purple backpack and Joey's workout bag. She nudges Joey from behind so that they both move toward the doors. "Duh," she says and I notice the wink she throws Jax. "It's initiation night, fishes. Upperclassmen drew names to collect you guys one by one since practice ended. We're in charge of y'all for the night. And you, dear Joey, are coming with me."

Joey shoots me a look that says something like, "Remind me

why we joined this team again?" as she is herded away from me and out the door. Then fingers are moving down my arm, sending goose bumps racing over my skin. Jax is beside me. Those blue eyes roam over me like a lioness after a capture of her prey.

Jax raises an eyebrow. "Looks like you're all mine."

CHAPTER FIFTEEN

So this is where you've been hiding."

Over my shoulder, I watch Joey slip into the bathroom behind me. "Nice leggings," I say, nodding at her tiger-striped legs reflected in the mirror before me.

She grins and carefully clicks the door shut. "You don't look so bad yourself. I'm digging the eye makeup."

I dry my hands on the sink towel and meet my own gaze in the mirror, squinting at the heavy winged eyeliner drawn in thick strokes around my brown eyes. My lips are an unfamiliar crimson red and I fight what has to be the ninth urge to blot more of it off.

"Thanks. Jax did it. She said she was going for something like 'Sexy Punk Vampire.'" I shrug and pull at the *Will Dance for Tips* midriff top, which lands a good four inches above the waistline of my jeans. Joey, meanwhile, pulls on my sleeve.

"This is Jax's, too?" I nod, now moving on to my hair, which I try to flatten after T. and Jax had teased it for an hour. "Surprise, surprise." Joey sighs, then she lowers the toilet seat and sits down.

Deciding to give up on the ungodly amount of makeup I have on, I turn around to lean against the sink. "Are you trying to hide out from everybody, too?"

"Me? Hide?" Joey puts her hands up, feigning innocence. "T. was just trying to get me to 'warm up' for the dance floor tonight. There was twerking involved." She shudders. "I told her I ate bad sushi at lunch. I think Emily took pity on me and let me run to the bathroom. Plus," she adds and pulls a small bottle of cherry-flavored vodka out from behind her, "I thought we might want to 'warm up' in another sense of the word. Just a little bit, before things get started."

I grin and she takes that as a go-ahead to open the bottle.

While she pours a small shot for me in one of Emily's glasses that she'd also brought with her, my eyes rove over her legs, and I wonder if a little liquid courage isn't such a bad idea right now. Just twenty minutes ago, I was dealing with a minor panic attack as Jax did my makeup. Her eyes had been glued to my lips between each application of mascara. Despite our proximity, I couldn't see past her gaze to figure out what she was really thinking. Perhaps with a little something in my system, I won't panic every time she comes near. Maybe I can loosen up. Maybe Joey and I can even have some fun.

"My lady." Joey pulls me from my thoughts. She holds the glass in front of me and I take it. In turn, she holds the bottle up between us in a toast.

"Here's to a night we probably won't remember," I say, taking her cue and clinking my glass against the bottle.

"And here's to spending it with someone I hope to never forget."

The shot almost comes back up as I sputter. Fortunately, I clasp my hand over my mouth fast enough, my eyes watering as the liquid rises, and I force it to fall again down my throat.

The bathroom door slams open. Jax stands in the doorway, a wild look on her face. She grabs my hand, making me almost drop the glass, and I'm being pulled out the bathroom and away from Joey.

"Come on, girls," she says over her shoulder. "It's show time."

CHAPTER SIXTEEN

"I don't feel very well." Callie wipes her mouth off on the leopard print poncho she's wearing, then fans herself. "Is it hot in here to you guys?"

I choke back my shot of rum and take a breath. Sweat coats my forehead.

"It is a little warm," Joey says. The three of us stand in a circle with Mary and Sarah; the five freshmen huddled together at the counter in Emily's kitchen. Each of us is in the most outrageous outfits the upperclassmen could find. Callie, for instance, looks sort of grandmother-meets-sexy-leopard. Meanwhile, Mary sports a giant glittering star in the middle of her forehead and a slick jogging suit. Sarah is the replica of an '80s cover girl.

For the last hour, we've been in the kitchen taking shots. "Five newbies, five rounds," T. had joyfully exclaimed before pouring rum into five shot glasses. Number four currently rolls around in my stomach as we set our glasses back down. T., Jax, and Haley pour us the final round. Emily comes up behind me, patting my shoulder.

"You guys are doing great," she says.

Callie burps. "Do we get kicked off the team if we puke?"

T. nods. "Absolutely."

"No," Emily says, shooting T. a look. "Nobody gets kicked off the team for puking."

"Drink up, ladies." Jax and Haley hand out the shots.

"Oh, God," mutters Mary.

"We can do it," Joey says, but even she seems wary of the liquor as we hold up the glasses in a quick cheer. "Last one."

We throw the shots back. Mary and I cough. The rest of the team, scattered around Emily's apartment, cheers as we gasp and hold on to the counter, chairs, anything to keep ourselves upright. Callie grips her stomach, while Joey tries to look calm, but her smile is anxious.

"Everybody ready?" Emily asks, and the team starts to file out of her apartment. I exchange glances with Joey. T. rinses the glasses while Haley grabs her keys. Jax saunters up to our group and throws her arms around me and Mary.

"I think they're ready." She turns to me. "Right, Kyle?" She's so close I can smell her perfume again. The scent mixes with the smell of lingering rum. All I manage to do is nod. "Let's go then!"

❖

Somehow, the fourteen of us pile into two cars and make it to the strip, the street everybody frequents on weekends located about a mile from campus. Bars and clubs line both sides of the small block. I'd driven down this street during the day and had to ask Emily if any of the places were actually open for business. She had laughed and taken me down it again after practice one night. The change was like a stadium come to life right before a game: the street was lit with neon signs, bands and DJs blared their music through open doorways, and the student body roamed like thirsty cattle. And now our soccer team, five of us in our outlandish regalia, take to the streets, and wander over to one of the bars.

Emily motions for all of us to follow her. Mary grabs hold of Callie, who has looked pale since leaving the apartment. I walk behind Joey and feel a slight push against my back. Jax smiles when I glance over my shoulder.

"How you feeling?"

"All right," I reply. "Though it doesn't seem fair we're the only ones drinking."

Jax laughs, nudging me past the doorman after flashing him a series of IDs. "Just you wait, cutie."

T. calls us over to a large table she's made by pushing three together. Haley and the other upperclassmen watch us with amused grins as we take our seats. I settle between Joey and Callie. Mary is on her other side, next to Emily. Sarah sits between her and Jax, who hands Emily a baseball cap.

"Please tell me we get to leave here and go play slow pitch," Sarah says, groaning and adjusting her pink skirt and leg warmers.

"Not quite," grins T.

Emily clears her throat. "Ladies. Inside this cap are five tasks. One for each of you. You will have until two a.m. to complete your task." She shakes the ball cap, and several slips of paper bounce around inside. "Once you have chosen your task, it is yours and yours alone. You may not switch with a teammate."

"Oh, God," Callie moans.

I look warily from Emily to Callie. Joey nudges my knee beneath the table. "We got this, short stack." She leans toward me for a second, then sways back. I laugh and blink a few times to keep her in focus, the rum starting to buzz inside my head.

"Feeling all right there?" I reach out to steady her.

"Never better."

Jax grabs the cap from Emily. "Joey, you first." She shoves it across the table. Her expression gives nothing away as Joey grabs a paper. When she opens it, she reads aloud: "Get five strangers' phone numbers." She flourishes the paper. "Easy breezy." Jax leans back in her chair and hands the cap back to Emily.

"We'll see," Emily muses, holding the hat out to Mary, then Sarah.

"Kiss the bartender," Mary reads, then blushes profusely.

Sarah grimaces. "Take two body shots. One off a teammate, the other off a stranger." I sit wide-eyed as they read off their tasks. T. and Haley giggle as Emily passes the cap to Callie. She unfolds a strip of paper and reads, "Dance on top of the bar two times."

More cheers from our table as Callie folds the paper and looks around the crowded bar. "Won't I get kicked out for that?"

"Nah," T. says, leaning back in her chair. "Trust me. I was up there three times my freshman year."

"Kyle," Emily says. I look across the table at her. "Good luck." She smiles gently, and I feel a small rush as I reach into the hat and grab the last paper.

I take a deep breath. Oh, God. "Don't leave the dance floor for thirty minutes."

T. and Haley high-five each other. I stare at my paper, then look up at Emily. "Really?" I ask. "Emily, I hate the dance floor. I hate dancing."

Emily just shrugs and goes to give the cap back to Katie at the other end of the table.

"At least you don't have to dance on the bar," says Callie.

There's a thud as five more shot glasses land loudly on the table, courtesy of Jax and T.

"Drink up, fishes. And get to it."

❖

"How are you doing?" Emily shouts over the music thumping around us. We're standing in one of the rooms off the main bar—a dimly lit black box with tall tables lining the walls and a dance floor in the middle. Multicolor lights strobe overhead, making the people on the dance floor look like they're moving faster and slower at the same time. My stomach is holding up surprisingly well, but my head spins when I walk. So I've parked at a table on the edge of the dance floor, dreading the time I step onto it and can't step off again for thirty minutes.

"I'm good," I holler back at Emily. "Not as good as Mary, though." I nod to the back corner, where Mary has been lip-locked for the last twenty minutes with some guy I recognize from my geology class.

Emily smiles. "See? Not all of our intentions from this night are bad!" The music changes. A fast, techno beat surges over the dance floor. A few people wander off, but the majority begin jumping erratically and throwing their arms up, somehow completely in sync with the music. "You almost ready?" Emily asks with a nod to the dance floor. "It's one fifteen. Almost out of time."

"Thank you, Time Master. I had almost forgotten."

Emily laughs then stands and gives my hip a nudge. "Go on. You look hot. You never know what might happen out there." Then she disappears into a crowd at the edge of the room. I watch the people on the dance floor. Even with all the liquor surging through me, I don't know if I can loosen up enough to dance like them. Not after spending the night trying to decipher Jax's smirks and flirtatious comments. It hasn't helped that every time I've tried to speak to her tonight she just laughs and disappears into a crowd. And then there's the fact that I've felt, I don't know, strange each time I've caught Joey off in some corner of the bar, saying whatever she's saying to get a phone number from someone. I know it's just the task, but I couldn't help feeling on edge each time I saw her talking to somebody.

"Hey."

I jump and turn to find Joey. "Sorry, didn't mean to scare you." She sits on the stool nearby. "It's the leggings, isn't it? I told T. they were too much."

"It's okay." I laugh. "I was just thinking about you, actually."

Joey's eyes, which had been roving the dance floor, turn to me. "Is that so?"

I bite my tongue. Damn rum. "Um, well, yeah. About you and Mary and all of this. Some night, huh?"

She nods, then gestures to the dance floor. "You heading out there soon?"

"Yes." I wave a hand dramatically toward the crowd. "Eventually."

Joey stands back up when she sees T. coming our way. "Crap, I better get moving. T. won't let me be until I've collected my last number." I nod and she walks past me. Her voice is low when she pauses next to my ear. "Save one dance for me."

She squeezes my shoulder before heading into the crowd. Feeling slightly dazed imagining what dancing with Joey feels like—our bodies flush against one another—T. walks up to me, a beer in her hand. She shakes me from my thoughts when she says, "I swear, for someone so tall, she sure knows how to lay low." Then she looks at me. "Better get moving, Kyle. No time to waste."

"I know, I just—"

"Am being a pussy?"

"That's not quite how I would put it."

T. rolls her eyes and drags me with her. My Converse shoes skid along the tile until they slip on the ledge that leads up to the wooden dance floor. Speakers rage over our heads, and the lights make me dizzy. "Have fun!" T. shouts before vanishing behind a group of girls who I've seen dancing since midnight.

I sway, shuffling my feet as the music changes again. This time it's rap, and several people start dropping low, doing things with their hips I didn't even know were possible. A group of guys scream the lyrics and several people pair up and begin to, for lack of a better description, grind on one another. I close my eyes and will time to move faster. Eventually, the music changes. A sensual pop ballad with a club beat mash-up throbs overhead.

Suddenly, a pair of hands snakes around my waist. My eyes shoot open. For a moment, I think it might be Joey. But the hands are smaller and feel greedy as they tug me closer, making our hips bump. Whoever she is, she stands flush behind me and holds me firmly, putting me in rhythm with her body. Heat rushes to my center as one hand roves up my waist and holds my exposed midriff. I move my feet to keep up and find it hard to breathe. After a few seconds, I brave a look over my shoulder.

"Having fun?" Jax grins. Her face is so close to my own, her eyes look like diamonds in their circle of black eyeliner. Her breath is bitter from beer, but her perfume is sweet. The lights whirl, and she spins me to face her. The dance floor is packed with bodies bumping into us on either side. Jax pulls me to her and my chest bumps hers as she sways her hips against mine. The music wraps around us and her fingers dance up my back, to the base of my neck, and into my hair. I feel like I'm in a dream. Her hips slow and her cheek presses against mine. I close my eyes, and she pulls me closer. My chin rests atop her shoulder as the music moves us. Her hand slides under the back of my shirt.

"Wait." I open my eyes and pull back.

"What's wrong?"

I stare at her, not sure what I want to say. Then I glance over her shoulder. Joey is standing just off the dance floor. Our eyes lock, and it's like a bucket of ice water soaks me head to toe. I step back.

"What is it?" Jax asks. I look from her to Joey, who turns to walk back toward the bar. Trepidation freezes the words in my throat when I go to call after her.

I move to chase after Joey, but Jax grabs me. "Not so fast." She shakes her head, smiling. "Time's not up yet."

"But…"

She laughs, her blond hair glowing under the pulsating lights. I feel sick. All I want is to go after Joey; it should be her I'm dancing with. I want to find Emily. Tell her I'm done. Tell her to take me back to my dorm. But Jax has a firm grip on one of my arms, which she wraps around her waist. "Dance with me," she purrs into my ear. My heart races and I'm sweating. I try to move again, but she keeps a tight hold on me. "Relax, Kyle." She runs a hand over my temple, then traces her fingers between my breasts. "We're having fun, aren't we?"

I swallow and look around the dance floor. I'm really not sure if I am anymore.

Chapter Seventeen

By some bizarre miracle, the events of initiation night become a quick and distant memory over the next few weeks. Nobody on the team speaks a word of what happened. Well, nobody except for Emily, who was thrilled at her unexpected matchmaking abilities.

"Can you believe Mary and that guy from your class are dating now? Who would have guessed?" she says one night after a game during the first week of October. "I guess you never know what will happen between two people."

Even though I'm pretty sure their meeting had less to do with Emily and more to do with alcohol, I let her go through our soccer season feeling accomplished. And boy, was the season moving along at record speed. After that night, I could barely catch a moment for myself, things were so busy. At first, I had been worried, believing an awkward run-in with Joey was inevitable. But the next morning, when we'd all woken up at Emily's apartment, she only exchanged bewildered looks with me about being strewn out on the floor with makeup smeared over both our faces and pounding headaches.

"All right?" I had asked as Callie groaned from somewhere near the corner of the room.

Joey had stretched. "Just a few bumps and bruises. Don't remember much of last night after that first shot at the bar."

I hoped then that she had forgotten all about what had happened on the dance floor. Admittedly, even I was starting to confuse the final few hours of that night with dreams. It was too hard to believe that Jax had been out on the dance floor with me. Her hands on my body were now only memories curling around the corners of my mind like smoke—too faint to hold for more than a moment.

And she wasn't giving anything away as the weeks rolled by. Fall played out like any other school semester. If I saw Jax on campus, she smiled slyly but continued on her way. Meanwhile, Joey and I chatted easily when we ran into each other in the dorm, but there were no more Spanish study sessions. By November, I was starting to feel as if the whole night might have been some crazy collective hallucination. Regardless of what happened that night, it certainly boded well for team chemistry. We ended the season 9–1 and now had a week off for Thanksgiving before playoffs. Coach Gandy gave us an encouraging end-of-season speech and sent us on our holiday with reminders to not eat too much turkey and to keep up our workout regimen.

With the university only giving us three days for the break, I opted to stay in town. But while I'm sitting in my dorm, reading over some notes for geology, I decide to call home.

"Hi, honey." My mom's voice sounds tired on the other end of the line.

"Hi, Mom. Happy Thanksgiving."

"Happy Thanksgiving, sweetie. Uncle Will and Aunt Stacy will be here tomorrow. With the dogs, of course. I'm making a ranch chicken casserole. You sure you won't be able to make it home?"

I flip through the pages of my textbook mindlessly. "I'm sure. Coach has us meeting on Friday for a team bonding exercise. We have a playoff game next Tuesday. I guess she doesn't want us to lose any momentum from the season."

There's a rustling on her end of the line. Kevin's voice sounds somewhere behind her.

"Do you want to talk to your brother?"

"In a second. How's Dad?"

"Oh, you know." She sighs, and I'm not sure if it's over the paperwork she's probably going through that warrants it or my bringing up my dad. "He's busy. Traveling a lot for his work. He'll be in Austin next week."

"Maybe he can swing by and watch our game." I consider mentioning he hasn't returned the text message I sent three days ago with the same request, then decide against it.

"Sure, honey. Maybe." Her voice is distracted, and I know I'm reaching for straws when I ask about my dad. "Here's your brother."

I change the phone over to my other ear.

"Hey, what's going on?"

"We're building a robot in Technology Club using old video game equipment."

"That's cool."

"Yeah." It's quiet for another second. "How's school?"

I close my textbook and stare at the ceiling. "It's going well. Soccer is fun."

"Is Emily making sure you don't get kicked off the team?" he asks.

I laugh. "I am a very dedicated athlete, thank you very much. Even with all of the team's complications."

"Complications?"

I scrunch up my face. "Did I say complications? Oh, you know. I just mean like fighting for starting positions and all of that."

"Oh."

I lay back against my pillow. I'm tempted to tell him. What could be so bad about letting Kevin know more? He already knows so much. Why not talk to him about the team? About Joey. Or whatever it is Jax is doing. He's been so wonderful, not saying a word to Mom and Dad since I've been gone. Maybe he would even have some uncanny advice, being so oddly sage for a sixteen-year-old.

Then, as if she knew I was thinking about her, there's a knock on my door followed by Joey poking her head inside. "Hey, Taco Night in the caf. Move it or lose it, short stack." She grins, then disappears back into the hallway.

"Sounds tasty," Kevin says from the other end of the line.

I nod. "Yeah. I had better go. Don't want to miss the good stuff."

"No problem. Well, see you at Christmas, then?"

I smile. "Absolutely. I won't leave you alone with Mom and Dad two holidays in a row."

"Better not."

After wishing him a happy Thanksgiving, I bounce off the bed and throw on my sandals. Then I race out of my dorm to catch up with Joey.

CHAPTER EIGHTEEN

"Will you pass the popcorn, Kyle?"

With my eyes still on the screen, I hand the large bowl over to Emily. She takes it, adjusting her legs to slide underneath her on the couch cushion next to me. I rearrange a bit to give her room.

"I'm so glad we don't play football," Sarah says from somewhere on the floor near the television. Half the room nods, and Joey says, "No kidding."

"It's weird to think that all that racism existed only, like, fifty years ago," Haley says through a mouthful of popcorn on the other side of the room. "I mean, I know racism still exists today, but this was so intense and was when our grandparents were our age. It's wild to think about."

I grab a handful of popcorn by reaching over Emily to where she'd propped the bowl up on the arm of the couch.

"I love this movie, though," Callie chimes in from the La-Z-Boy to our left. "Such a sports classic. I'm glad Coach suggested we do this."

More heads bob in agreement throughout Emily's dark living room. The team has gathered in her apartment for Coach's "strongly encouraged" team bonding night the weekend after Thanksgiving. Our first playoff game is fast approaching. And her grand idea: movie night. Specifically, something sports related to get us motivated for the upcoming game. Emily has a fairly healthy collection of DVDs, and after a ten-minute debate about what to watch, we decided on *Remember the Titans.*

We all watch in silence until the bathroom door opens off

the side of the living room, filling the space by the TV with a momentary rectangle of light.

"Sorry," Jax mutters before clicking the light off, and stepping carefully through our teammates, she makes her way back to her seat. Which is on the couch. Next to me.

I had to give myself a pat on the back, though. We are about half an hour into the movie, and I haven't yet sweated profusely, turned an obnoxious shade of red, or said anything I'd regret. Since initiation night, I haven't known how to act around her. She's been like a book written in a language I don't know, shrouded in mystery despite the letters screaming at me.

Taking a breath, I try to get my body to maintain its composure as she settles into the couch. Like Emily, Jax folds her legs underneath her, but instead of leaning toward the arm of the couch, she leans toward me and rests her right arm on the back of the couch so that her forearm stretches behind me.

There are more minutes of silence while we all watch the film. My throat is dry, so I reach forward and grab my Gatorade from the coffee table. When I lean back against the couch, I feel fingers brush the back of my neck. My eyes flicker over to Emily, but she is practically hugging the popcorn bowl, and her eyes are glossed over, lost in the movie.

Jax's fingers don't move for a second, then it is as if a thousand pins prick every inch of my body. The tips of her fingers sweep lightly along my neck, moving down toward the line of my T-shirt, making soft circles on my skin.

My breath quickens, and I don't dare move to put my drink back after taking a quick sip from it. I look over at Jax, but her eyes are still on the TV, although her lips are curled up in the slightest of smiles.

That's how we spend the rest of the movie. Eventually (and thankfully) my body relaxes against her fingers, which never stop their movement on my neck. At times, she would move them up into my hair, massaging the top of my neck, and I couldn't help but enjoy the way her fingers weaved themselves in and out of the base of my ponytail. Occasionally, my neck rolled back involuntarily at Jax's touch, and I swear I heard her snicker slightly at what she was doing to me.

When the credits roll at ten o'clock, I practically leap on top of Emily when T. flicks on the lights.

"Whoa," Emily says, "you okay?"

I look sideways at Jax, who has her head low to tug her shoes back on.

"Yeah, sorry," I mutter as everyone stands up, a few girls stretching and moving around to find their things.

She clears her throat. "All right, everyone," Emily says, looking from me to the packed room. "Big game next week. I hope this helped motivate you guys. See y'all at practice. Coach said no weights tomorrow morning, just a field day at four."

I walk past Jax and into the kitchen to toss my Gatorade bottle in Emily's recycling bin. I hear some of the girls say their good-byes before they file out of the apartment.

"Thanks for coming over," Emily calls, her voice at that octave where I can tell she just got a huge rush from hosting a successful night.

"Yeah, thanks for letting us crash," Joey says from behind me in the doorway. Then she adds, "See you, short stack." I walk back into the living room and give her a wave.

"See you, Joey."

She smiles and her hands slide into her pockets. For a second, I think she's about to say more, then she decides not to and turns to head out behind the others.

"I'm gonna make sure they can get out the apartment gate," Emily says, throwing on a jacket over her blouse before moving toward the door. "Be back in a few."

I pick some pillows up off the floor. "I'll help clean up."

"Thanks," she replies happily before closing the door behind her.

I rearrange some of the couch cushions, punching out the indentions where we'd been sitting before bending over to pick up some of Emily's bed pillows she'd let everyone borrow. A voice behind me makes me jump.

"Hey."

I whip around, and Jax is walking out from the hallway. She holds her cell phone up. "Forgot this in the bathroom." I nod as she moves toward me. I take a step back until my heels bump into the couch. She doesn't stop until she's right in front of me, in what most people would consider their personal bubble.

She slides her phone into her back pocket and leaves her hand resting back there so that she's posed like some casual-looking model in the window of a department store. "Did you enjoy the movie?"

"Um, yeah," I stammer, realizing I am close enough to see that her lips are glossed and that she has a cluster of freckles on her left shoulder next to the strap of her black tank.

"Good," she says, and I meet her eyes only to see them flicker down to my lips. "Me, too." She takes another step forward (which I didn't think was possible) and I smell her perfume—sweet, like cotton candy this time. She reaches out and brushes away some strands that have fallen loose from my ponytail.

I think I stop breathing when she leans forward.

"I *swear,* Katie really should have to do that driver's test again. She about rammed the gate when—"

Jax takes a big step away from me, and I turn to find a wide-eyed Emily standing in her entryway. "Um, sorry," she says, her eyes going from me to Jax. "Did I interrupt…something?"

"No, of course not," Jax says so nonchalantly it makes me wonder if everything that just happened was just my extremely vivid imagination.

I look at Emily, then back at Jax as she grabs her sweatshirt off the kitchen counter and moves past both of us.

"Thanks for tonight. Was fun," she says, then shoots me a smile over her shoulder. "See you, Kyle." Then she's gone, the door clicking shut behind her.

Emily stares at the door, then turns to me. "What the hell was that?"

I blink a few times, my head still whirling. "I have no idea."

"Want to talk about it?"

I run a hand over my hair and down my ponytail. My hand lands briefly on the base of my neck, where Jax's fingers had spent the better part of the evening. My stomach flutters at the thought of it.

"Kyle?" Emily says, pulling me out of my thoughts.

"She's just…so confusing!"

"Who is?"

"Jax."

Emily nods, crossing her arms. "I hear she has a knack for that."

I brush more hair from my face, agitated. "It's just so hard to understand. And Joey—"

"Joey?" Emily perks up. "She's great. Did you see the video she and Sarah posted online the other day? The one where they call out the guys' team because they said we wouldn't make playoffs this year? I died laughing."

The video of Joey doing her original rap song did make me laugh. It came out four days ago, and I *may* have watched it several times since then. "She does know how to pull off a backward cap."

Emily winks at me. "So, what's the big deal, then?"

All I can do is shake my head, my thoughts too worked up. Yes, Joey and I have been in a really great place lately. After all the run-ins and almost kisses since the semester started, she and I are back on track. Things have calmed down after initiation night. *The night Jax found me on the dance floor…*

"It's just that…Jax is acting strange toward me," I finally say, fidgeting next to the kitchen counter.

"Who doesn't Jax act weird with?" Emily replies, shrugging. "That girl is a mystery wrapped in an enigma."

"I wish she wasn't."

Emily puts one hand on her hip. "What do you mean?"

But I'm overwhelmed again. My face is hot and my head feels as if it's stuck in a blender, whirring a mile a minute with no one around to unplug it. My breath comes too quickly and my eyes start to water.

"Whoa, Kyle. Take a breath." Emily reaches out, running her hands down my forearms.

"Um…I'm good. Really. I'll call you, okay?" I say quickly, hurrying toward the door. As I open it, Emily grabs my arm, making me pause.

"Hey," she says softly, her eyes meeting mine. "Don't forget," her grip turns gentle, "you can talk to me. School problems. Family problems. Girl…problems," she adds. "Okay? It's still you and me."

I smile, and my shoulders relax. "Thanks, Em." Then I open the door. "I'll see you tomorrow, okay?"

She pulls me in for a quick hug. "See you tomorrow." Then she lets me go and closes her apartment door.

CHAPTER NINETEEN

I finish the final practice response on my geology study worksheet, then lean back in my blue plastic library chair. Fluorescent lights give the impression it's two p.m., not almost eleven at night. Now that the first week of December is here, it seems the entire student body has stopped sleeping and bathing and has taken up permanent residence in the campus library.

I am one among many zombie-like students, having officially dived into my first foray of "Blackout Week" on campus—a time when there are no parties, no athletic events, just studying. I remember calling Emily around this time last year with a question about the soccer team's schedule before I had signed on to play. I got her voice mail three times before finally she called me back at one a.m., four cups of coffee into an all-nighter with her mass communication class. How anyone survives their freshman year of college is pretty impressive, especially those who are student athletes. Between preseason and then actual season workouts and games, I'm not really sure how I've managed to juggle everything. Or where my first semester has gone. It seems to have turned into a blur of early morning runs, weekend buses to games, and unresolved hormonal confusion. Though that last part might just relate specifically to me.

Things have, thankfully, been calm in regard to my constant need to avoid any and all feelings and emotions. The season helped, I think. With Coach Gandy's strict schedule, there wasn't much time to think about everything since August. If I wasn't in class, I was in the weight room. If I wasn't in the weight room, I was on the field. If I wasn't on the field, I was in the library. Now, though, with the season having just ended in a heartbreaking semifinal loss, here I am, ignoring my confused libido with two days left before winter finals. Just another ordinary member of the student body nestled between thick stacks of musty textbooks piled atop brown laminated tables, coffee cups, and energy drinks glistening under the bright lights.

I started the evening with a few of my classmates from geology. We went over a review packet Professor Kaufman handed out last week. We each took a section, spending an hour poring over our semester notes for the answers. Eventually Roxanna, a girl who usually sat next to me in class, decided we should call it a night at around ten thirty. But I wasn't ready to pack it up just yet. Mostly because Coach Gandy's emphatic postseason emails about good grades and work ethics continue to echo in my mind.

I rub my eyes, lean back again in my chair, and roll my neck to stretch it. My tired eyes rove over the rest of the students littered across the second floor of the library. Many sit scattered throughout the old brown tables, their plastic chairs occasionally dragging along the old blue carpet. Lines of computers glow softly to my left. To my right, ten rows of bookshelves stretch thirty yards toward the other end of the room, where large windows face out to the Student Union. Through the books, I spot the occasional browsing student meandering down the aisles. The sound of beanbags shifting on the floors can be heard from behind the shelves. This was a new idea from the university to stay modern and create "healthy, student friendly study spaces." Of course, it's mostly just led to couples reinforcing the tried-and-true tradition of making out in the stacks. I glance to the back wall a few feet behind me when another shifting sound draws my attention, and my eyes land on a familiar pair of tennis shoes.

Leaning back a bit farther, my neck stretches to confirm my suspicion. Joey lounges in an oversized, purple beanbag to my right. Her long legs stretch toward me, and I can just see the top of her forehead while the rest of her face is buried in a calculus textbook. Several journals and stray papers are strewn next to her, along with a water bottle. I grin, then set all four chair legs back on the floor.

I close my notebook, collecting it and my geology books into a pile before sliding them under my arm as I stand.

"Room for one more?" I ask, using my toe to poke the bottom of her foot.

Joey moves the book down onto her chest, her clear eyes sparkling when she greets me. "I've actually started charging," she replies, gesturing to an empty collection of beanbags nearby. "Five bucks for thirty minutes." She sits up, adjusting so that her legs are crossed. Then she pats the now empty indention in the beanbag next to her. "But I might be able to offer you a discount," she adds with a grin, and I join her.

"So," I say, leaning back against the cool faux-leather, my legs out in front of me. I throw one arm behind my head. "I see you read Coach's motivational email today, too?"

Joey snorts. "Sure did. 'Great season, ladies,'" she begins, quoting our coach's email. "'Third place is something to be proud of, but also something to improve upon. So work hard and keep an eye out for the winter workout schedule before you all head home. And don't forget to study!'" Joey finishes our coach's speech with a fist pump across her chest.

"She certainly respects the importance of grades," I say. "Not always a common trait amongst coaches."

Joey nods and fingers through the textbook splayed out in front of her. She sighs. "Yeah. If only I could get my head around this stuff." I sit up as she thumps on the pages. "I was fine at math in high school. I mean, I was no star, but I could get by. I really didn't think I would need a math credit as a political science major, but I guess when you do mediocre all your life, they want to make sure you can still count to ten."

I watch her frown at a notebook she pulls closer to us. The lines on her forehead surprise me. Joey is usually the epitome of confident, especially on the soccer field. She hasn't wavered all season, and she never let on if she was struggling with something.

I reach out, nudging her knee with my hand. "Well, hey, if you like, I'm happy to help you out."

"Yeah?" she says, still focused on her notes. "I'm sure you've been here awhile. You probably want to go home."

This is more like the Joey I know. The lone wolf at the end of the field. The "I can take care of it myself" goalie, who never lets anyone help her.

"I don't mind," I say with a shrug. "I actually took calculus as a junior. Math has always made sense to me."

Joey sits back against the beanbag, leaning on her left arm so that she mirrors me. She glances at her sports watch. "I don't know. It's already late. We'd only have an hour before the library closes, and I don't know if that's enough time to help me." She looks down sheepishly. "It may be futile."

I hold her gaze when she looks back up at me, and wonder at her stubbornness. "You don't have to do everything on your own, you know."

Joey raises an eyebrow, and for a second, I see that look again. The same one she gave me all those months ago. And I feel myself returning it. But, as if she senses us falling back into its grasp, the look vanishes, and she lowers her gaze. But she's smiling. Genuine. Bright. The smile I saw when we first met in my dorm room in July.

"All right," she finally says. "But it won't be easy." She sits up, pulling her textbook and notes closer.

"Good," I reply, stealing a sip from her water bottle. "I like a challenge."

❖

I reach over Joey to glance at her notebook, where she's answering one of the practice problems I wrote for her. Scanning the page, I nod.

"Yeah. And so, to find the derivative, you have to—"

"Multiply the number with the exponent."

"And then…"

"And then." Joey bites her bottom lip in concentration. "Subtract one from the exponent?"

"Exactly." I shift, bumping her shoulder as I straighten my back. It's been so long since I've done any of this math, I've forgotten how much I actually enjoy it. "Think of it like this," I say, and Joey leans back to listen. "Math is a lot like poetry." I ignore her raised brow and continue. "Poetry likes to use a lot of flourishing language to say very little. Take Shakespeare and his sonnets, for example. They're beautiful, but they all essentially talk about the same thing: love. And he uses a lot of words and fancy metaphors to basically say 'I love you,' to whomever he's writing about." Joey's gaze is trained on me instead of her notebook, an inquisitive eyebrow raised. "What I'm trying to say is, all of those flowery words are simply the means to an end. They're the path that gets you to the final message. Math, or calculus, in this case, works the same way. All formulas, like this one," I say, gesturing to her notebook, "are just road signs pointing you where to find the answer. So don't get hung up, stay focused on where you want to end, and it will be easy to follow."

After a moment, Joey looks back at her notebook, her lips pursed. "Okay, so if that's the case," she mutters, starting to scribble under her practice problem, "if I do this…" I watch her scrawl numbers into a formula, then work a couple minutes to solve it. As she writes the final answer at the bottom, I can't contain my excitement.

"Joey, that's it!" I grab her knee and lean into her shoulder, my excitement bubbling over.

She bumps me back. "Really? I got it?"

"Yes! That's the right answer."

Joey grins at her notebook, then turns to me. "Thanks, Kyle."

I notice then how similar the shade of her eyes is to the fluorite crystal we examined in geology the other day. Not the whole crystal, I decide, but the tiny sliver toward the end where the rock transitions from light blue to translucent. The lump in my throat threatens to race up and over my tongue, spilling out all of the ways she has made my heart skip in the last hour. "Um, you're welcome."

After clearing her throat, Joey adds, "Though, I have to say, I doubt you've read many of Shakespeare's sonnets. You do know they're not all about love, right?"

I shrug. "I slept through most of English senior year."

Joey nods. "I can tell. Remind me to never ask for your help when I take British literature next semester."

"Hey, my analogy helped, didn't it?"

Joey is still watching me, her eyes bright.

My throat tightens again.

She shakes her head in disbelief, and I fight the urge to brush back her hair that's fallen loose over her face.

Once we pack up, we take the elevators down and walk outside.

The bracing night air feels good on my face as we stroll quietly side by side across campus. Each step we take is so charged that gloved hands tremble, creating a force that drifts our hands closer. When my pinkie bumps hers, Joey turns to me.

"Race you back?"

Our dorm is only fifty yards away now. I hadn't even realized how long we'd been walking. I exhale, the mist warm when it passes my lips. "Loser has to try the Jell-O in the cafeteria?"

"You're on."

Then, like two shooting stars, we speed into the night with billows of laughter streaming behind us and across the lawns. An exhilaration fills my body and threatens to pick me up and carry me faraway. And as I watch Joey dash ahead of me, I wonder if I might ever touch the ground again.

CHAPTER TWENTY

"All right, so we've got *Elf* or *White Christmas*."

I glance up at Emily from the other side of the kitchen counter. "Seriously? Those are, like, the two most opposite of Christmas movies."

"They both feature singing," Emily counters, arranging herself against one of her couch cushions.

"And that's where the similarities end." The microwave beeps behind me and I grab the fresh popcorn before pouring the contents into a bowl. "The question really is: do we want a modern-day funny take on Santa and his elves, or a holiday classic with a killer soundtrack and Bing Crosby's signature crooning?"

"Well, Zooey Deschanel isn't bad to look at," Emily says as I join her on the couch. "Don't you agree?"

I give her a look. "Yes, I have to agree. She looks pretty cute in this one."

Emily picks up both of our cocoa-filled mugs from her side table and hands one to me. She carefully clinks our cups together. "Congratulations, Kyle."

I take a sip. "What in the world for?"

"That is the first time you have openly admitted to finding another woman attractive."

I chuckle and enjoy the warm feeling of the mug between my hands. Real winters—believe it or not—do actually blow through Texas every once in a while. Sure, we don't get piles of snow up to our waists, but we get the occasional falling of white stuff that turns into slush with which we happily form lopsided and sad-looking snowmen. And it can get cold. Really cold. So, thanks to this current winter weather and the fact that it is still a couple days until I head home for winter break, Emily and I are taking advantage of the end of the semester to indulge in a movie night.

The wind lets out a howl as Emily breaks me out of my musings. "Okay, Zooey takes the cake. *Elf* it is."

I snuggle deeper into her apartment couch. Emily pops the DVD in, and a soft *ding* goes off underneath me. My phone has found its way under my legs, and I fish it out to find Joey's photo on my screen. I open up the message.

Hey, short stack. Did you already leave for Xmas? Just knocked on your dorm room but no answer.

Quickly, I type out a response.

No. I'm still here. At Emily's. Will be home around eleven. What's up?

Her reply comes in just as Emily plops down next to me and presses play.

Nada. Just curious :) Have a good night.

"Jax?" Emily asks me.

"Joey," I say and Emily's face goes from vague disdain to excitement in half a second. "Oh," she says with a smile. "How's she doing? You two going to get together over the holiday?"

I glance at Emily as the previews play onscreen. Emily always insists on watching them despite the fact that the menu options allow you to skip them. Ever since I spilled the beans back in August on what happened at Alex's party, every time Joey is mentioned, Emily lights up like the Fourth of July. And even though she says she understands my trepidation following the events of that evening, I feel like she still doesn't quite get it. Even though I've explained to her over and over that, while I enjoyed the kiss, I'm still not ready to take that leap. Not with Joey. Not with anyone, really. Still, Emily continues to be supportive of whatever Joey and I are…or aren't.

"Em, Joey and I are just friends."

She rolls her eyes. "Yeah, because 'just friends' eat breakfast together in the corner of the cafeteria every day, giggling like they've got a dirty little secret."

I scoff. "We do not giggle!"

"Fine. Call it a chuckle." I shoot her a look, but she continues.

"And, *amiga*, I see those eyes of yours roaming down her legs during warm-ups."

"Wow, Em, she's not a piece of meat."

"Aw, that's so sweet of you. Defending her like that."

I thwack her with a couch pillow, and she nearly spills her cocoa before crying out. "Okay, okay! I was just saying. And who knows," she adds, "maybe it would be fun for you guys to get together over the next few weeks. She's only an hour and a half from your hometown."

"Mm-hmm," I mumble as the opening credits finally roll.

Emily throws up her hands. "It's just a suggestion. You know, just doing the best friend thing and all that."

"Sip your cocoa, best friend, before I get my hands on another pillow."

"Such force," she replies. "I can see why Joey likes you."

Emily has just enough time to set her cup down before a yellow throw pillow hits her square in the face.

❖

About two hours, one pillow fight, and four consumed cups of cocoa later, we say good-bye, and I hurriedly run six feet out to my car that's parked outside her apartment. My bare hands fumble with my keys, and then I collapse into my seat and start the ignition. Traditional holiday music starts while I let the engine warm up. Clicking on the defroster, I sit back for a minute, enjoying the warm air coming through the vents.

After a little while, I go to put my car in reverse when I notice something sitting on the other side of my windshield. The defrosted, watermelon-sized space through which I can now see outside frames something sitting on the opposite side of the glass. I step out carefully onto the frozen parking lot, glancing around and finding nobody, I pick up a small white box, quite cold to the touch. I think back. It definitely was not on my car on the drive over to Emily's. I misplace things from time to time, but I'm not so bad as to leave something on the front of my vehicle.

The engine purrs while I hold the box, which is no bigger than my hand, up to the slivers of moonlight peeking through my windows. I click on the overhead light to get a better look and notice my name written on the top. When I open it, there's a small leather pouch, and underneath that, a folded piece of paper. Setting both the box and pouch down in my lap, I unfold the paper to find a slanted but neatly handwritten note:

> *Kyle,*
>
> *Since you have a strange (but oddly endearing) fascination with rocks, I thought you might like this. It's an amethyst with hematite inclusions—whatever that means. I still say stars are better than rocks, but according to this little stone, it looks like the two can coincide with one another pretty beautifully. Anyway, I was just thinking about you. Merry Christmas.*
>
> *Joey*

Setting the paper down in the passenger seat, I grab the pouch out of the box. Untying it, I turn it over, and out falls a gemstone about the size of a quarter, wrapped intricately in a silver frame that's attached to a chain, creating an absolutely stunning necklace. I hold the stone up to the moonlight. I don't think I've ever seen anything like it. Clouds of purple and black whirl around each other while flecks of gold and white are splashed across its many faces. Faint swirls of brown give the impression that some faraway galaxy has been captured and compacted to fit onto this one tiny, triangular stone.

Rocks and stars.

I slip the necklace around my neck. The chain feels cool and the heavy stone settles neatly onto my chest. From where it lands, a heat radiates outward, making every part of me feel as if I'm packed with fireworks ready to burst. My fingertips dance along the steering wheel and I actually squeal before leaning back into my seat, completely giddy. Then I rev the engine and turn up the music until I'm swimming in a sea of blue light all the way back to campus.

CHAPTER TWENTY-ONE

Fiddling with the necklace around my neck, I resist the urge to text Joey while Mr. Kaufman flickers on the oversized projector to begin our first class since the new semester began. Now would be perfect, I think, to send her a picture of my actually quite full Geology 102 classroom, demonstrating that there are others like me who have an appreciation for the subject. I imagine Joey's sarcastic response as the familiar sound of backpacks being unzipped and students shuffling their feet on their way to their seats echoes off the bare, high walls and tiled floor. The noise actually brings me a weird sense of comfort. I have to admit that I am glad to be back. Not that my holiday break wasn't great or anything. Our family Christmas dinner featuring my mom's brother and sister-in-law, Uncle Will and Aunt Stacey, was actually pretty fun. They brought their three Yorkies, of course. Kevin and I played video games. My parents even managed to tear themselves away from work for the day to indulge in some turkey and stuffing.

Yet, while I was home, I found myself missing everyone from school. Well, okay, I found myself missing certain people. I did see Emily on New Year's, despite her urgings that I call Joey up to see what her plans were. For some reason, though, just the thought of being around her on a night involving champagne and turning over new leaves made me nervous. Instead, I opted for a night of movies and watching the ball drop at Emily's with her family and friends.

"I hope you all enjoyed your holidays," Professor Kaufman says from the bottom of the small auditorium, breaking me out of my thoughts. "We're going to jump back into things with a brief review of last semester's items."

My phone vibrates in my back pocket, and I pull it out to find Jax's photo gracing the screen. Despite the fact that I'm halfway up in the auditorium and fairly obscured in the small sea of faces, I glance up to the front of the room, then swipe open the message.

Hey cutie. Can't wait to see you at practice tonight ;)

I don't realize I'm biting my lip until the gaze of my classmate to my left makes me look up. A girl I recognize from last semester's lecture is staring at me like I've got some deep, dark secret. My face flushes and I set my phone in my lap, trying to think of a response. Jax always makes me feel like I have no power for words, even with something as simple as crafting a thought-out text message. She had messaged me three times over the holidays. Each nothing more than a quick *Hey cutie* or *Miss me?* but they were enough to confuse me even more and left me spending hours trying to decipher what she wants with me.

My professor's booming voice pulls me back to reality. "So, we have three main types of rocks, if you will remember." Mr. Kaufman is a tall, lanky man whose only remaining hair seems to be on his face in the form of a Santa Claus–esque beard. "And those three types are…"

Several people in the auditorium raise their hands. After a moment, Mr. Kaufman calls on a guy sitting to my right. I half listen while continuing to stare at my phone screen.

"Igneous, sedimentary, and metamorphic."

"Very good," Mr. Kaufman responds with a smile. Meanwhile I fiddle with my pen, doodling circles in the margins while glancing back at my phone, wishing desperately that I knew what Jax was up to.

Mr. Kaufman continues. "Let's start with igneous rocks." He gestures to a slide on the projector screen behind him. "These are formed when the molten lava, or magma, from beneath the earth's surface cools and solidifies. There are also two types of igneous rocks. And those are?"

More hands raise.

"Intrusive and extrusive," the girl who'd side-eyed me earlier answers.

"Excellent." Mr. Kaufman beams, then clicks to another slide. I look up finally and see *Intrusive* and *Extrusive* written at the top of the screen, followed by some bullet points beneath each. "First, there's intrusive. Intrusive igneous rocks form from the solidification of magma beneath the Earth's surface. Second, we have extrusive. Who can give me some characteristics of this type?"

Rereading Jax's message, I hear the rustle of more hands going up.

"Ms. Lyndsay? Care to rejoin the class?"

I look up, realizing Mr. Kaufman is staring right at me. *Crap*. I rearrange myself, hoping to hide the cell phone in my lap.

"Sorry," I mumble.

"Extrusive igneous rocks," he says. "Some characteristics, please."

Thankfully, I remember these well from last semester's exam. I sit up then clear my throat to speak. "Extrusive igneous rocks form when magma reaches the Earth's surface, like from a volcano. Most extrusive rocks tend to have small crystals due to their quick cooling process. Some examples include basalt, rhyolite, and obsidian."

Mr. Kaufman nods, and my shoulders relax a little. "Can you expand upon one of those examples?"

I glance down at my phone when the same picture of Jax pops up with a message beneath it. "Sure," I say, meeting Mr. Kaufman's gaze. "Obsidian." I remember reading about this one last semester. It was fierce looking. Dark. Bold. "It's a dark rock, usually black, made of volcanic glass. It's formed when the magma from a volcano cools extremely quickly. In fact, the cooling process is so rapid that crystals aren't actually able to form. And since it's considered a glass, obsidian is very chemically unstable. Also, due to its sensitive nature, it's rare for an obsidian to reach old age. Oftentimes the rocks are damaged and destroyed by outside factors like weather, heat, or other processes."

"Beautiful but unstable," Mr. Kaufman says with a smirk. "Sounds like some people I've dated."

The class chuckles as he moves to click a new slide. "Very good, Ms. Lyndsay, thank you."

I sigh and open up the message from Jax as Mr. Kaufman continues with the lecture. *Sedimentary* is on the screen now, and I briefly hear him go into this one before reading Jax's text.

Saw some Facebook pics of your holiday. You look better than ever.

My stomach does a flip-flop. Jax is picking up her flirting game. Why she's choosing to direct that game at me, I still have no idea. I mean, she's stunning. She's the type of person to draw a crowd just by walking into a room. And what am I? Regular old Kyle, with her plain T-shirts and confused libido. What the hell can someone like me offer someone like Jax?

Staring at her message, I imagine those piercing eyes under their dark sheet of eyeliner. That knowing grin.

Why in the world is she so interested in me?

"And finally, we come to our third type of rock," Mr. Kaufman says, and I force myself to refocus. But just as I look up, my phone vibrates. This time, though, it's Joey's photo that pops up. "Who can tell me the third type?" Mr. Kaufman asks.

"Metamorphic," somebody calls out from behind me as I slide open her message and read the text.

Where do geologists like to relax?

I can't help but grin at the screen, waiting for Joey's second message, and the subsequent answer, to come through. Sure enough, about five seconds later, there it is.

In a rocking chair!

I cover my mouth to stifle my laugh, then type out a reply.

It ain't easy being cheesy.

Joey replies quickly.

Oh, there's more where that came from, short stack.

Mr. Kaufman clears his throat, and I force myself to listen to the lecture. "Metamorphic rocks arise from the transformation of preexisting rock types. So, in layman's terms, you have something stable, some rock formations that already exist, but then it is transformed through what we call metamorphism into something new, something different. And how does this occur? Mr. Willis?"

I glance over to a guy a few seats in front of me. "Metamorphosis occurs when the original rock is subjected to heat and pressure, which then causes physical and/or chemical changes."

"Very good," Mr. Kaufman replies. "Metamorphic rocks are usually formed deep within the Earth. They can take longer to form before they reach the earth's surface. Can somebody give me an example of a type of metamorphic rock?"

I force myself to close my phone, despite wanting to send another quip back to Joey. But instead I slide my phone back into my pocket and turn my attention to the class.

"Marble," a girl from my row says. "During metamorphism, the calcite within the rock we know as limestone recrystallizes and the texture of the rock changes. In the early stages of the limestone-to-marble transformation, the calcite crystals in the rock are very small. So small, in fact, that they really only look like a sugary sparkle reflecting from the surface when the rock is held up to light. It's kind of like a preview of what's to come."

"Very good. And then," Mr. Kaufman says, "as metamorphism progresses, the crystals grow larger and become more easily recognizable. This recrystallization process is what marks the separation between limestone and marble. Marble that has been exposed to low levels of metamorphism will have very small calcite crystals. The crystals only become larger as the level of metamorphism progresses. And eventually, the rock transforms into what it was always meant to be. Something strong, complex, and ultimately beautiful."

I jot down Mr. Kaufman's ability to make even rocks sound poetic. Without thinking, I fiddle with my necklace as I write, smiling over sharing the lecture with Joey next time I see her.

CHAPTER TWENTY-TWO

Joey holds open the locker room door for me. "You know you don't have to wear the necklace all the time."

"Are you kidding? It's beautiful."

"She hardly takes the thing off," Emily adds behind us.

I shoot Emily a look, but catch Joey smiling as we walk into the locker room for the team meeting Coach Gandy has called. Joey shrugs. "I'm just saying. It's been a few months; it's almost April. I wouldn't be mad if you switched it out for something different after a while."

We take a seat in front of our lockers on the other side of the room. Emily gives my arm a squeeze, then goes into Coach's office. I watch them start to go over the meeting agenda as Joey stretches her legs. She peels off her jacket and puts it over her backpack. I sit cross-legged on the bench next to her, my sweatpants baggy over my knees. I grab hold of the pendant dangling over my university T-shirt.

"Joey, relax." I nudge her shoulder with my own. She brushes back her hair with one hand. "I love it."

T. and Haley wander into the room with a few other upperclassmen. Jax strolls in behind. "Hey." T. waves. "I'm starting to think you two are glued at the hip." She smirks at me and Joey. Haley throws her backpack in her locker and plops down next to me. Her leg brace is gone; the only hint that it was ever evident is the faint tan lines running down her leg. She leans over, grabbing my necklace and turning it in her hand.

"Whoa. This is gorgeous."

I smile and carefully pull it back. "Thanks."

T. settles next to Haley. “Gift from your girlfriend?”

I blush and run a hand through my hair. Joey clears her throat and sits up. “We’re not girlfriends,” she says, her voice low. I catch her eye for a second, then Jax makes a show of throwing her own bag next to Joey before sitting. Eyeing us, she says, “Cute,” then leans back, one leg up in front of her on the bench, her wrist resting casually on her knee. Her eyes stay on me as Coach Gandy, in her traditional sweatpants and fitted T-shirt, follows Emily out of her office. Emily takes a seat while Coach moves over to the whiteboard on the wall near her door.

“Good afternoon, ladies. Thanks for coming. I know finals are fast approaching and you have a lot of studying to do. But I wanted to get together since the off-season is winding down.” She hands a stack of papers to Emily, who starts going around the room, handing each of us a sheet while Coach continues. “These are your summer workouts. I know it’s a little early, but we can’t afford to lose any time. The second your classes end in May, I need you girls taping this to your fridge, to your car window, to your forehead—whatever is necessary to ensure you’re doing these between then and July.”

“We know a lot of you all go home for the summer,” adds Emily, handing me my copy. “But when you’re not with family, or working, or whatever it is you do,” she pauses at Jax, who snatches a copy from the pile, “please keep yourself ready for next semester. There will be a conditioning test once we’re back in July. And I don’t know about y’all, but I’d rather not be regretting a lazy summer when that test rolls around.”

“Don’t worry, Cap’n,” T. says, leaning back against her locker, “I’ll be here all summer, making sure the young’uns hit the gym.”

Callie and Sarah share nervous glances in the corner, but Joey scoffs. “By gym, do you mean bar?”

There’s stifled laughter around the locker room. Emily looks ready to jump between Joey and T. when Coach clears her throat. “I’ll pretend I didn’t hear that.” She places her hands on her hips. “You ladies did well this year. Each and every one of you. So don’t let yourselves down over the summer. Keep working hard. We’ve got two weeks left of practices. That means two weeks to get to where we want to be before summer hits. And it’s up to you ladies to get there. What do you say?”

Cheers fill the locker room and Coach looks pleased as the noise dies down. "Wonderful. Also, before you all go, a quick announcement." Haley sits up next to me. When I glance at Emily, she throws me a wink. "First, a round of applause for Joey Carver, who stepped up this year as a rookie and did big things for us in the goal when we needed her most."

Joey sheepishly waves while a few people whistle over our cheers. T. and Jax applaud a few times but quickly fold their arms over their chests. "And congrats to Haley for being cleared by the doctor and trainers with a clean bill of health on her knee." This time, louder cheers from Jax and T. "However," Coach continues, holding up a hand, "we can only have one starting goalie. And as of now, that honor will stay with Carver going into the summer."

The freshman, including myself, whoop and holler while Joey gets pats on the back from Emily and a few others. Jax stays seated, as does T. Haley leans over me and gives Joey a handshake. "Congrats." I feel a little bad for Haley as they share a hug but am grateful for the respect she shows regarding Coach's decision.

"Thanks," Joey tells her. "I learned from the best."

"Congratulations, Joey," Coach adds after everyone sits back down. "All right, ladies. That's it for now. See everyone in the morning."

"Let me know if anybody didn't get a copy of the workout!" Emily shouts over the commotion as everyone stands and moves toward the door. "See you at practice tomorrow!"

I stand with Joey, who grabs her backpack. "Congrats," I tell her. "That's so awesome." I stand up on my toes and wrap her in a hug. She pulls me closer. The hug is quick, but I can't ignore the small rush that comes with being so close.

"Thanks, Kyle. It is pretty cool, huh?"

"Lucky break," mutters T. as she walks by, not looking back on her way out of the room. Jax moves over. She glances between Joey and me, sizing us up like two art pieces she's not sure are worthy of her gallery. As she's about to say something, Emily hops over to us.

"Joey, congrats!" They share a hug, then Emily turns to Jax. "Sorry about Haley. But she'll still see the field. Seniors always get a respectable amount of playing time."

Jax raises an eyebrow and nods. "Sure."

"Well," Emily says, bouncing anxiously as more of the team streams out of the locker room until only the four of us are left standing. "See you at practice tomorrow. And don't forget about the end of the year party. I'll send out evites next week!"

"Right," Jax says slowly, then turns to go. When she's out of earshot, Emily sighs.

"Just a bundle of sunshine that one, isn't she?"

Joey and I laugh and follow Emily outside.

Chapter Twenty-Three

"Kyle, I love you."

I turn around and Emily stumbles toward me, an unmistakable wobble in her step. She's on the arm of Haley, who helps her over to where I'm standing alone at the edge of the basketball court at Emily's apartment complex during our end of season party.

"She's a little tipsy," Haley says, struggling to place Emily against the basket. Emily adjusts her glasses and throws a hand up.

"I am not." She hiccups. "I'm just trying to let everybody know how much I love them. And I want to talk to my future neighbor. Did you know Kyle is moving into that building over there next semester?" Emily sloshes her drink.

Haley pats her back. "That's great, honey. Well, I've got next at beer pong," she tells me. "And she's your best friend. Do you mind keeping an eye on her? She keeps hugging everyone. It's kind of distracting."

Emily gives a retort in Spanish, and they get into a brief exchange. I try to follow it but only catch bits and pieces. When I recognize the familiar, playful warning of "*Ay, cuidado*," as Emily pulls her shoulders back, I step between them.

"Easy, tiger," I say, wrapping one arm around Emily. Then I tell Haley I can take it from here. She nods gratefully and heads back over to the group.

"I've got you." Emily manages to stand herself upright against the basket. While I'm not super sober myself, I can't help but laugh at Emily as she takes another drink and stares up into the coral-colored sky. The spring wind brushes past.

She hums to herself, then says, "Kyle, you made it."

I sip my drink, eyeing Emily as she sways. "Made it? Yeah, I didn't really have much trouble finding your place. Been here once or twice." I smirk and even through her blurry eyes Emily manages to give me a look.

"No." She draws the word out. "I mean you made it through your freshman year." She holds out her arms again. "I'm so proud of you!"

The music coming from our team's stereo system set up under a patio awning isn't loud enough to cover up the excitement in Emily's voice. A few of our teammates turn and holler excitedly back at Emily from around the pool, returning her enthusiasm. Emily cheers back at them, then spins closer to me. She grabs me by my shirt, tugging me closer so that our faces are only inches apart.

"Um, Em?"

"You know, I bet Joey asks you out soon."

I blush. "Emily, come on."

She grabs the pendant that dangles in front of my chest. "She's awesome."

My eyes drift across the pool, over to the patio. There are several chairs scattered around the beer pong table, where most of my teammates lounge lazily, enjoying the soccer-free weekend that is our end-of-season party. Joey sits next to a table we've packed with coolers of beer, chatting with Callie and Sarah. One ankle rests on her opposite knee. She's in a purple cotton V-neck under a brown jacket. Her hair falls down over her shoulders. It waves hypnotically when she laughs at something Callie says.

My stomach flutters. "She *is* pretty amazing."

Emily's voice is low, even though no one is around. "You guys should date."

I look down, shaking my head. "I'm not arguing that Joey isn't awesome. I'm just not ready for that. Not yet." *And whatever connection she and I have terrifies me*, I almost say.

"I know." She sighs dramatically, then pulls me into a hug that makes our drinks slosh in their cups. "I just want you to be happy."

I hug her tightly. "Thanks, drunk Em."

She shoves me off her and I laugh. "You're lucky you're my best friend." Then she waves good-bye before calling after Katie and making her way back over to the crowd. A voice behind me makes me jump.

"We're friends, right, Kyle?"

I turn to Jax as she struts up to me. Her black jeans sit low on her hips, exposing her midriff. Her signature tank top seems tighter on her chest than it's ever been before. Laughter from the beer pong table pulls my attention. Emily is hugging people again.

"Kyle?"

"I'm sorry?" I ask, realizing my gaze had drifted back over to Joey.

"I asked if we were friends."

"Oh," I swallow some more of my vodka-cranberry mix. "Yeah. I mean, I guess so." I consider telling her about how she's done nothing but confuse me all year long. But I think better of it when she smiles, and I see something forming in her eyes.

"Good," she says. "Because you see that guy over there?" Jax points to a group of students walking toward us from the parking lot. I squint into the fast fading light but can't figure out which guy she's referring to. Out of the five people approaching the volleyball court, three of them are guys. So I just nod. "He's my ex."

I'm not sure what my face does in reaction to this statement. But suddenly Jax is tugging at my elbow. "Hey," she practically purrs, her face close to mine, so close that I smell the beer on her breath. "Don't worry. We're friends, okay? You and me."

"Sure," I say more to my cup than to her, "because you flirt with all of your friends, right?"

My comment surprises me as much as it does her. She takes a step back. When I finally look up, her eyes have shifted, and it looks like Jax is seeing me for the very first time since last fall. I force myself to take another sip just as the newcomers, including Jax's ex, stroll up to us.

"Jax, you're looking good," says the lanky, unshaven guy in the middle of the group. Through my now slightly blurry vision after chugging half my cup, he resembles one of those emo-pop band members that hit it big in the early 2000s. Someone from a group with a name like Two-Car Garage Door Depot or Idiot Glitter at the Disco. He wouldn't be the lead soloist, I decide, eyeing him over my cup. Maybe the bassist.

Jax scoffs at him. “And you look like shit.”

Everyone in the group laughs nervously, and I do my best to maintain my upright stance against my basketball post as a wave of nausea hits me. I take a deep breath to calm myself. I don’t exactly know why I feel so worked up all of a sudden as Jax’s next comment pulls me back into their conversation.

“What the hell are you even doing here?” she asks, one hand on her hip. The rest of the newcomers take this as a cue to start their search for a drink. The bassist is smirking and turns to me.

“Please excuse Jax’s lack of manners.” He sticks his hand out. I take it firmly. “I’m Steven. Jax’s—”

“Ex-boyfriend. As of seven months ago,” Jax finishes for him, her eyes narrowed.

“Was it really that long ago?” Steven muses, his eyes locked on Jax. “Seems like it was just last week when you and I were in the back of Rayner’s truck. You remember that night?”

“Oh, was that with you?” Jax frowns as if trying to recall. “I could have sworn it was the chick from my chem lab.”

I nod to no one in particular and take another drink. Maybe if I stare at the bottom of my cup long enough, I can crawl down into it and away from this drama.

A hand gently touches the small of my back. Joey appears beside me, and I’m thankful for the break in the tension that has built up around the three of us.

“Hey,” she says to me, with a small nod to Jax and Steven. “I put us down for the next round of beer pong. I’ll find you again in about twenty minutes, okay?”

I’m about to reply when Jax tosses her arm around me and pulls me close. The gesture is quick, and my feet skid in front of me to keep from crashing fully into her. “Sure thing,” she says to Joey. “I’ll take care of her until then.”

Joey raises an eyebrow, glancing between the two of us.

Steven snorts. “What are you, her girlfriend or something?” He pops open a beer can.

Jax, her arm still around me, grins. And that grin is all I have time to register before she turns and crashes her lips against mine. My heart picks up its pace and I struggle to breathe. I have to be dreaming. There’s no way this moment is actually happening.

This moment I had played in the dark recesses of my mind when I first saw Jax on the practice field almost nine months ago. This moment that, ever since initiation night, Jax had helped slip into quiet moments when I least expected it. This moment that, despite myself, brings a rush of heat to my lower body when her slick lower lip brushes against my own.

I taste the beer on her tongue when she pulls back. Her eyes meet mine. I try to focus on those pools of blue. They're swirling with—what is that? Excitement? Lust? Satisfaction?

"Great," Steven mumbles before walking away into the crowd near the pool.

Jax gives me a quick kiss on my neck, followed by a wink. Then she calls out after T. and runs off to the beer pong table.

I turn around, still flushed. Everywhere I look, Joey is nowhere to be found.

Part Two

Chapter Twenty-Four

I roll onto my side as the bathroom door opens. She's silhouetted in the light, allowing my eyes to trace the curves of her body. It's dark in my room, but the light from the streetlamp outside my apartment pours through the blinds, and I can just make out Jax's face amongst the shadows when she crawls back into bed with me. The makeup is smudged around her eyes, and her blond hair is disheveled. I swallow as she lies down, one hand behind her head.

"So..."

"So," she echoes, turning on her side to face me. She traces her fingers up and down my arm. "That was fun. As usual."

"It was fun." My voice cracks, and I clear my throat. Now I feel like that silly streetlamp outside; my entire body buzzes, and I swear my legs are tingling, just like they have every other time we've done this. Even now, as I watch Jax watching me, I struggle to recall how all of this began. After that kiss in May, things became a little gray. I remember her cornering me again that night of the party, both of us several more drinks into the evening. I remember looking for Joey but Jax finding me instead. There are flashes of us stumbling into Emily's bathroom, her hands roaming over my body, my own hands touching Jax in ways I never imagined. From there it's a collection of dark, scattered nights that fill my mind, where every moment felt like a camera shudder, focusing in and out as we end every night tangled in each other's arms. Nights spent around campus, in her back seat, at a bar, almost anywhere. Nights where I forced the image of Joey from my mind. She wasn't returning my calls, so what else could I do? Then Jax became this thing I couldn't say no to. All summer long. Until I came to the conclusion that maybe I'd found what I was looking for in Jax. Somebody to hold. Somebody who didn't ask questions. Somebody who could make me feel what I was so afraid to feel before.

"Water?" Jax offers, reaching past an empty bottle of wine on my bedside table for the glass she'd brought in once we'd come back from dinner. Practices don't start for another week. So Jax and I passed the day on my couch until we ventured out to TJs, the local Mexican joint, for margaritas courtesy of some fake IDs. After a couple of hours, we'd stumbled back to my place and, like every other weekend this summer, ended up in bed.

"No thanks," I reply, watching her take a sip before replacing the glass on the table. The sheet slips, exposing her midriff. Jax turns to face me, resting her head on her hand so that we're face-to-face again. Her blond hair is a messy halo around her head.

"Kyle," she says, her eyes lowered. "This summer has been fun. I really like you."

I blink a couple of times, not sure if I heard her correctly. "You do?"

She hums, low and deep, and her eyes flicker up. "Yeah. Obviously." She laughs, running a hand absentmindedly over my shoulder.

"Oh," I stammer. My stomach leaps into my throat. "Uh… thanks."

Jax laughs again. She leans forward and kisses me quickly. My head rushes as her lips part from mine. "Want to be my girlfriend?"

I stare at her for a moment. She seems amused as I search her face. Then my eyes fall to the sheet draped over her; I envy the way it clings so effortlessly to her curves. My stomach twists, but I figure it's just the margaritas from earlier talking back to me. Did I really just hear Jax ask me that? She wants to date me? *Me?*

"Jax…I…"

I don't know what to think. My mind drifts back to last year. To all of those moments on the field, in the weight room, in that ice cream shop. Was she getting at this all along? Then there's Joey. I bite my lip as I think about her. She hasn't spoken to me since the party, since Jax kissed me. I understand why. I understand she deserves somebody who can give her what she wants. I had begun to think that could have been me one day. But now…maybe I was meant for this instead.

Jax grabs my waist and pulls me closer. My thoughts falter and trip over themselves as she traces her fingers down my arm and along my body.

"Say yes, Kyle." She grins again, pushing her hips forward so that they bump mine. My body reacts in kind, and I can't help but grab her, removing the sheet from around her waist. Then, in one smooth motion, she moves so that she's on top of me, straddling my hips. Slowly, the friction from her own hips moving over mine leaves me gripping her thighs, my fingers pressing desperately into her skin. Instinctually, I thrust up into her. She cups my breasts in her hands. My back arches, and her hips quickly put us into an easy rhythm. The groan that escapes my throat makes her laugh. Then she's leaning over me, one of her hands snaking down my stomach, moving lower, then lower. Then her other hand reaches up to cup my face. "Say yes," she whispers next to my ear.

I moan and kiss her. "Yes," I finally say between breaths. She smiles into my kiss, and I lose myself once again in Jax. I let the night fold its dark blanket over us and we slip down into its folds, deeper and deeper until there's no one and nothing else but us.

CHAPTER TWENTY-FIVE

After a quick kiss, I say good-bye to Jax while trying to wriggle myself from her grip on my shorts. Our impromptu scrimmage with half the team, organized by Emily, has just ended. The evening air holds the last few hints of summer, and a warm breeze blows a few strands of hair across Jax's face. She leans into me as I brush them out of her eyes.

"I'll see you tomorrow?" she asks before biting her bottom lip—a gesture she knows turns me into nothing more than a puddle of helpless hormones.

With a sigh, I reply, "Definitely." Jax gives me one more kiss, then grabs her bag she'd dropped at our feet five minutes earlier. As she turns away, the spell of her begins to fade, and I can suddenly feel somebody's gaze burning the back of my head. I turn to find Emily making her way over to her car two spots away from where Jax and I had been standing.

I glance back at Jax, who saunters over to a car that pulls into the parking lot. She leans down to chat up the driver through their rolled-down window. When I hear the trunk of Emily's car slam down, I jump.

"Sorry," she says. "Didn't mean to scare you. I was trying not to interrupt you guys."

I look back at Jax once more to see her join the driver in their car for a ride back to campus. Then I walk over and pull open the passenger side of Emily's car, throw my cleats and bag into the back seat, then plop down as she starts the engine.

The radio plays a recent Top 40 tune while Emily and I sit in silence pulling out of the lot. Which, really, is fine by me. The quiet means I have time to relive the past few months with Jax, to go through those all-consuming moments that leave me reeling each morning. I close my eyes and am once again standing at a bar we took to frequenting over the summer. I can feel her hand slide into my back pocket before she pulls me against her in a dark hallway. The camera shutters and my memories flicker to a new image: Jax is crawling toward me on the couch in her apartment on a lazy Sunday. Her breath is sweet, with traces of an empty bottle of wine. *Click.* I blush, thinking of being with Jax in the shower after a workout—

"So," Emily says, yanking me out of my thoughts. I brush a few sweaty hairs out of my face. "It seems like things are going... well."

I nod. "Yeah. They really are."

"That's wonderful."

I glance over at Emily when we pause at a light. She's staring straight ahead, her index fingers tapping a persistent beat onto the steering wheel.

"Em."

"Hmm?"

"You're doing it."

She raises an eyebrow. "Doing what?"

I shoot her a look. "What do you want to ask me?"

Emily shakes out her shoulders as we take a right and head toward our apartment complex. She narrows her eyes—a sign that she's weighing what she wants to say to me before speaking. A habit I've witnessed since we were kids. I'd watch her make that face for decisions such as what to buy from the ice cream truck, or how she was going to tell her mom we had broken a rather expensive pot in her family's green room after a rambunctious game of hide-and-seek.

"It's nothing," she finally says.

I reach forward and turn the music down, then turn in my seat so that I'm facing her. She glances over at me before rolling her eyes in defeat.

"It's just...Okay, I'm happy for you, Kyle. I am. I'm just curious about Jax. I mean, she had you missing calls from me all summer long. I didn't even realize you weren't going home over the break."

"I called you about that."

"You did…in June, after I went by your house thinking you'd be home and your parents told me you were staying out here to work out through the off-season."

I sigh. "Okay. I could have mentioned that a little sooner. I just…was busy."

She licks her lips, another familiar nervous habit. "That's okay. I guess, if this is really happening, I want to know more. I want you to be able to talk to me about this. So, why don't you tell me a little bit about her?"

My brow furrows. "You just want to know more about Jax?"

With a nod, Emily says, "Yeah. What's she like? Because, you know, despite playing with her for two years, Jax has always found a way to fly under the radar. She…she never shares much."

I watch a group of students, who must be incoming freshmen, hurry past our car, looking a little lost at a crosswalk before Emily turns into our sprawling apartment complex. "Okay," I say. "Well, she's from the Houston area. She's a year ahead of me, which you know, obviously. Played soccer since she was five."

Emily turns to steer us toward her building in the back of the complex. "Does she have any siblings?"

I frown. "You know, I'm not sure. I never thought to ask. She's never mentioned any."

"What's her major?"

"She was pre-med. But she just recently changed. I, um, I can't remember what she is now." I flash back to the night she told me she was "giving up the doctor gig." She had insisted we celebrate her liberation with a bottle of wine. The rest of that night, I realize now, is blurry.

Emily nods. "Does she have a favorite class?"

I furrow my brow, thinking back. "Jax doesn't talk much about school."

"What about her parents?"

"I know they're both doctors. Or surgeons? Something like that." I pause. "She doesn't mention her family very often." My throat feels dry, and my face grows hot as Emily fires off another question.

"What does she want to do after college?"

I swallow. "I don't know."

"What about—"

"Emily!" I snap and throw my hands up as we pull into a parking spot. Emily puts the car in park. Her hands fall into her lap, but she keeps her gaze forward. "Okay, Em. I get it."

"Kyle, you're my best friend."

"Is it a best friend requirement to give me the Spanish Inquisition about the girl I'm dating?" I feel anxious, like suddenly I'm ten again and have been caught sneaking cookies out of the pantry with Kevin. "All right, so, I don't know everything about her. Is that so weird? We haven't been dating that long, you know."

Emily nods and turns to me. Her face is conflicted, like the time in middle school when I dyed my hair blue, and she wasn't sure how to break the news that I had made a terrible decision. Still, her eyes are soft, though her voice doesn't waver when she finally speaks. "I know. I'm sorry. I was just hoping you could shed some light on the girl that had you disappearing for days at a time all summer long. I mean, it isn't like you to miss my calls. And you didn't even tell me until last week that you guys were together." She pauses. "And honestly, I thought you and Joey were heading that way."

I glance down at my hands. Maybe we were. But I wasn't sure what I wanted with Joey. Part of her scared me. The way she could see into me. Nobody could do that. "Joey deserves better than me," I say, finishing my thoughts aloud.

Emily shakes her head. "Kyle, come on. That's not true. You two—"

"Are friends." I look out the window. "We were friends. I don't know."

"She hasn't returned your calls?"

"Can you blame her?"

Emily nods. "She comes back to town next week when practices start. Kyle, what happens when she hears about you and Jax?"

I pick at my nails, unable to make eye contact. "I'll tell Jax to keep a low profile."

Emily laughs, loud and sharp. "Because that is definitely her style."

"Em, come on. I'm finally with somebody. Isn't that good news? Things are easy with Jax. Just let me have this, okay?"

She sighs. "I'm sorry about all of the questions." She licks her lips, then adds, "I just want to know that she's good for you."

My eyes meet hers. "Do you think that she isn't?" I ask, agitated.

Emily looks at me. "I'm not saying that."

"You kind of are, though." I unbuckle my seat belt. All of a sudden, I feel the desperate need to defend Jax. "You know what, I don't want to do this right now, Emily. I'm tired. And I have homework."

"Kyle."

But I'm already out of the car. I open the back door, grab my stuff, and then shut it a little harder than I normally would. Emily gets out and stands next to her open driver's door. I start off down a paved sidewalk path lined with geraniums, toward my apartment building. All I want to do is forget about this conversation. I don't want to think about Emily, or Joey. I just want to see Jax. I want to feel her arms around me. I want her to tell me everything's fine.

"I'll see you tomorrow, Emily," I huff over my shoulder.

She calls after me. "Wait, Kyle."

But I just keep walking and reach into my workout bag for my phone.

CHAPTER TWENTY-SIX

"I don't understand why she's being so negative all of a sudden." I grab the beer Jax hands me before she joins me on her couch and pops open the top. Right away she swallows half of it.

"She's probably just jealous," Jax replies, licking drops of beer from her lips and tucking her legs beneath her.

I frown and take a sip. "Jealous? Emily's not the type. Besides, she's happy with Alex. What's there to be jealous about?"

Jax shrugs, her eyes wandering to her cell phone on the coffee table in front of us. "Some people are like that. You know, when two friends are close for years and one of them meets somebody new and starts spending more time with that other person, the friend left behind just freaks out." Her eyes are wide as she speaks and takes another swallow from her beer. "Emily is used to having you around. Now that she doesn't, she's losing it. She wants you to herself."

I frown over the top of my beer. "That doesn't really sound like Emily, though." I mull Jax's words over in my head. Emily has never been the type to monopolize anyone's time. And sure, I'm her best friend, but I am definitely not her *only* friend. Not by far. If anything, she spent most of last year encouraging me to meet new people.

"That's the funny thing about people," Jax says, nodding. "You never really know them. Even if you think you do."

I take another gulp, the bitter liquid sliding easily down my throat. My conversation with Emily reverberates in my mind. Her claims that I hardly know Jax sting behind my eyes. Yes, she was probably just being a concerned friend, but it still had hurt.

"Maybe she just needs to spend more time with you," I wonder aloud. Jax's eyebrow raises. "With us," I add quickly. "She probably just wants to know more about you. Like…how many siblings do you have?"

Jax laughs and throws back the final drops of her beer. "That's what she wants to know?" She gets up to toss the can into the trash, then grabs another from the fridge.

I watch her wander back over to the couch and shrug. "Well," I say, "I don't even know the answer to that."

Jax opens her drink and takes a sip. She's watching me over the top of it as if she's considering what she wants to say. "One brother. But he's seven years older. He's married to a woman he met on a business trip. He sells tubing parts to companies. They live in Tennessee together. I don't see him much." She looks down for a second, then clears her throat and sets the beer can on the coffee table. She sits back with one arm up on the couch. "Happy now?"

I can't help from blurting out another question. "What about your parents, do you get along with them?"

"Sure," she says, crossing her legs so that her left foot can bounce the way it does, I've noticed, when she's in a conversation. "As much as any college kid does, I guess. Not much else to say."

"Are they the ones who wanted you to be pre-med?"

She nods. "Since my brother was kind of a drifter from the get-go, I guess the pressure to follow in their footsteps fell to me. Not like they were around much to show me how to do it." I nod, the lack of a parental presence all too familiar, and she continues. "I was mostly raised by my grandmother, till I was, like, fifteen or so. She lived near my parents, so it was just easier with them working so much, you know?"

"How was that, being brought up by your grandmother?"

"It wasn't half bad. Thanks to her, I can name every movie starring Cary Grant or Debbie Reynolds."

I look down into the opening of my beer. I must sound ridiculous, having all these questions lined up for her. "Thanks… for sharing all of that. I, well…Emily just thought maybe you and I didn't talk enough. That maybe we spent too much time…"

"Not talking?" Jax grins. She reaches out, two fingers creeping up my leg toward my waist.

I wriggle beneath her touch and fight the urge to lean toward her. "She's a concerned friend. She wants to make sure I'm with somebody—"

"Who makes you feel good?" Jax finishes, her fingers completing their trek at my hipbone, where she rubs against me for a few seconds. I let out a sigh, and she leans back, a satisfied glint in her eye.

"She's just being Emily. I'm sure T. is the same way whenever you start dating somebody and she does the overprotective best friend thing." I pitch up my voice before continuing, mimicking Emily with a shake of my finger, "*Mira*, you better bring home a girl who treats you right!"

Jax's demeanor changes then, like a troupe of clouds has just rushed into the room and settled over her face. She sets her beer next to her phone on the coffee table. She eyes it, then picks it up. Her phone is in her lap when she slowly says, "So…she thinks I'm not good enough for you?"

Her sudden shift in mood throws me. "What?"

"Is that what you think, too, Kyle? That I'm not good enough for you? Is that why you feel like you need to ask me so many questions all of a sudden?"

The blood drains from my face. *What is happening?* "Jax, that's not what I said. That's not what I said at all."

"Well, it sure sounded like it. I mean, gee, Kyle, why don't we just call up your good pal Em and invite her over. She's clearly the one feeding you all of these lines."

"No," I reply quickly, my ears hot. "Jax, she hasn't said anything about you."

"Sure, sweetheart." She sits up and takes another drink before setting the can back down. Her voice is raised when she wipes her mouth and says, "Come on! Let's get her over here. She can transcribe the whole thing."

"Jax."

"What? It'll save a lot of time. You won't have to report back to Captain Emily and give her the play-by-play."

"That's not fair."

She's typing something into her phone now, her gaze down at the screen. "Well, if you think I'm not good enough for you, Kyle, maybe we should take a break."

"Jax, no." How did this conversation turn into this? I move next to her. Part of me wants to throw her phone across the room so that she'll listen to me. Fortunately, the rational side of me wins out, and I reach out to touch her wrist. "I didn't mean any of it like that," I say, trying to keep my voice steady. "I'm just trying to get to know you. Emily just wants to make sure I'm happy. Okay?" I reach up and tug her chin forward to look at me. "Hey, Jax, please."

Her blue eyes are clear when they meet mine. Her voice is as vulnerable as I've ever heard it when she says, "I just want us to be happy, Kyle. Don't I make you happy?"

"God, yes, Jax. You make me so happy." I'm kissing her then, hard, and passionate. Tears well in the corners of my eyes. Jax puts the phone down onto the couch and grabs my face, returning my kiss.

Eventually, I pull back, breathless. My mind races as I look at her. I never imagined dating anybody like Jax. What was I thinking, bringing that up to her? Of course she got defensive. What kind of girlfriend says what I said to her?

"I'm new to this whole dating thing," I say. "And I'll talk to Emily. I'll tell her that she has nothing to worry about. You and I are great." I run a hand over her face, cupping her cheek in my palm.

And just like that, the clouds vanish.

"Thanks, babe. I think it'll help to hear it coming from you."

I nod. "Absolutely."

Jax places the phone back onto the coffee table, then pushes me back onto the couch. "Tell me," she whispers, "why are you so good to me?"

I kiss her briefly, then pull back. "That sounds like one of your grandmother's movies."

"Cary Grant in *North by Northwest.*"

I chuckle and she kisses me again. Then, as quickly as it began, our conversation fades into the back of my mind. Jax is right; she always is.

Chapter Twenty-Seven

The open-air patio outside TJs is heavy with the smell of grilled vegetables, and the sharp sizzle coming from the waiter's tray nearby makes my stomach rumble. Jax and I sit with a few teammates at the hole-in-the-wall Mexican place a few blocks from campus. The breeze kicks up a napkin from our table of six. T. grabs her half-empty margarita and clamps it down on the runaway napkin. She sits across from me and Jax, who sits with one arm up the back of my plastic chair. I wrap my hand around my margarita, the bright liquid running up and over one side of the glass as I do so, and bring it to my lips.

"Pretty delicious, aren't they?" Haley motions to me from the other side of the table next to T. The cold drink takes some of the salt with it as it passes my lips and slides down my throat. I remember the first time Jax bought me one; I had cringed at the smell of tequila. Funny how things change.

I nod to Haley, and Jax answers for me. "She's a natural."

"So is this one." Haley nods toward T. before dipping a tortilla chip into our shared bowl of salsa. T. downs the remnants of her drink, slapping the glass back down onto the table.

"Hey, it's not alcoholism until after graduation." We all laugh as the waiter comes around collecting our empty glasses. Mary hands hers to the young man, but Elaine—a new freshman from Michigan—keeps hers close and doesn't make eye contact. When the waiter heads back into the restaurant, Jax nudges Elaine's shoulder.

"Relax, Frosh, you're good."

Elaine grimaces, lifting the drink to her lips carefully. Watching her, I can't help but think about first meeting Elaine two weeks ago at the beginning of August. I hadn't imagined her as the type to go out drinking on weekends, especially underage with a fake ID. She's not even close to being twenty-one. But for whatever reason, she really took to T., and T. is not one to turn down a drinking buddy.

The waiter comes back with two margaritas, placing one by T. and the other in front of Haley, who finishes the last of hers.

Suddenly, Jax whispers into my ear. "How about you? Another?" Her hand snakes down my thigh. The alcohol warms my face when she kisses my ear.

"I still have half of mine," I manage to say, and take another gulp. The warm buzz of the liquor begins to swim in my head. Jax's fingers dance along the bottom of my shorts and I feel light-headed.

"So that's a yes." She grins and signals for another drink to the waiter.

"I think somebody's trying to get you drunk." T. leers gleefully, her own drink toasting us. She winks at me. I blush.

"You know what, I think I'm gonna run to the restroom," I say, pushing out of my seat. I sway a little and close my eyes for a second to regain my step. Two margaritas in, and I'm already feeling it. Better to go freshen up before the third one gets here. I smile, imagining this is just what Jax had in mind. The image of another Sunday tangled up in her sheets makes me float through the restaurant.

I stumble a little when I exit the bathroom stall and walk to the small black counter. I grab hold of it and glance up into the mirror, adjusting the stray hairs that have come untucked from my ponytail. There are small bags under my eyes, but I brush it off as evidence of a busy soccer schedule and never-ending studying now that the semester has started. When the bathroom door opens as I turn to leave, I almost run right into Emily.

She stops once she's inside the door. I straighten up as best I can. At the same time, the buzzing in my mind decides to up the volume a notch. Emily lifts her head a little higher, then crosses her arms, which bunches the coral green sleeves of her sweater at the elbows. "Hi, Kyle."

"Hey."

"I, um, I didn't realize you were here." She adjusts her glasses quickly, then resumes her stance.

I nod. "Yeah, I'm here with some of the girls. And Jax." Emily stiffens for a moment at Jax's name. She nods but doesn't say anything. So I continue. "Are you here with Alex?"

"I am. And a few of the people from my PR class."

"Good."

Silence falls between us. I think back to the message I left on her voice mail three nights ago. After realizing how crazy I was to spit off fifty questions at Jax, I had downed a few beers, then called Emily to clear everything up. However, thanks to the buzz I was feeling at the time, the message geared less toward friendly banter and became frustrated ranting. But, I reasoned afterward, it was justified. I wasn't trying to rail into Emily, but how could she think that Jax wasn't treating me right? Or that she and I weren't a good pair? I mean, I am *finally* being open about who I am. And Emily is my best friend, for crying out loud. Shouldn't she be supportive?

"Well," I say, starting toward the bathroom door, "I won't keep you."

Just as I walk by, Emily grabs my arm, turning me gently. "Kyle. We should talk."

I swivel around. Emily squares up to face me, my back now to the door. "We really don't have to," I say.

Emily sighs. "Kyle, please. That voice mail…I've never heard you like that; you didn't sound okay." I look down, a flush creeping up my neck. Maybe I had been a bit overzealous in what I said. "We're best friends," she goes on. "I can tell when you're not being yourself."

"Really? When *I'm* not being myself? Em, I would think now more than ever I'm being who I really am. I mean…I'm out! I'm dating!"

"Kyle, you know that's not what I'm talking about." She watches me through her glasses. I sway and reach out for the sink to steady myself.

"What then? You don't like that I'm using a fake ID, or that I'm enjoying myself before soccer gets going?" I throw up my hands. "Heaven forbid a college student drinks underage. *Dios mío!*"

Emily's jaw clenches. "You're mocking me now? That's rich, coming from you, *la borrachita*."

"I don't know what that means," I reply, moving backward. "And I really don't care."

"Jesus, Kyle. Listen to yourself! What happened to you?"

"I'm spectacular, Em!" I practically shout to be heard over the buzzing that grows louder with every passing second. "But thank you for your concern."

At this, Emily only shakes her head, and the look on her face makes my stomach churn. She's never looked at me the way she is now. I find the word for what I see in her eyes immediately but try to force it away, drive it from my mind. But it persists in the way her lip curls up. Complete disgust is impossible to ignore.

"Great, Kyle," she finally says. "Well, I'm glad you're fine. I'm so happy to hear that not only are you letting an unhealthy relationship get between us, but you're also turning into a complete and total bitch."

My head jerks up. "Unhealthy relationship?"

Emily throws a hand up. "*Of cours*e that's all you heard from that."

The flush on my neck turns into a heat wave and the buzz in my head roars. The instinct to defend Jax leaps to the front of my mind until it's all I can see. My fists clench at my sides. "What did you say about my relationship with Jax?"

Emily just stares at me. "You heard me."

My head feels light and the words come out before I can stop them. "Well, it's not like what you say really matters. You're not my family, are you? We're not sisters; what gives you a right to say all this?"

"Oh, I don't know," she replies, her voice growing louder. "Maybe because I've taken care of your ass for almost thirteen years! I've covered for you more times than I can count."

"Is that why you brought me to this school? So you could watch over me? Make sure oblivious little Kyle doesn't stray onto the wrong side of the tracks?"

"Well, apparently, I need to because you have no idea what the hell you're doing. I mean, really, Kyle, you pick Jax?"

My shoulders heave, and my breath comes in heavy bursts.

"You still don't think she's good enough for me, do you?"

Emily and I stand quietly. Tension crawls out from the cracks in the tile floor and engulfs us, inching its way up our legs until my chest grows tight. Emily searches the room as if the right response may be written on the walls around us. She's about to speak when I cut her off.

"Emily. Come on." I step forward, the rush of alcohol surging confidence inside me. "Say it. Go on."

"Kyle, please."

"Say it. I want to hear you say it."

Now we're standing in the middle of the bathroom. The walls seem to close in on us, the air overwhelming me until I start to sweat. Emily stares back at me. I can see her biting the inside of her cheek. I wonder briefly if she feels it, too: the anger, the confusion, the years of friendship crumbling as the moments pass by. After a few more seconds, she sighs. "Fine, Kyle. You want me to say it? I don't like Jax. And I especially don't like her with you."

I stumble but regain my footing and cross my arms over my chest.

Emily's voice grows soft. "Happy now?"

I take a deep breath. There it is. My best friend finally admits that she hates the girl I'm dating. I wait for relief to come. I wait for the breath to return to my lungs. But, maybe because of the alcohol or the suffocating air inside this bathroom, I only feel nauseous.

Emily steps forward and takes my hand. "Kyle. I'm sorry. I just don't think she's right for you. But that…we can't let that change our relationship."

I look at her through bleary eyes. "Doesn't it, though?" Emily's eyes search my own. "I don't think this can be good for us. I mean, God, didn't you just hear everything we said to each other?"

"Kyle."

I shake my head. "Until you are on board with Jax, maybe it's best you and I take a break for a little while."

She watches me a moment longer, seeming to search my face for the Kyle she used to know. The Kyle I used to be before Jax. The Kyle she played soccer with for years, who she recruited to come to this school. I'm not even sure who that Kyle was. But how could I go back to her now?

Eventually, Emily drops my hand. "Okay. If that's what you want."

I nod, biting my lip to keep from crying. My head is reeling; the floor tilts beneath my feet. "I think that would be best."

Before Emily can say anything else, I run and push through the bathroom door and back out into the restaurant, unable to look back.

Chapter Twenty-Eight

Back in my bed, I roll onto my stomach. The pillow is warm from my having been in bed all morning. I flip it to the cooler side and drop my face down, letting myself sink lower into the mattress. With a sigh, I stare out my apartment window, thinking about the conversation with Emily in TJs bathroom. It's not like we've never fought before. We've been friends since we were little. Of course we've fought. What pair of friends hasn't?

But that fight wasn't like any of the others. This one made me sick to my stomach. After storming out of the bathroom, I had forced myself to sit through another hour of drinks and food, but even Jax's ever-roaming hands couldn't ease the unrest in my gut. When she took me back to her place, Jax must have sensed my unease. Because instead of our usual Sunday fun day in bed, she told me to rest until I felt better. Then she went to the library to pick up some research books for her biology class, and I collapsed into her bed as soon as her apartment door closed.

This morning, after excusing myself quietly once Jax got home in the early morning hours, I drove to my little apartment and haven't gotten out of bed since. Not even to touch the homework I have due on Tuesday. All I can think about is that ridiculous fight. Not that I'm second-guessing defending Jax. It's just that I never imagined getting into it like that with anyone. Especially Emily.

My eyes rove over to my bed table. The cell phone on it lies dark and heavy next to my lamp. I don't have the guts to reach out to Emily yet. I feel foolish. Like a little kid who lost control of her temper when she didn't get what she wanted. And I would normally run to my best friend in a situation like this to tell her all about it, but now I can't because my best friend was the target of my tantrum. It's probably better to let things cool off.

My next thoughts, before I can stop them, go to Joey. Thanks to my doing, it's been ages since she and I have had a real conversation. She finally texted me a few days ago, asking about Coach Gandy's meeting that's scheduled next week. But it was short, and I could tell she didn't want to really talk yet. But it was progress. I couldn't help but miss her. And now, despite my best efforts, I want to tell her about me and Emily. I hear her calling me out in that sarcastic way of hers while still managing to make me laugh. She would probably know exactly what to say to make all of this better.

My wandering mind runs in circles until I drift off to sleep. When I look at my digital clock over on my dresser, it reads 3:47 p.m. As I stretch, I hear a distant thumping coming from my living room. I imagine one of the giant black crows who likes to squawk outside my window pecking around my barely stocked cabinets. A few more seconds of the thumping, and I realize it's not the noise of a criminal bird but somebody knocking at my apartment door.

"Hey, cutie," Jax says when I open it. Her expression quickly falls at the sight of my unwashed hair and baggy sweats. "Oh, still not feeling great?"

I shake my head and move aside to let her in. She sets a couple of grocery bags down on my counter and places her backpack on the floor. "I brought you some pick-me-ups. Nothing a little beerita mix can't fix." I groan at the sight of the cans she puts onto a shelf in my fridge next to a half-empty carton of milk. "No problem," she adds at my wary look. "That's why I also have wine." She displays a cheap bottle of red and leaves it next to the sink.

"Thanks," I say. "But I think I just want to try to get some reading done before practice tomorrow morning."

Jax nods and makes her way over to where I'm leaning against the couch in the middle of my living room. "Babe, I'm sorry you're not feeling well." She reaches out and grabs the bottom of my T-shirt. "Still upset about Emily?"

I had drunkenly confessed to Jax about our argument on the way home last night. I don't remember much of Jax's response, but it must have been okay if she's bringing it up again now.

I nod. "Yeah. I still can't believe that we're fighting."

Jax pouts and pulls me closer. "I know, baby."

I let her wrap her arms around me and try to lose myself in her touch. Our bodies pressed against each other give me a feeling of hope that things will be okay again. I take a deep breath to calm myself down. As soon as I do, I pull back, keeping Jax at arm's length.

"What?" she asks.

"You…you smell like a guy."

For half a second, her eyebrow tilts up, then she rolls her eyes and shrugs. "Oh, God. I'm sorry, I know." She laughs and runs her hands down my back, holding me tight at my waist. "I went to the library again today. When I was heading out, I got stuck in the elevator with half of the guy's soccer team. You know how they are." She mimics spraying cologne around us. "They don't know when to stop with the body spray."

Coughing, I say, "I guess so. It smells like they tackled you on their way out."

Jax laughs. "Something like that." She winks, then goes to grab her backpack. "I should actually hop into the shower, if you don't mind? I was at the weight room earlier, too. So between my workout and those smelly jerks, I smell less than stellar." She saunters over to give me a quick kiss, then disappears into the bathroom.

After grabbing my geology and history books from my bedroom, I flop onto the couch to start reading. In the middle of a paragraph on tectonics, Jax's ringtone goes off.

"Just leave it!" she shouts from inside the bathroom, the sound of the water blurring her voice slightly.

"You sure?"

"It's just T. with questions about the practice schedule this week!"

"I can answer those," I shout back. But the only response I get is the steady drum of running water. Shrugging, I get up and grab Jax's backpack off the floor. Searching in the front pocket, I find her phone. When I go to answer it, the name on the screen makes me freeze.

My stomach drops. I try not to jump to conclusions. I try to stay calm. I haven't seen them together since the party. I'm sure it's nothing. But there he is, his name dark and bold on her screen: *Steven.*

I let the call go to voice mail and a text message notification pops up. I'm tempted to read it. My finger hovers over her unlock key. But I think better of it and tuck the phone back into the front pocket of her backpack. As much as I hate to admit it, it's not like they couldn't have just run into each other. Like at the library. Or even when she was on her way there, after the weight room.

Then it hits me as the shower water shuts off: Jax didn't have a stitch of athletic clothing on when she walked in the door.

CHAPTER TWENTY-NINE

The second Thursday of August I'm on campus, sitting in the soccer locker room, officially a sophomore member of the team. I'm one of a handful of girls already here for Coach's meeting, sitting along the newly carpeted benches below our designated lockers. Three freshman girls sit in a huddle in the corner. Elaine, who arrived first, has her raven hair pulled back in a ponytail, and her charcoal-colored eyes flit around the room while she talks. The two girls on either side of her, I learned from Mary ten minutes ago, played together in private school in Dallas. Carrie and Allison give off more confidence than Elaine, which made sense when Mary told me they were recruited as attackers. The three of them make small talk while I sit back against my locker.

The other person in the room, Mary, has her nose in a chemistry textbook a few feet to my right. My own textbooks seem to glare at me from inside my backpack sitting at my feet. Personally, I haven't felt motivated to do much schoolwork lately. This summer seems to have done me in more than previous ones, especially after my fight with Emily. So instead of reading for the past week as I should have been doing, I've been with Jax. Or thinking about Jax. Like I am now, reading over a text she sent me two minutes ago.

Hey, tell Coach I'm going to be ten minutes late to the meeting. Chatting with prof after class.

I type a message back, fighting the odd feeling that's settled in the back of my mind since I found that message from Steven last week. That afternoon I casually brought him up to Jax. She laughed and asked me what even made me think of him. And I couldn't very well tell her I'd dug into her backpack. As a result, the conversation ended up going nowhere. As I look down at my phone screen now, my mind floats back through memories of Jax and me from the summer. I remind myself I'm silly to worry about anything.

During my reverie, more of the team trickles into the room. When Emily walks in with Coach Gandy, I sit up but can't manage to look at her. A soft buzz of conversation fills the room, and I'm grateful that everybody seems too distracted to notice the fact she and I aren't sitting by each other, let alone making eye contact.

"Hey, short stack." Joey pulls me from my miserable thoughts when she sits down beside me. "How was your summer?"

Seeing Joey again for the first time in two months shakes me more than I expect it to. I had heard T. telling Haley that she had missed the first few weeks of practice because of her summer job and didn't come back until school started. Joey's hair is a little shorter but still the perfect shade of red to complement her fair skin. Her clear eyes seem even brighter. She sits cross-legged in skinny jeans on the bench, relaxed and radiating positivity.

"Hey," I say. "My summer was good. Busy," I add, realizing just how much has happened since I saw Joey last. I briefly wonder why she's acting so casual with me. Maybe she hasn't heard yet. She did just get back into town. I swallow and try to push the conversation along. "Did you have a good break?"

Joey leans back. "I did. I worked at a youth soccer camp. Which is why I'm back later. The kids were insane. But it was a lot of fun. Plus, who better to shape the goalies of tomorrow than me?" She grins and I can't help but smile.

"That's awesome. And way more productive than my summer."

Joey nudges me. "You and Emily hole up playing video games with your brother for two months?"

She definitely hasn't heard. How is that even possible?

"Um, not quite."

"Please. You don't have to hide it, Kyle. I know you're a closet gamer. You were probably locked in a room, piles of bagels and energy drinks all over the floor, yelling at twelve-year-old boys through the microphone during *Call of Duty*. You do look pretty pale," she adds with a grin.

I shove her and she laughs. Then I glance across the room at

Emily, who's deep in conversation with Haley. "I, um…I haven't actually talked to Emily in a few weeks."

Joey leans forward, stretching her legs out. "Is everything okay between you guys?"

I scrunch up my face. "Things are a little rocky at the moment."

Joey lowers her voice, leaning closer. "Must be. You guys are always inseparable during season." She watches Emily with me for a moment then says, "It seems like there's an ocean between you guys."

I nod. "Or maybe two."

"What happened?"

Coach Gandy, today in black jeans and a Nike polo, stands near her office door, and the chatter in the room begins to die down. I shake my head. "It's a long story."

Joey looks curious but doesn't press the matter. As Coach begins her preseason speech, welcoming the new girls to the team and announcing position changes for the roster, my mind wanders. What if this is how the rest of the semester plays out with Emily? What if she doesn't talk to me all season? I imagine our games: silence in the locker room and forced congratulations after a good play on the field. Just the idea of not getting along as teammates makes me reel. I have to talk to her. I have to make things okay again.

While Coach explains new league regulations, the locker room door swings open, and in strolls Jax.

"Finally," T. calls out next to Elaine.

"Jax, thank you for joining us. Take a seat." Coach gestures to the room, and Jax gives a mini-salute before shooting a look at T. Then her eyes are on me. I shift on the bench. I had told her over the summer we should keep things low-key once season began. I guess now I'm about to find out if she heard me.

Coach Gandy begins again about a rule on offsides as Jax plops down on the other side of me. I feel Joey's eyes on us. When I look back at her, her eyebrows are raised and she nods toward Jax. I can hear the "What's up with her?" question bouncing in the air between us.

For the next twenty minutes, we sit through the rest of Coach's rule updates, league changes, and team introductions. Jax, meanwhile, uses the time to bounce her knee against mine while we listen. From time to time, she even reaches out and runs her fingers briefly down my forearm. I sit frozen as she does, petrified. And even though nobody is paying attention, I can't shake the feeling that I'm under a microscope.

Finally, Coach's speech ends. There's applause and cheers as everybody gets up to leave. Coach shouts a final reminder about practice at seven o'clock tomorrow morning. Jax pops up from her bench without a look back in my direction. She bounds over to T. and starts chatting with her and Elaine.

Joey stands up slowly. "Somebody is feeling friendly."

"What?"

Joey nods toward Jax. "She must have had a lonely summer. What was up with her?"

I turn to Joey. Her eyes are cautious. I can feel that she wants to know what happened after that kiss last spring. And I realize then just how much has happened since that night. Since that unexpected kiss from Jax at our team party. Why didn't I have the guts to text her about it? We're friends after all. Now her eyes are locked on mine, the slightest of smiles in them as she runs a hand through her hair. What am I so afraid of when it comes to her?

"Joey, about my summer..."

"Joey, hey!" Haley skips up to us, and my courage deserts me. "Coach wants us to go over corner kick plays before heading home. Hi, Kyle!" she adds, giving me a quick hug. "Good first week back at school?"

I feel like a fast-wilting flower. "Yeah," I mumble. "It was fine."

"Great," Haley replies. "Joey, you ready?"

Joey nods. She turns to me. "Hold that thought, yeah? We'll catch up soon." She squeezes my arm. I feel guilt growing inside me, though I'm not exactly sure why. I watch Joey walk off with Haley and wonder how I'm ever going to tell her about my summer, if the news doesn't get to her first. How do I tell Joey I'm sorry for never leaving her a voice mail or sending a text message? How do I tell her that she kept running through my mind but that I spent all summer washing our memories away with wine-soaked days that blurred into hazy nights? How the hell do I tell Joey that I'm dating Jax?

Chapter Thirty

I lace my cleats and stand to look for my lucky athletic tape. While I dig through the top shelf in my locker, Emily begins a pep talk behind me in her best motivational speaker voice.

"Okay, ladies. Start visualizing the game. See yourselves out there. Feel the ball flying from your foot with practiced ease and watch it soar into the back of that net."

T. groans. "Emily, you do know this game is against Itasca, right? They were 0 and 8 last year."

"I am aware, thank you. But you can never underestimate your opponents," Emily replies.

I unzip the same pocket for the fourth time, wondering where I left my tape. I bite my lip, then decide there's only one person I can ask about where it may be. "Emily," I say before turning around. "Have you seen my tape? The blue tape I always use around my cleats?"

She frowns for a second, either at my bringing her inspiring words to a quick halt or my simply talking to her. "It's not in your bag? You always put it in there. And you always have, like, two spare rolls."

"I know," I say, pulling my bag out from my locker onto the bench beneath it. "But I can't find any of it, anywhere."

"You can play without it, can't you?" Sarah asks from where she's pulling up her socks on the bench next to me.

I give her a look, then glance at Emily.

"Kyle has been playing with blue tape since she was seven. It's her thing," Emily replies for me.

"Okay," Sarah says. "Well, I've got some black tape you can use if you like."

"It's got to be blue," Emily states simply. I give Emily a grateful look, and she almost smiles. But then she turns and jumps into a conversation with the freshman.

With a sigh, I plop down onto the bench. "I can't believe I forgot it."

"Relax, short stack," Joey says, sitting up from a leg stretch she'd been in across the room. "I'm sure you'll be just as mediocre a player without your special magic tape."

"Hush," I say before tossing my extra pair of socks at her, warranting a grin.

"Girls, come on, let's focus," Emily calls, her ponytail bobbing enthusiastically. "Coach will be here in a minute." She glances around the locker room. "We're all here, right?" She starts to count under her breath. "Wait. Has anyone seen Jax?"

"Did somebody say my name?"

The heads in the room all turn as Jax ambles in through the doorway, her bag over her shoulder and the rest of her still in street clothes.

"Jax, what are you doing?" Emily asks, her voice frantic. "We take the field for warm-ups in three minutes."

"Relax, Cap'n," Jax says before making her way toward me. "I'll be quick."

"What was keeping you anyway?" Emily presses. "Did Coach know you'd be late?"

Jax shakes her head, and I realize she's not looking at anyone but me. "I had to make a quick drugstore run."

Joey scoffs from her seat on the floor, and Jax's eyes flicker over to her for a half a second before returning to me. "I had a feeling my girlfriend was out of her lucky tape, so I went to pick some up. Blue, right, baby?"

My face flushes as Jax presents me with a still-packaged roll of blue athletic tape. Emily's eyes are on me, and when I glance at her, her eyebrows are raised so high I feel like they might disappear into her ponytail.

Finally, I manage to mutter my thanks.

"No problem, cutie," Jax replies. Then before I can move,

she gives me a quick kiss and says, "I'll just be a second," before moving over toward the bathroom to change.

I pick at the edges of the plastic encasing around the tape and try to ignore the pairs of eyes focused on me in the suddenly very crowded locker room.

"All right, ladies! Game time!" Mercifully, Coach wanders in, clipboard at the ready, and the eyes shift from me to her. I exhale as the shuffling of bags and cleats start around me, and I force myself to focus enough to open up the packaging before quickly unpeeling two lengths of tape.

"Let's go, let's go!" Coach exclaims, motioning for all of us to get up and moving. She claps, the sound echoing around the tiled room as she hurries back out toward the field.

My teammates run out, and I look up to find Emily eyeing me, then she follows the group outside. Jax, true to her word, has changed and is out of the bathroom. She drops her bag in front of her locker, gives me a wink, and jogs out behind the others.

I finish placing the second ring of tape around my right cleat when the sound of a ball bouncing on the other side of the room makes me jump. I look up. Joey is standing across the room, a ball pressed between her two hands like she's trying to squeeze the air out of it.

"You scared me," I say through a relieved laugh.

"Sorry."

I stand slowly. "You aren't waiting for me, are you?"

"Well," Joey starts, moving the ball to rest under her wrist against her side. "I was. I actually was," she says, smiling a little, her gaze down. "But it seems like I've just been wasting my time."

I furrow my brow, confused as to what she's talking about. "Joey, I'm not sure what you mean."

"No, it's fine," she says, looking back up at me. Her eyes gleam as if she's fighting back tears. "I mean, it's my fault really. I was being ridiculous, thinking that you'd wake up out of your little fantasy and realize that…" She stops. "No. You know what? This is on you. Not me. You chose to keep that from me." Her voice lowers, and the terseness in it takes me aback. "You said it, Kyle. You told me you weren't ready. Those were your words, don't you remember?"

It hits me then what she's talking about. Of course, Jax had to make a very public display of the fact that she and I are girlfriends before I had a chance to tell anyone else. But I didn't think…

"Joey, I'm sorry. I'm sorry I didn't tell you. I was going to. But I thought…I thought we were friends. What are you trying to say?"

"I'm saying that you weren't ready, Kyle!" she shouts. "God. What was I, just some little experiment to make sure you really did like girls? Somebody to keep around in case you felt like giving something different a try?"

My face flushes, but I force myself to reply. "Joey, I never meant—"

"That night, Kyle! We kissed. And you said you weren't ready for anything. And I accepted that. Because that was fine. You weren't ready and that was okay."

"Then why are you so upset?"

"Because!" she cries, her left arm up in exasperation. "Now apparently, you *are* ready. When it comes to Jax, you're ready now."

"Joey," I start, the words fumbling out, "when you and I… that was a long time ago. Over a year ago. I didn't know…I wasn't sure…"

"Of what you wanted, I know."

I watch her, and for the first time in over a year, for the first time since I met her, Joey is crying. The pang in my chest at the sight of her with tears glistening from the corners of her eyes nearly knocks me out. But I force myself to go on. "You can't be angry at me for this, Joey. It's not that simple. Not for me." As we stand there with the sound of bleachers creaking overhead, the air between us feels as if it's slowly being sucked out. Like whatever Joey and I had between us is being drawn out, piece by piece, and every moment we once shared is being stolen away to a place I'm not sure either of us will be able to get it back from.

She looks down again before rubbing at both her eyes. "I guess it's like you said. That instinct people have when they see a rock on the ground? They kick it aside without giving it a second thought."

"Joey," I start, but she ignores me. She just grabs her water bottle from the bench and jogs out of the locker room and up onto the field.

Chapter Thirty-One

"Hello?"

"Hi."

"Kevin?"

"Yep."

I switch my cell phone to my other hand and turn my wrist to see the time on my sports watch. 4:17 pm. "What's up? No Technology Club after school today?"

"It was canceled."

I glance out the window when our team bus pulls up to a stoplight. The city limit sign sits beyond it, nestled between trees on the lush roadside. The dry leaves curl at their tips, and I wonder if they feel as beaten down by this past summer as I do.

"Oh, okay," I say. Across the aisle, Emily tilts her head in my direction—her curiosity warranted since she knows my family well. Rather, she knows us well enough to understand how we communicate, which is never. Then she lowers her gaze and dives back into the marketing textbook in her lap. Meanwhile I mumble into the phone, unsure how to proceed with my brother. "Um, well, are Mom and Dad working?"

"Yeah," replies Kevin. "Mom's in DC and Dad is in Houston. They're traveling a lot lately."

I nod. "How's school?"

"It's okay. Senior year is a lot easier than last year so far." I nod while he tells me about his anatomy class. I realize I haven't spoken to Kevin since my semester started after the summer holidays. And since Jax convinced me to stay in town all summer, I haven't seen him since he came to a playoff game last spring with Mom and Dad.

I didn't think I'd be missing much by not going home. Just an empty house. But now a pang of guilt hits me.

"How are you?" asks Kevin. "How's school and soccer?"

"It's fine. I'm with the team now. We're on our way to a game." I glance over at Emily and know she's listening. If I wasn't on the bus, I wonder if I would tell Kevin about everything that's going on. He probably wouldn't even believe that Emily and I haven't spoken much over the last month. Or that I'm dating a teammate now and have become a hot point for team gossip. I grimace, everything from the last few months sitting on the tip of my tongue. But I choke it back. "Things are fine. They're…fine," I finally say. I clear my throat and force a smile. "Classes are fun." I practically hear Kevin's smile. "But you always were the smart one between the two of us."

"Yeah, but at least *you* can catch a football."

The memory of us three years ago at a neighborhood Fourth of July party makes me smile. All the kids had been corralled into a touch football game. Our neighbor's son Andrew McCauley was quarterback for our team. Before a play, I tried to tell Kevin where to run, and Andrew said he'd get the ball right to him. Somehow, Kevin made it to the spot on the field, but as soon as the ball came toward him, he put his hands up like some sort of shield. The ball went right through his arms and we spent the rest of the day tending to his bloody nose.

"Hey, that was just my way of getting Andrew's sister to talk to you," I say finally.

"Sure," he replies.

Laughter escapes my mouth before I can stop it. The sound feels distant and unfamiliar; I realize it's been ages since a lighthearted thought caught me off guard. Especially when it came to my family. The memory of that holiday, featuring my unfortunate brother, lingers next to me on the bus, and then shifts into an image from later that same evening.

My mom had taken Kevin to an urgent care to patch up his nose, which left me and my dad alone for the evening. That was the summer before everything became complicated with Beth. It was also a rare night when my dad was home. I replay the evening: I'm at home with my dad, watching bad sci-fi movies after ordering pizza. Fireworks crackle down the street, and together we laugh at the goofy costumes and special effects from a bygone TV era.

I move the phone away from my ear as a swell of noise comes from the other end. "Sorry," Kevin mumbles. "The rest of the club just walked past. We're heading over to Joe's for ice cream since our meeting was canceled. And the rest of them will be, too, I guess, for a while."

I blink, shaking loose my thoughts and bringing myself back to the present. "What do you mean?" I ask, my eyes floating to the tattered cloth on the bus seat in front of me. "They're not making school cuts again, are they? I remember when they cut the water polo teams. The pool was dyed purple a week later in retaliation. Remember me telling you?"

Kevin chuckles. "I remember. But it's nothing like that."

Cars pass by outside on the highway we've merged onto. I shift the phone to my other ear as T. and Jax turn up the volume on their speaker that's blaring pop songs in the back of the bus. I wait for my brother to continue. The metal clanking of lockers opening and closing echo in the background on his end.

"Mr. Collins died."

"What?" I say after a few seconds. I press the phone closer to my ear.

"Mr. Collins, my technology teacher. He died. He didn't come into school today, and we just heard the news that he was in a car accident last night. He was hit by a drunk driver. The driver was fine. But Mr. Collins…" Kevin's voice fades and cracks like an old radio. The news seeps into me, slowly at first, then crashes into me head-on.

"Oh, God," I finally say. Emily shifts in her seat, her eyes flickering over to me. But I can't bring myself to catch her eye. "Kevin, I'm so sorry. I know how much you liked him." Kevin had found his niche in Technology Club since entering high school. He'd always been good with gadgets and read a lot on video game design. He spoke highly of Mr. Collins whenever we managed to sit down to a family dinner. It was clear the man had impacted my little brother.

"I'm so sorry," I say again.

Kevin's shrug seems audible before he says, "Thanks. I just..." His voice falters. "I wanted to call you when I heard. I didn't really know who to talk to, since Mom and Dad are never here."

My eyes well up, and I turn to face out the window. I swallow. "I'm sorry I wasn't around this past summer."

His silence on the other end magnifies the guilt creeping over me. My mind replays the phone message he had left me in June. Kevin had offered to teach me how to play *Assassin's Creed* while our parents were away for work. If I came home. But I was too busy to even return his call. Running a hand over my face, I rack my mind, wondering why I thought it was okay to ignore him. Was I really that selfish, so caught up in Jax?

"Kevin?" I ask, the line still quiet.

"It's all right. I get it."

"I'm still sorry." I run a hand over my ponytail. Then I take a deep breath. "Hey, Kevin?"

"Yeah?"

"I love you."

The line is quiet again, and someone shouts my brother's name. "I gotta go," he says.

I swallow my tears and nod. "Okay, yeah, sure."

"I'll, um, call you again soon."

"Yeah," I say, trying to smile. "I'll let you know how our game goes tonight."

"Okay." Silence for a moment. "Kyle?"

"Yeah?"

"I love you, too."

I hang up the phone and lean back against my seat. Staring out the window, I run the last few months over in my mind. The shining star in almost every memory is Jax. I didn't think spending time with her would cost me so much time with everybody else. But that's how relationships work, isn't it? It's normal for things to change. People can suddenly fade into the background. I just didn't realize it would be the people I held dearest.

"Scoot."

I turn and find Emily nudging me closer to the window, sliding one leg onto the seat next to me and tucking it beneath her.

"What are you—?"

"Kyle, I am the *only* person on this planet who understands your family as well as you do. So, spill."

I wipe my eyes and shake my head. "Em, you don't have to do this." Her mouth falls into a frown, but her eyes are bright and determined. "Really," I say, tucking my legs closer to me. "Besides, I don't deserve your help."

At this, Emily sighs dramatically. "Come on." She waves a hand in the air. "Kyle. Please. This has gone on long enough, don't you think?"

I glance over my shoulder. Jax is deep in conversation with T. at the back of the bus. Then I look sidelong at Emily. "By 'this,' do you mean my acting like a complete jerk or your silent treatment and frustration over who I'm dating?"

Emily purses her lips, then says, "Well, both." I smile. "Kyle. Look, you had a point about my acting like your big, bossy sister."

Slowly, I shake my head. "I didn't mean what I said that day."

But Emily interjects. "Still, there was some truth to it." She looks down at her hands. "I've always seen you as a part of my family, Kyle. And I think I was afraid to say good-bye to you once I graduated high school." She shrugs and adds, "Getting you to come here was a way for me to hang on to us."

"Em, you didn't *make* me come to this school. I wanted to."

"Well, even so. I'm sorry for acting like the one in charge of what you do. I know you can make your own decisions." She pauses, "I can't very well go on pretending things are like they used to be. There's no use in it. And I'm not saying that I've changed my mind about everything. I can't do that." My gaze falls and I nod. "But that doesn't mean we can't agree to disagree on some things. You and I are adults. That's the mature thing to do about all of this, don't you think?"

Our eyes meet, and once again Emily amazes me with how wonderful she is. I nod in agreement.

"Good." She sits up straighter. "So, enough of this nonsense between us. Things always work themselves out in the end anyway. And in the meantime, it sounds like something's up with Kevin. So, let's hear it."

The rest of the bus ride I tell Emily all about Kevin and my parents spending less and less time at home and all of my guilt about not being there for him. While I talk, I feel something stir inside me. Like the feeling right before a corner kick: the familiar excitement of what's to come, even if you're not sure what that something will be. The feeling spreads as Emily nods, listening. I've got my best friend back. And I make a promise to myself to never lose her again.

Chapter Thirty-Two

All right, ladies, corner kick time!" Coach Gandy hollers at us from atop the goalie box.

"Ugh, I swear these water breaks are getting shorter and shorter," T. grumbles in our scattered huddle along the sideline of the practice field.

I swallow more of my Gatorade and water mix, then inhale deeply. Now in September, Coach seems determined to work us harder than ever. And this practice has been rough. Callie actually puked once. Even T. had to take a break after our second round of sprints. All of us are dripping in sweat, and my legs are killing me. We hit the weight room yesterday and Coach demanded we do an extra set on top of our normal amount. I literally had to fall out of bed this morning, my legs were so stiff.

"Come on, ladies," Emily chimes in, though it's clear her usual chipper demeanor has been deflated a bit. "Big game next week."

She tosses her water bottle down onto her bag and jogs back over to where Coach is standing. A few others follow behind her. I bend down to relace my cleat when a hand grabs my backside. Wide-eyed, I look up as Jax walks away from me, her face straight but her eyes mischievous. "Don't be the last one, babe," she calls before turning to run over to the cluster forming near the goal box.

I watch her jog off when a sudden, sharp *rip* turns my attention to the bleachers. Joey stands up, tightening her gloved hand. Her eyes are down, looking at anything but me.

I open my mouth to say something—though I'm not sure what—as she hops down off the bleacher. But before I can, Joey speaks first.

"Come on," she says. "I don't feel like running more gassers after practice."

I open my mouth to reply, then decide against it and jog a few feet behind her back over to the others.

"Okay," Coach Gandy says sternly, "just like Tuesday's practice. Emily, you're on the corner," she says, tossing her a blue pinnie. Coach moves quickly, her sculpted arms cutting through the air as she hands a few more out, including to Jax, T., and five others, all of whom pull on the mesh tank top. "Blue, you're with Emily. And if you can put two and two together, which I sure as hell hope you can, you guys are on offense. You girls without a pinnie, mark up, you're defense."

Before I can even move, Jax is beside me. "Found my girl," she says, linking her arm through mine.

I chuckle. "I thought I was supposed to look for you."

She shrugs and gives me a playful push before we wander over to the goal box. "I found you first." She finishes with a hip bump.

As Emily grabs the ball and runs over to the corner, the rest of us line up along the top of the goal box. Jax tugs at the base of my T-shirt, and I give her a bump of my hip in return. We exchange grins as Emily raises her arm up from the field's corner, signaling she's ready.

The ball sails up and curves just slightly. Half of the team moves forward while the rest of us hang back, including me and Jax. The ball falls and bounces off Sarah's chest before she taps it in our direction.

I move forward for it, but Jax is one step ahead of me. I reach for her pinnie but I miss and end up watching her whale a kick off her left foot toward the goal.

Joey dives to her left. The ball just grazes off her fingertips and falls behind her into the net.

Everyone in blue cheers and goes to high-five Jax.

"Nice one," Coach says before blowing her whistle for us to reset.

"Lucky shot," Joey says after she hurls the ball back over to Emily.

"Please," Jax says, and there's suddenly a knot in the pit of my stomach. "That was pure skill."

Joey rolls her eyes, and Jax shoots her a look, but the whistle is blowing again and we move back to our original places.

Emily's arm is up once more, and then the ball is flying at us, this time more directly and faster. I move in front of Jax, ready if it comes our way. Then suddenly, it's like everything is on fast-forward. We all crash in toward the goal, and as the ball reaches us, I find myself near the bottom of a pile that's jumping for a header. Shoulders crash and legs get tangled, and I'm shoved downward. But my eyes are still up on the ball as Jax leaps up to make contact. At the same time, Joey has jumped up from her mark with her hand balled into a fist.

The sound of her fist making contact with Jax's temple reminds me of the ball smacking right into the goal post. There are a lot of "oooohhs" as Joey's fist, Jax's head, and the ball all ricochet off each other in opposite directions. The ball lands on the other side of the goalie box behind us. Joey lands on her feet, shaking her fist out, and Jax is bent over, her hand on her temple.

"Holy shit!" she cries. "What the hell was that?"

I move away from both of them as T. rushes over to Jax.

Joey stands upright, pulling her shoulders back. She shrugs. "I was making sure the ball didn't get past me."

"And, what, you temporarily mistook my head for the ball?" Jax bites back.

"Okay, okay," Coach says, moving between everybody and standing between Joey and Jax. She lifts up her sunglasses and her dark eyes rove over her players. "Reset, ladies, reset. Jax, are you all right?"

Jax stands up and rubs at the side of her face. It's red but doesn't look swollen. She nods, reaching out to grab my hand. "Yeah," she finally says, "I'll live."

When Jax releases my hand, it's like a button is pressed, opening an invisible door from where unspoken words crawl out from behind Jax's eyes and move slowly toward the goal line where Joey stands. Imagining all of this, the hairs on my arm stand straight up. Joey and Jax have never been close as teammates, but this was slowly starting to feel like some sort of territorial showdown. Sure, some words had been shared on the field over the last few months. I know Joey becoming the permanent goalie has Jax wound up.

Between that and the stress of Coach's workouts, it makes sense they're a little on edge. But there's no reason, I think, as Emily shoots me a look over her shoulder, for them to do something crazy, like throw punches.

I watch Joey in the goal. She cracks her neck and swings her arms across her chest, and her eyes are locked on Emily standing on the corner. We reset again at the top of the box. Jax gives my arm a brief nudge, and I smile. She'll be fine. I was silly to worry. It's all just friendly competition.

This time, when Emily fires another kick off from the corner, I'm two steps ahead of everyone. The ball falls toward us with a high, sloping arc. I hear the thunder of cleats behind me, but my eyes are trained on the ball.

"Got it!" I cry.

"Mine!" I hear half a second later. But I'm already jumping and so is Joey. My forehead collides with the ball, and I direct it away from the net. Joey's body is flush against mine, and then one of her legs tangles with mine while we're still in midair.

I fall. Hard. My leg that had been caught with hers lands a second after my right one, and I know what happens as soon as I hear it.

Crunch.

The rest of my body follows my ankle and I flop into a heap on the ground. The whistle blows from somewhere behind me, but all I see is an obnoxious collection of stars as I clench my eyes shut and roll onto my back.

"Dammit," I grumble.

There are hands—big hands—suddenly on my arm. It takes me a second to realize they're not hands but gloves. I open my eyes. Joey leans over me, her usually clear gaze clouded with panic.

"Oh my God, Kyle, I'm so sorry!" she says, her eyes moving down to my ankle and back up to me. "I heard you call it, but I was already jumping, and then I couldn't stop myself, and then my knee got caught under yours, and I'm so sorry!"

She's kind of cute when she's flustered.

Wait. What?

A jolt of pain runs from my ankle up to my knee. I grimace.

"I'll be fine," I finally say, looking up at Joey. The rest of the team has circled around me. "Really," I say, letting Joey help me up. I put my weight on her after a quick try of my ankle proves useless. "I'll be fine." Jax appears on my other side. Her right arm slips under my left and around my back, and she pulls me toward her.

"I've got it," Jax says, more at Joey than to me.

"It's no problem," Joey says, "I've already got her."

"I think I can help my girlfriend over to the bench."

I limp between them and my face flushes as we walk through the rest of the team and over to the sideline. Neither of them concedes, and the three of us finally make it over to the bleachers. I fall down onto the first metal bench with a wince and prop my foot out in front of me.

"She needs ice," Joey says, looking through the trainer's cooler.

"I know she needs ice," Jax calls back. My ankle is throbbing so much I have to close my eyes to try to block it out. "She's *my* girlfriend," Jax says. "I think I know how to take care of my own girlfriend."

The whistle blows. "Ladies," Coach shouts from across the field. "Get ice on Kyle, stat. Carver, get back out here!"

My eyes are still shut, but I hear Joey take a deep breath, followed by the sound of her footsteps fading as she heads back to the others on the field. Then there's a rustling from the trainer's cooler followed by a shadow over me. I hood my eyes and open them to find Jax. Her eyes—bold, surrounded with their signature black eyeliner—are focused on the ice pack in her hands. She cracks it and sets it against my ankle.

"Thanks," I mutter, turning slightly to face her.

Jax coos something into my ear, but the throbbing makes it hard to hear. She kisses my temple. The sweat from her chin mingles with my cheek, and the sweetness of it lingers when she sits back up.

"I've got you," she says. There's a hint of something in her voice, but my ankle is pulsing so much I can't gather my thoughts enough to pinpoint it. "Whatever you need, babe, just tell me."

I swallow, my throat parched, and close my eyes again. "I'll be fine, Jax, don't worry. It's just an ankle sprain."

I take a deep breath and relish the feel of her fingers as they move through my hair and down my face. Of course it'll be okay, I tell myself. My ankle, my lingering concern about Jax and Steven. I was silly to even worry. Jax will take care of me. She would never do anything to hurt me.

Chapter Thirty-Three

"You should do something about this."

I glance at Emily from where I'm sitting on my bed, my left leg out in front of me with a bag of frozen peas resting on my now very swollen ankle. I lift the bag briefly and my face falls at the shade of purple that's sprung up around the bone. The wind howls as an evening storm brews outside, the bare branches scraping against my bedroom window.

"Yeah." I grimace and try to rearrange the pillow behind me to keep myself propped up. "I know, Emily. Hence the ice pack."

"No," she says, swiveling my desk chair around so that she faces me. "I mean, you've got to do something about the whole Jax and Joey situation."

"Oh." I frown, leaning back with a huff against my wall of pillows. I was hoping what had happened at practice hadn't been as obvious as it evidently was.

Emily looks at me, her eyebrows raised. Then she glances back at my laptop, which I notice is open to Facebook. She speaks in a slightly higher voice, her fingers up in air quotes. "'Ugh…some people just can't appreciate other people's happiness and have to drag them down,'" she finishes, her eyes back to me.

I shrug. "One of your professors upset about exam grades?" I ask, feigning ignorance.

Emily shuts the laptop and spins around fully to face me, her dark curls now a mane framing a face of disbelief. "No, that's Jax's latest post."

I nod. "Ah."

Emily takes a deep breath. "I'm going to start this by saying that I love you. You're my best friend, and I'm so happy that you're here and we're playing together and that everything from this summer is water under the bridge. But…" She trails off, looking at me as if I should know where this will end.

I stare back at her.

"Seriously, Kyle. Last week in the weight room Jax practically dropped the barbell on Joey's face."

I fiddle with the bag of peas but don't say anything.

"And have you completely forgotten about the time Joey slid for the ball and cleated Jax's thigh?"

I give her a look. "Come on, that's just part of the game."

Emily's hands fly up. "Really, Kyle? You really don't see what's going on here? It's like the freaking novellas I watch for Spanish class."

"No, I don't see." Her eyes are still pinned on me. Eventually, I sigh. "Well, maybe."

She nods. We're quiet for a moment, then she asks, "Do you love her?"

I don't know why, but the question makes me reel. Obviously, the answer should be an immediate, unwavering yes. I'm with Jax. Me. I'm actually dating the girl whose first words to me knocked me off my feet. Jax, who is stunning. Fun. Full of life. But that little voice in the back of my mind begins to whisper. Yes, she can drink too much. And she's the type to post our dirty laundry on Facebook and Twitter. But all of that doesn't make her a bad person.

And maybe things haven't been as great as they were when we first became girlfriends. The first two months were magical. Pure bliss. Things aren't bad now, by any means. It's just that now…I can't seem to ignore the other thing that has followed me like a shadow for so long. That one person who's always been there, even when I tried to forget her.

As if she knew my thoughts had drifted to her, my phone dings. I reach for it resting on the blankets by my knee. Sure enough, there's Joey's face—captured in a hilarious smile with her face covered in colorful splatters after a paintball fight. I open up her message.

Hey. Just making sure you haven't had to chop your leg off or anything. Let me know if you need more frozen peas.

I smile, but then Emily clears her throat and brings me back to reality.

"Which one?" she asks, her brow raised.

I look up. "Joey."

"Uh-huh," she says, and I see the wheels turning in her head. "Put the phone down."

"What?"

"You heard me." Emily stands up. "Put the phone down. Don't reply."

"I'm sorry…what?" I ask, entirely confused as Emily walks over to my bed and plucks the phone out of my hands. "Wait. Hold on," I say. "What are you doing?"

"Saving your skin." She looks around the room before her eyes settle on my mini-fridge. She walks over to it, opens it up, and sets my phone next to a bottle of blue Gatorade. "There." She smiles at herself as she closes the door and straightens back up.

"What does chilling my phone have to do with saving my skin?" I ask, wincing at the pain that shoots up through my foot.

She sits down on the edge of the bed and gives me a look. It's one of her classic Emily looks, and I know it means I'm about to be in for it.

"Listen, Kyle," she says, "you're with Jax. And Jax, apparently, makes you happy, right?"

I raise an eyebrow, realizing I'd never answered her earlier question. "She does," I say, picturing Jax wrapping her arms around my waist when she sneaks up behind me on the field. I feel her hands on my hips, and I smile. "She really does."

"Right," Emily says. "Well, then, if she makes you happy, then that's what counts. I am glad that you're getting out there. And, sure, I thought maybe you'd have leaned toward a taller, more levelheaded 'out there,' but hey, that's up to you." I give her a look, but she presses on. "The thing is, Kyle, now that you're with Jax, you have to be *with Jax*."

"I'm not sure I follow you."

"Okay, it's like this," she says, brushing some stray hairs out of her face. "I'm dating Alex, and there's this guy in my communications class who's attractive. He just is, I can't deny that. And one day he asked for my number, claiming it's in case he has questions on one of our class projects. So I gave it to him. We spent a week chatting through messages, mostly about class stuff, occasional random banter here and there. Then I could tell that he was trying to get at something else. Something…more," she says, pausing to make sure she still has my attention. "So I stopped. I would respond to his messages when I needed to, but they'd be short and direct. I didn't want him to get the wrong idea that I was flirting. Because I'm with Alex."

I look at her, trying to line up the pieces of her story. "So," I say, "you put my phone in the fridge because in this situation, I'm you, and Jax is Alex and…"

"Joey is the guy in my communication class."

I shake my head. "But…no." My thoughts refuse to give in to what I know Emily is trying to get me to see. "It's not the same. Joey and I are friends. We've been friends since my first day here. We play on the same soccer team, for crying out loud. And she *just* started talking to me again."

Emily shifts on the bed, then adjusts the bag, which had started to slide off my ankle. "That's the thing, though, Kyle," she says, still focusing on the frozen peas. "You and Joey were never just friends."

"Sure we were," I say. "We just…we're just…"

"Complicated," Emily finishes for me. I slump back against my pillows as rain begins to beat against my window. "I'm sorry, Kyle. But you're not being fair to Joey."

Once again, Emily's right. "Okay." I frown. "I guess that makes sense. I just didn't see why Joey and I couldn't still talk."

Emily looks at me then. "I've seen those text messages you guys used to send. Y'all's talking is like Alex's and my foreplay."

I laugh, blushing. Emily grins. "Fine." I sigh. "So, what do I do? Just cut Joey off completely?"

"Yes," Emily says without hesitation, surprising me with her authoritative tone. It's amazing how easily she can shift from best friend to the older sister role in one move. "Well." Her face softens. "Just for a little while. Give it three weeks."

"Three weeks?" I ask, my ankle shooting pain upward.

"Yes, three weeks. No texting. No calls. You guys can make nice at practice, but no talking outside of soccer."

"And if I see her at a party?"

Emily stands up then and pats my ankle, making me grimace. "Good thing you're about to be bedridden for a few weeks."

I lean back and groan.

"I know you, Kyle," she says, grabbing her workout bag from off the floor and pulling it over her shoulder. "You're a good person. But you can miss what's right in front of your face sometimes. And if you really do care about them—Jax and Joey—you'll do this to make things right." She pauses, then adds, "One of them deserves your full attention. So you should give it to them."

I glance up at her as she stands in my bedroom doorway. "You mean Jax deserves my full attention."

Emily just smiles back at me. "Take some ibuprofen and try to rest. I'll come back in the morning to check on you."

Then she's out of sight, and a few seconds later I hear my apartment door open and close. I throw one of my arms behind my head and stare at my mini-fridge, trying to ignore how much I want to write Joey back.

CHAPTER THIRTY-FOUR

Bring it in, ladies!" The team jogs into the middle of the field, surrounding Coach Gandy in a huddle while I watch from the sideline. With a sigh, I reach for my crutches at the end of the bleachers. Carefully, I half hop, half fall onto the grass, landing with a thud on the sideline before bracing myself with my metal companions. The team huddle is still in formation, so I throw my small workout bag over both of my shoulders and start off for the parking lot.

Over the last week and a half, I've missed one game against Aledo. Coach gave me two days of full bed rest after my injury—which turned out to be nothing more than a good, old-fashioned sprain. I was determined to be back out quickly to watch the drills and plays the team had to run through so that I wouldn't be completely lost when I rejoined everyone next week.

As I walk, making sure to put the tiniest heel-toe pressure on my bum foot, a small *ding* sounds from inside my bag. I know it's Jax sending me a message. She had to skip practice today thanks to a chemistry lab. When she and I met up for lunch earlier today, she told me she was going to check in on me after practice, to make sure I didn't fall down a sewer or sprain my other ankle while getting from Emily's car to the field. I conjure up the image of her concerned face while we shared some fries in the Student Union. And then my own face heats up at the memory of her comment after she kissed me good-bye.

"Good thing it isn't your wrist that you sprained." This, of course, was followed by her signature wink.

I have to admit, Jax was being unusually great when it came to my lack of mobility. She brought me coffee over the weekend and we hung out all day watching movies, rotating frozen veggies on my ankle every few hours. During the week, she made sure I had a ride to campus and then to my evening with the trainers for therapy. She even helped to carry my backpack on Tuesday during her free period.

"Anything for my girl," she said, dropping me off in front of geology.

I glance over my shoulder, pausing at the ramp leading down into the parking lot. Emily gathers her stuff from the sideline and gives me a quick wave. After a deep breath, I start down the ramp.

Eventually I make it to Emily's car and gingerly lean on the crutches against the passenger side. I let my body relax against the car for a moment. With my head back, I close my eyes, congratulating myself on another mini-journey completed.

"Hey."

I pick my head up and open my eyes. I don't see anyone, then turn to look behind me. Joey walks up to the far side of her car, which I hadn't even noticed was parked next to Emily's.

For a second, all I feel is panic, which sends an excruciating throb through my foot and up to my knee. "Shit." I grimace, stumbling slightly.

Thanks to her long stride, Joey rounds both of the cars between us quickly. "Whoa, easy." She helps me straighten back up. "Are you okay?"

"Yeah," I mumble, the pain subsiding just as quickly as it came. "Thanks."

She nods at my crutches. "The robot arms suit you."

"I hear they're all the rage in Europe," I say. "Decided to bring the trend stateside."

Thanks to a lot of willpower and several *CSI* marathons to distract myself, I've actually managed to follow Emily's orders and not talk to Joey for the last twelve days. It helped that I wasn't really able to leave my apartment much since rolling my ankle. But after I didn't respond to her text the first day when Emily placed my phone in the fridge, Joey sent me another message two days later, asking if I was going to be at practice. I waited two hours to respond, eventually only saying yes. I was pretty sure she'd taken my shortness as a cue to leave me be. And since I'd been sidelined the last few days of practice, we hadn't talked at all. Which, to say the least, was weird.

I shift my weight, then say, "I'm, um, just waiting for Emily."

Joey nods. She's watching me, and I can tell that she wants to talk about it. I don't blame her. Of course, she's curious to know why I'm ignoring her, especially right after we started talking again. I would want an explanation, too.

I take a deep breath. "Listen, Joey. I know I've been kind of AWOL lately." She doesn't say anything, just moves to lean against the car next to me. "And I'm sorry about that. Thinking about it, if I were in your place, I would be pretty confused and hurt if one of my friends just stopped talking to me. Twice," I add with a cringe.

Joey nods. "Brilliant deduction, Sherlock."

I can't help but laugh at her very Joey response. "Yeah, well, I should…well, I should be more honest with you about why I haven't talked to you at practice or anything."

"Mm-hmm," Joey says, crossing her arms and eyeing me carefully.

For a moment, I consider telling her. I consider telling Joey that she and I aren't just friends, which makes everything between me and Jax complicated. I consider telling her that I still think about that kiss. But if I spend more than a moment on those thoughts, I start to think too much. And I can't give into those memories now that I'm with Jax. I consider telling her how confusing things are. And that things only get more confusing when she and I are around each other.

"Kyle?"

"Yeah?"

"You were going to tell me something?"

I blink, realizing I haven't actually spoken yet. "Sorry." I adjust my weight onto my right leg. "The reason we haven't been talking. It's, well, it's because of Jax."

Joey raises an eyebrow. "Jax?"

I nod. "Yes. I mean, she's not, like, making me not talk to you or anything. It's just that, well, things always seem to be a bit tense when the three of us are together, and it was suggested to me that maybe you and I take some time apart, since I am, you know, with Jax."

It's quiet for a moment, the only sound the scraping of cleats behind us signifying the girls have made their way over to the parking lot.

"Is that it?"

Confused I ask, "Is what it?"

"That's why you stopped talking to me?" She reaches out, running a quick finger along my collarbone, "Why you stopped wearing the necklace? There's no other reason?"

I swallow. Again, the urge to tell her overwhelms me. What if I did admit all of those things? I gaze up into her light blue eyes. What if I told Joey that part of me wishes I was brave, like her? What if I told her the truth?

"No," I finally say, looking down. "There's no other reason."

Joey stands up. "Okay. I get it."

"You do?"

Joey looks down then, scuffing her cleats along the asphalt. "Sure," she says softly. Then she pauses. "Though Jax, I have to admit, isn't my favorite person."

I chuckle. "You don't say?"

She laughs and shrugs. "Is it that obvious?"

"Only most of the time," I say, smirking.

"Hey, you two."

Our conversation is interrupted when Emily opens up the trunk of her car. She piles her soccer bag and some cones into it before slamming it shut.

"Hey," Joey and I say in unison.

"Ready to go, Kyle?" Emily asks, giving me a look that I know means I'll have to spill about this later.

I turn to Joey. "I'd better go." Then I reach for my crutches. Emily clicks the car unlocked, and Joey pulls the passenger door open for me. "Thanks," I say before slowly falling not-so-gracefully backward into the seat.

"Very nice," Joey says once I finally get my seat belt on.

We exchange grins as she hands me my crutches. Emily opens up her driver's side door then slides in. "All set?" she asks, starting the engine.

"Yep. Thanks," I say again to Joey.

"No problem." Then she leans down so that she's eye level with me. Emily fiddles with the radio when Joey lowers her voice and says, "Call me when your babysitter lets you out again."

I stare at her for a second, then her face breaks out in a smile and she stands up, shutting the door. Emily puts her car in reverse. It's quiet except for the pop music as we pull out onto the road. Then Emily finally breaks the silence.

"I heard that."

Chapter Thirty-Five

"You know, I would have had that shot today if Katie hadn't blocked my view." Joey hands me another beer from the fridge.

"Sure, keep telling yourself that."

"Hey," she says, hip pushing the fridge door shut. "I'm serious. You're good, but not that good." Her eyes twinkle, amused.

I shrug, then say, "All right then. I'll be sure to use my freshly healed left foot next time. You know, to go easy on you."

We cross the living room and drop down onto one of the cushions on Emily's couch. The apartment door stands open, and Elaine and T. stand just outside the doorway, calling into Haley's open apartment across the hall. Haley, who moved in over the summer, has created a communal gathering space at our apartment complex. Now Emily shares the hosting burden each time we get together. Music from Haley's drifts over to us with the brisk November air coming through the open door. Initially, I pitied the notoriously uptight swim team members who had to live next door when these team parties began, but Emily insists that with a healthy schedule of freshly baked cookies, they let our get-togethers slide as long as things don't get too loud.

Emily sits with Callie, Sarah, and a few other upperclassmen out on her patio. There's laughter coming from Emily's bedroom, where Mary and the new freshmen have been watching cat videos on the Internet for the last hour. I take a sip from my beer and stretch my left foot out to rest on the coffee table in front of Joey and me. Joey crosses one ankle over her knee, and I shift to lean against the arm of the couch, facing her.

"Hard to believe another season is almost over," I say as Katie runs in from the hallway to grab another drink from the fridge.

"I know." Joey stretches out one arm up onto the back of the couch. "Before we know it, we'll be juniors."

I nod and we both stare at the TV for a little while. Emily has the old movie channel on with the volume off. As a result, the characters in the mobster flick speak vehemently but silently at one another in black and white. When the movie cuts to commercial, there's an advertisement for holiday decorations.

Joey clears her throat. "So, are you going home once finals are over?"

I nod. "I think so. Since I wasn't home over the summer, I'd like to be there for a few weeks. Kevin mentioned that my parents aren't home much. And I don't want to leave him alone again, especially over Christmas."

"Such a good big sis." Joey smiles.

"Well, I don't know about that." I look down, fiddling with the bottom of my blue button-down. "I still feel bad about the summer. I think Kevin's had a rough time this semester. And my parents... well, my family isn't great at the whole communication thing."

Joey tilts her head. "Never would have guessed."

I give her knee a bump with mine. "All right. That was a fair shot."

She grins and takes a drink. My eyes flicker down to her lips for a moment, but I force them back onto the TV when she meets my gaze.

"Um, any New Year's plans?" I ask her.

Her fingers play with the rim of her beer as she says, "Actually, there's this group of people from my economics class getting together in Dallas." She shrugs. "They're pretty cool. And sometimes it's nice to hang out with people who aren't on the team, you know?"

I don't really know, but I nod anyway. "That sounds fun."

"Yeah," she says. "We'll see."

Our eyes meet over the tops of our respective beers. Then I feel two hands snake over my shoulders and down my chest.

"Hey, babe," Jax whispers next to my ear.

“Hey,” I say, clearing my throat. Joey shifts away from me on the couch. I didn’t even realize we’d inched closer to one another over the last ten minutes. Nor did I realize how cold I would feel when she excused herself to leave.

CHAPTER THIRTY-SIX

Jax and I pull up in front of Emily's house. I rub my hands together and tug my coat closer to me, then undo my seat belt in the passenger seat. The street outside is bright: every house on Emily's block awash in holiday lights lining the two-story roofs and front lawns. Jax turns off the engine and reaches across me into the glove compartment.

"What are you doing?" I ask as she pulls out a flask. "How long have you had that in there?"

Jax smirks, then takes a long gulp. "Ease up, Kyle. God, you think I just pulled out a weapon or something."

I frown as she takes another drink. "Jax, we're going to a party. There will be alcohol there. It's New Year's Eve, for crying out loud."

She holds up the flask in a toast to me. "Exactly." She lets out an exaggerated "ah" and wipes her mouth after another sip.

My mouth hangs open, frustration fizzing up inside me. But I can't find any words, so I just reach to open my door. Jax grabs my arm, pulling me back. "Hey," she says, the flask recapped. She tucks it into the inside pocket of her black pea coat. "Jesus, Kyle, I'm sorry. I just…" She releases my arm and looks past me to the homes outside. "I just thought I'd loosen up a little bit. We are going to a party at Emily's house, after all."

"Yeah. Emily." I cross my arms in a huff. "My best friend."

"Your best friend who doesn't like me."

I roll my eyes. "Jax, I told you all of that blew over. She doesn't hate you."

"She doesn't like me either."

I sigh. Jax isn't completely wrong. But when Emily invited me to her party back in November, she actually told me to invite Jax. She told me there was no better time to get to know her, telling me it would be an opportunity for them both to turn over new leaves with one another. However, as I watch Jax adjust her meticulously drawn eye makeup in the mirror, I'm not sure how that will go now that my girlfriend is the equivalent of two drinks in before we even reach the front door.

"Ready?" Jax turns to me. I hesitate and she leans forward, grabbing me and pulling me into a kiss. "Hey, relax, Kyle. I'll behave." She winks and we both get out of the car. I take a deep breath, stepping onto the front walkway. Jax rounds the car and takes hold of my waist as we walk up and ring the doorbell.

Callie opens the front door. "Hi, guys!"

"Oh my God, hi," I say with Jax holding tight to my waist still. "I didn't know you'd be here."

Callie smiles. She looks wonderful in a blue dress with black tights. It always makes me double take seeing my teammates outside of practice or game attire. "Emily invited me," she says, stepping back to let us inside. "A few other girls are here, too. Mostly our year," she says to me.

"Great," Jax says as Callie closes the door behind us. "Where's the bar?"

"Jax." I tug on the sheer black blouse she reveals as Callie takes our coats to hang up in the corner of the entryway.

Callie laughs. "There's a bunch of stuff in the kitchen." Jax follows Callie and they move into the crowded living room filled with people I recognize as Emily's parents' coworkers, along with several people I went to high school with.

"Jax," I call after her.

"Yeah?" she says, and I already see the sparkle in her eyes courtesy of whatever she had in that flask.

"Just...let's have fun, okay?"

Jax walks back over to me. "But not too much, right?" She kisses me hard. I'm blushing when she strolls back through the living room.

"Kitchen's that way!" I call out, pointing to my left. Jax turns and throws me two thumbs up, then disappears around a corner.

"Hey, about time you showed up." Emily skips over to me through a throng of people in the open living room. Alex follows behind her, and he wraps an arm around her shoulder once they're in front of me. "It's already ten thirty," Emily adds.

"Hi, I know. Sorry." I pause. "You guys look great."

Emily beams, flattening out her black dress that shimmers under the house lights. Alex is in slacks and a blazer, his beard trimmed close to his face and his hair slicked back. Together they look like the top of a wedding cake from the 1960s. Emily adjusts her red-rimmed glasses and nudges my arm.

"You look great, too, Kyle."

"Yeah," says Alex, nodding approvingly. "Leather pants. Props for pulling them off."

I shift my weight, looking down at my outfit. I pick at the sleeve of my forest green button-down. "Thanks. The pants were Jax's idea."

Emily quirks an eyebrow. "Where is she, anyway? I thought she was coming."

"She's here," I say, scanning the room. "I think she's in the kitchen."

"Wasting no time." I give Emily a look for her comment, and she holds her hands up. "Sorry, sorry. New year, new leaf." She pauses, patting Alex on the chest. "Come find us in a little while, Kyle. My aunt has a hot game of charades going on in the dining room."

I grin. "Sounds good." Emily hugs me, then heads off with Alex back into the crowd of people. I brush some hair away from my face then wander through the double doors leading into the kitchen. I say hi to a couple of people I recognize and grab a beer from a tub of ice on the counter when I hear my name.

"Kyle?"

When I turn around, Beth is standing with a few of my old Tornadoes teammates at the other end of the kitchen. And she looks exactly the same. Her light hair is in a mermaid braid that falls to one side of her freckled face. She's wearing leggings and a deep red dress that makes her eyes shimmer.

"Oh my God," I say, setting my beer down on the counter.

"Oh my God is right." She smiles. "How are you?" She pulls me into a hug. I stare, awestruck, when she steps back.

"I'm…I'm good," I finally say. "How are you?"

"Great," she says.

I nod slowly, taking everything in. Beth. My high school crush is actually here. Standing in front of me again after, how long has it been?

"God, what is it now, almost two years?" She answers my question for me. "Funny how time goes so fast."

My words fumble, coming out in short bursts. "What are you… how did you…why are you here?"

Beth chuckles. "Well, Liz keeps in touch with everyone from the Tornadoes," she says, gesturing to one of my old teammates who nods at me, then continues her conversation on the other side of the counter. "And she mentioned that Emily was throwing a party. I thought it might be fun, figured a few people from the old gang might be here."

"Yeah," I say, taking a sip from my drink. I feel like I'm in a dream, standing here with Beth again.

"I see you're still friends with Emily," she says, moving a little closer as laughter roars from the living room.

"I am. We actually play together at Meadowbrook."

"No way." Beth takes a sip from her glass of white wine. "That's so fun."

I smile. "What about you? You still playing?"

"I am." She nods and tilts her head back to Liz and a couple of our old teammates. "The four of us actually play together out in Boulder."

"As in Colorado?"

Beth laughs. "That's the one."

"Wow. That's amazing."

We share a smile. I take another drink when Liz comes and grabs Beth by the elbow.

"Oh, looks like it's our turn up at charades," Beth says, turning back to me. "It is so great to see you again, Kyle." She pulls me into another hug.

"You, too."

When she pulls back, she squeezes one of my hands for a moment, then hurries out past the double doors. I stand watching the spot where she stood, trying to process the last ten minutes. Beth: the girl I couldn't get enough of back in high school. The girl who stirred something inside me I didn't even have a name for. The girl who started all of this. Here again. But this time, I didn't swoon. I didn't sigh at the mere touch of her. I take a sip of my drink and can't help but smile at how far things have come.

"Who was that?" Jax sidles up next to me. Her eyes are unfocused and she leans one arm against the counter.

"Who?"

Jax leans forward, one finger tracing down my cheek. "Don't play coy with me, Kyle. That strawberry-haired girl you were just talking to."

"Oh, Beth. She's just a girl I used to play with back in high school."

Jax takes a drink of the beer in her hand, downing it and making a show of tossing the can into the sink across from us. It clanks around, and I wince as everyone in the room turns to look at us.

I lower my voice. "Jax, tone it down a little, okay?"

"Sure, babe," she slurs, grabbing another beer from the tub next to us. "Whatever you say." Then she saunters off into the living room, motioning for Callie—who gives me a sympathetic look over her shoulder—and Katie to follow her. I sigh and walk out into the backyard where a lot of Emily's parents' friends rove around the patio. I end up in a conversation with a man who's a mutual friend of her parents and mine, but I struggle to concentrate. I keep glancing inside, afraid I'll find Jax stumbling over furniture or breaking lamps. At eleven forty, I finally excuse myself and head back inside. I scurry past Alex and some of his friends in the kitchen and close the guest bathroom door behind me.

Closing the toilet seat, I sit down and lean my head back. When did parties become like this? When did every outing turn into babysitting Jax? Wasn't I supposed to be having fun, too? I fish into my pocket and pull out my cell phone. Before I can think about it too much, I scroll to my messages from Joey and begin to type a new one. After several tries, I finally send her one that doesn't feel weird to write.

Happy New Year!

I tuck the phone back into my pocket, nodding in approval. No harm in saying that, right? Everybody's sending those tonight. No big deal. With a deep breath, I adjust my shirt in the mirror, then step back out into the party.

"Hey," says Alex. "You okay?"

I nod. "Yeah. I'm good, just freshening up. Fun party."

He beams. "Emily is an amazing hostess. I just try to help where I can."

I smile. "You do wonderfully." He nods and takes a drink from his beer. "Have you seen Jax lately?" I ask, looking around.

Alex raises an eyebrow, then points to the living room. I say bye to him and walk over to lean against the doorjamb, looking into the crowded room. The lights have been dimmed slightly, the countdown to the ball dropping showing fifteen minutes left on the TV next to the fireplace. I scan the room, my eyes roving over people milling around, wineglasses in hand while conversation floats through the room. I spot Callie on one end of the couch, typing on her cell phone. Then I nearly cough on my beer when my eyes land on Jax. Her legs are crossed toward Katie, who herself looks like she's had three too many. They both giggle, and Jax runs her hand over Katie's thigh.

My face is hot when I push through everyone on my way to the couch. When I stand over Jax, I'm practically seething.

"Kyle, hey," Katie says, giving me a sloppy wave.

"Jax, can I see you for a minute?"

"I'm talking to Katie," Jax replies, rolling her neck back to look at me.

"Jax, please."

"Fine." She gets up, throwing a wink to Katie. "It's getting warm in here anyway."

I follow Jax to the front door. She swipes her coat off the rack in the corner, and I grab mine before we step outside. Jax fumbles as she pulls on hers and falls over the front step. I rush to catch her.

"My savior," she says, pulling me closer as we stumble in the grass. She tries to kiss my neck, but I step back.

"What the hell were you doing in there, Jax?"

"What?" She wobbles but regains her footing and holds out her arms. "What are you talking about, Kyle?"

"In there with Katie. What were you doing?" Jax rolls her eyes. Then she reaches into her coat pocket. "Don't," I tell her, stepping forward. But she rushes backward, yanking the flask away from me.

"God, who are you, my girlfriend or my mother?"

Just then the front door opens, and Emily steps out, her coat wrapped tightly around her.

"Oh goody," Jax mutters before taking a long drink. "My favorite teammate."

Emily's wide eyes go from Jax to me. "Everything okay out here?"

"Just peachy, Cap'n." Jax sways and gives Emily a salute.

"Maybe we should go," I say.

"But it's almost midnight," Emily says softly, moving toward me.

"I know, but I don't want to make a scene," I tell her, my voice low.

"Too late for that!" Jax shouts, swaying before she falls onto the frost-covered grass, cackling into the cold night air.

"God," I say, moving forward to help her up.

"Kyle, let me help." Emily grabs Jax with me, but Jax jerks away from Emily once she's standing back up.

"Please. Don't act like you care about me."

Emily holds her hands up in front of her. "I'm just trying to be helpful."

Jax scoffs. "You're a piece of work, you know that? You, with your never-ending Goody Two-shoes act, and you," she snarls, pointing at me, "my girlfriend, flirting the night away with anyone who walks by."

Emily turns to me, and I stare back at Jax.

"What the hell are you talking about?" I say, my jaw stiff from the cold.

"Please." Jax laughs. "Like you don't know. You and Shirley Temple in there. I saw you two." She gestures to the house, stepping closer. I choke back a cough at the smell of liquor on her breath. Jax sneers and runs a hand up my thigh, slipping it under my shirt. "You could've lit a match with all that tension."

I force her hand away. "Jax, there was no tension. There was nothing!"

"What is she talking about?" Emily asks, her voice still low as she stands next to me.

I sigh. "I was talking to Beth."

"Beth! That's the one," shouts Jax. Then she turns to Emily. "Thanks for inviting her, by the way."

Emily pulls back her shoulders. "That's enough, Jax."

"I agree," I say, reaching out to steady her, but she stumbles backward again.

"Oh great, two against one." Jax laughs, then reaches for her keys inside her coat pocket.

"You're not driving," I say, stepping forward.

"Sure I am." Jax makes a move for the car, but I step in front of her. Cheers erupt from inside the house, and a countdown from ten begins.

"Em, please, go back inside. I'm sorry. This is my fault."

"It's not your fault, Kyle," Emily says as Jax, her arms still out, jingles the keys in front of me in a taunt. Emily sneaks around and grabs them from her, and she spins around. Emily tosses me the keys as the countdown hits five.

"Thanks," I say.

Emily smiles, but her eyes are brimming with tears. My face is hot, and I bite my tongue not to cry. "Happy New Year, Emily."

I grab Jax, who continues to holler absurdities into the night as I get her into the passenger seat of her car. The house explodes in cheers, the sound of champagne bottles popping a boisterous welcome to the New Year.

In the driver's seat, I tug Jax's seat belt over her while she laughs hysterically. No longer able to hold them back, the tears roll down my face as I start the car and drive away.

CHAPTER THIRTY-SEVEN

Finally, I pull into the dark parking lot of our hotel fifteen minutes from Emily's house. I turn off the engine, slump into my seat, and glance at Jax next to me. She's slipped in and out of consciousness since we left the party. One of her arms is splayed against the window, her head resting in the crook of her elbow. With a sigh, I pull down the overhead mirror. I hardly recognize my reflection; my makeup runs in staggered streaks down my cheeks, my face is flushed, and my eyes are puffy. I grab a used Kleenex from my cup holder and try to wipe away some of the shame from the last few hours.

After several minutes, I take a deep breath and pull myself out of the car. When I open the passenger side, Jax groans and falls forward. I undo her seat belt and pull her upright to stand next to me, one of my arms around her waist.

"My knight in shining armor," she mutters, barely opening her eyes as we stumble into the hotel lobby. The lone concierge eyes us with a grin from behind the desk as we shuffle over the tile floor that echoes our footsteps into every inch of the room. Jax waves at him, and I adjust my grip on her, practically dragging her behind me into the elevator. After I hit the fourth floor button, Jax pushes out of my grip and tumbles into a corner, squatting with her head leaning against her knees.

I stare at nothing but the doors until they open. Then I pick Jax up, and she lets me lead her to our room. I dig into my pocket for the key and push the door open. Once we're inside, Jax falls into the bathroom and retches. I close the door for her and collapse into the desk chair next to our open window that overlooks my hometown.

The sobs seize me like a fist wrapping its fingers deep around my lungs. I clutch my stomach and tug my coat collar up around my face to quiet my cries. Heat flicks at my legs and neck as I weep, and eventually I have to shed my coat, the top of it now soaked in tears and makeup stains on one sleeve. Jax continues to throw up in the bathroom and I cry out at the sound of it, flinging my coat against the window.

When my breathing finally slows, I gather myself enough to text an apology to Emily, telling her that I made it to the hotel. Sniffling, I scroll to the message I sent Joey earlier. The "read" checkmark underneath it glares back at me. My throat tightens and I cough before setting my phone down. I'm sure Joey's out having fun. No need to respond to a mess like me anyway.

After another deep breath, the bathroom door opens behind me. Jax staggers out into our room. She doesn't even look at me as she strips off her top and collapses into the queen-size bed in the middle of the room. Her face hits the pillow and she's out immediately.

I run a hand through my hair, watching her breathing turn steady. I go over and pull off her heels and set them next to the bed. When my phone rings, I dig around in my coat pocket and fall back into the desk chair. I clear my throat when I see my brother's name on the screen.

"Hey, Kevin."

"Happy New Year, sis." Sounds of a party on the other end buzz through the phone.

I choke back another sob at the sound of his voice. "Thanks, Kev. You, too."

"Are you okay?" I purse my lips, trying with everything I have to keep from crying at the concern in his voice. I cough and nod. But no words form and I stare out the window. "Kyle?"

"I'm fine," I stammer. "Great, actually."

"Are you sure?" Kevin asks after a few moments.

"Yeah, all good here." I sniffle and wipe my eyes, then readjust in the chair. "Did you have fun ringing in the New Year? I didn't realize you were going to a party."

"I wasn't," Kevin says. I frown and switch the phone to my other ear. "I was at home, but…I had to leave."

"What do you mean?"

"Mom and Dad."

"They weren't home?"

"Oh, they were home." He clears his throat as somebody shouts Happy New Year and pops confetti in the background. "We were watching the countdown. Then at around eleven, they blew up. They had both gone into the kitchen to get more pizza. And then all I heard is shouting."

"What was going on?"

"I don't know," he says. "Something about Austin. Maybe Mom doesn't like Dad traveling? Whatever it was, they couldn't agree on it. Dad slammed the bedroom door and Mom told me good night, then went into the office."

"God," I say, my head leaning on my hand against the desk.

"Yeah. I called Mike and I came over to his parents' house. They were throwing a party. Mostly a bunch of old people. But more fun than being home."

I shake my head, my eyes fixated on the city lights stretched out like stars below our fourth-floor window. "I'm sorry, Kevin."

"Not your fault," he says. "It was honestly kind of nice."

"It was?" I sit back in my chair, one knee tucked to my chest.

"I mean, you know how they are. They never talk about anything. It was kind of a relief for something other than school or work or the weather to come up. Of course, the neighbors probably heard. But…"

"I guess I know what you mean. We do have a tendency to bottle things up, don't we?" I ask, glancing over at Jax passed out on the bed.

"Maybe they'll work it out," Kevin says after a minute.

My eyes are still on Jax, her back slowly rising and falling. "Yeah. Maybe."

Somebody yells my brother's name on the other end. "I guess I should go," he says.

Tears well up again, and I rub one hand over my eyes. "Sure," I say, doing my best not to sound like a trainwreck. "Thanks for calling."

"Happy New Year."

I cough again as the tears run down my cheek. "Happy New Year, Kevin."

Holding tight to the phone after we hang up, I drop my head down while my whole body trembles. Slowly, I drift off into a dark, dreamless sleep, wishing that everything from tonight was nothing more than a terrible dream.

CHAPTER THIRTY-EIGHT

My grip slips on the bench press bar, and Emily reaches out to catch it before it falls onto my chest.

"Easy, Kyle." She helps me pick it up and set it back onto the holder above my head. My arms collapse on either side of the bench I'm lying on in our weight room. "I think it's time for a breather," she adds.

The sound of metal clanging against iron bounces around the mirrored walls as our team hits the thirty-minute mark early on a January Monday morning. Callie is spotting Mary on the leg press machine to our right, and Elaine and Haley are on the other side of me doing tri-dips. The rest of the team sits in wall squats across the room.

"I want to go again," I tell Emily, drying my hands on my shorts and reaching back up for the bar.

Emily's hands fly to her hips and she tilts her head at me. "And you will. In a few minutes, *after* you've let your muscles rest."

I heave a sigh and slide out from under the bar so I can sit up. She hands me a towel, and I wipe the sweat from my forehead. "Sorry," I say, taking a drink from my water bottle next to me. "Guess I'm a little tense."

"Yeah, just a little." Emily leans forward, lowering her voice as Coach Gandy walks up and down the line of girls against the opposite wall. Her dark hair is pulled into a high ponytail and her jaw is set while she nods approvingly at my teammates, a few of them straining against the wall to fight the quiver in their legs. "Are you doing okay?" Emily asks me.

I glance quickly over at Jax, whose back is flush against the wall between Katie and Sarah. My jaw clenches. "I'm fine."

Emily follows my gaze, then quickly scoots around the bench and slides next to me. "Are you sure?" I brush the hair off my sticky forehead and shrug. "Are you two okay? You haven't talked about her much since New Year's."

"We're fine," I say, running the towel around my neck, my eyes falling back down to the scuffed floor. "I mean, she apologized for everything. She's done nothing but apologize over the last three weeks."

"Good. She has a lot to apologize for," Emily states matter-of-factly.

"Trust me, I know. Though I'm not sure she even remembers what happened. She knows I was mad at her. And she's sorry. But…"

"But it's hard to feel guilty when you don't even know what you should feel guilty for."

I nod. "Exactly."

"Keep those legs bent, ladies!" Coach Gandy barks to the group of girls against the wall. Most of their faces are flushed, sweat dripping down from their temples. A couple of the freshmen have collapsed onto the floor. I notice Joey at the end of the line, her face stoic in concentration. My eyes drift down to her calves, and then trace up her knee, following the noticeable line of her hamstring until it disappears into her shorts. "Ladies!" I jump and Emily hops up off the bench. "If you want to gossip, go join the cheerleading squad. If not, get back to work!" Emily rushes behind the bar to spot me, and I lie back down.

"Sorry, Coach," Emily apologizes, holding out her hands as I lift the bar and start a new set of reps.

"Yeah, no slacking, Captain," Haley adds from the mat on the floor.

"Oh, like you haven't spent the last thirty minutes divulging your trip to the Bahamas with Elaine over there?" Emily replies with a playful grin.

"Don't blame me for having a fun time over the holidays," Haley says, switching to lie on her back and starting a set of crunches.

Elaine moves to hold Haley's feet down and says, "Speaking of holidays, did you guys hear about Joey?"

The bar wobbles above me, and Emily helps me set it back into the holder. "What about her?" I ask, glancing up at Emily, who just shrugs at my curious look.

Elaine lowers her voice, glancing quickly at Joey and the others who are dipping back into another wall squat. "Well, T. was out at Georgina's on New Year's Eve, you know, the gay bar in Dallas? And T. said that she saw Joey with Andrea Webber draped on her arm the entire night." Elaine punctuates the end of every sentence as she speaks, like a news gossip reporter relaying the latest breaking headlines.

"Andrea Webber?" Emily asks, stooping to ensure no one can hear her. "As in Meadowbrook swim captain Andrea?"

Elaine nods, her eyes wide. "And they apparently spent the whole night together. Dancing, drinking, you know." She gives us all a suggestive look.

"Well, good for Joey," Callie says, pulling up into another sit-up.

I huff and grab for the bar again. "Yeah, good for her."

❖

"Kyle, I think you've scrubbed long enough." Emily's voice floats over from the other side of the shower curtain.

"Just a few more minutes!" I shout back over the flow of the water.

"Well, make it quick. You've got Spanish in twenty minutes."

I dip my head under the showerhead for another minute, turning off the water once I can't stand the heat anymore. I wrap my towel around me and step into the changing stall, quickly throwing on my clothes. Scrubbing at my hair to get it dry, I walk out into the bathroom of our locker room. Emily is at the mirror applying lipstick when I move up next to her. She looks at me over the top of her glasses while I run my fingers through my hair, attempting to make it look as presentable as possible for class.

Emily sighs. "Do you want to talk about it?"

"What's there to talk about?"

She squints in my direction, then glances around the bathroom. Finding no one, she turns to me, one hand on the sink. "Kyle, I saw your face when Elaine mentioned Joey earlier. It looked like somebody kicked your puppy."

"I don't have a puppy."

Emily hits my elbow. "You know what I mean."

I smile slightly but shake my head, tossing my gym clothes into the bag at my feet. "It's fine. I'm fine. Besides," I say, zipping up my workout bag, "I don't have room to talk. And I'm happy for her. She deserves to be happy."

"Who deserves to be happy?" Joey strolls into the bathroom, a towel over her shoulder, nothing more than shorts and a sports bra covering her body. My eyes fall briefly to her taut stomach, but I force my gaze back onto the mirror, though the grin on her face doesn't escape me.

"Oh, nothing," Emily says. "We were just talking about, um, Coach Gandy." Joey quirks an eyebrow at us as she walks over to the shower stall I'd previously occupied. "You know, we were discussing, um, how she deserves to be happy because she works so hard. You know, with us."

Joey's incredulous gaze drifts from Emily to me. I just blush and bite my lip, looking anywhere but at her. "Sure," she finally says, then disappears behind the shower curtain.

I let out a breath, and Emily turns to me. "Thanks for the help, Kyle."

I grimace. "Sorry."

Emily sighs, tucking her makeup away into her backpack. I swing my bag over my shoulder, and we head back into the locker room, tossing our workout bags into our respective lockers.

"Come on, Kyle," Emily says, looping her arm through mine. "I'll make another attempt at getting you to spill after class. How about a movie night tomorrow? Just you and me?"

I lean my head on Emily's shoulder as we push through the locker room doors and walk out onto campus. We both pull closer to one another as the chill winter air hits us. I smile. "That sounds perfect."

CHAPTER THIRTY-NINE

Are you all right?" I ask, glancing sideways at Jax.

She shifts next to me on the couch, staring down at her phone screen. I change the channel again, landing on one of those cooking competitions that always seems to be on every Sunday afternoon. An angry, middle-aged man yells at a handful of terrified pastry chefs as they run around a cluttered kitchen.

"Yeah, I'm fine," she says without looking up.

I nod and resist the urge to glance down at her phone. Ever since New Year's, Jax has yo-yoed between borderline smothering me with affection one day and being completely glued to her phone the next. Since we woke up today, she's run to her phone each time it goes off, and once the conversation begins with whoever's on the other line, it's like I'm not even here anymore.

"How's T.?" I ask after a few minutes. Okay, I'm fishing. But she is my girlfriend. Shouldn't I be able to know some things?

Jax doesn't respond for a moment, until finally she clicks off her phone screen and sets it on the far side of her. "What? T.? Oh, she's fine. Why?"

I shrug. "I figured that was her."

Jax takes a breath and focuses on the TV. I watch her, my head leaning against my hand that's propped up on the arm of the couch. "No," she finally says. "That was Steven."

My jaw clenches, but I fight to maintain a straight face. "Oh. Steven."

The chefs on TV scramble over themselves. Somebody misplaced the sugar.

Jax crosses her legs, then reaches for the beer on the side table.

She takes a sip from it then says, "Yeah. He keeps bothering me about the paper we have coming up in chem. You know, since we're in the same class."

"Right," I mutter. "Well, why don't you just call him back to talk about it?" My face grows warmer by the second, but I don't let my voice waver.

Jax shrugs and takes another chug from her beer, finishing it off. "Because. Why would I want to talk to that jerk?"

"I don't know," I say, "maybe because you guys were together for, like, two years. And he needs help."

Jax stands up. "Please. He's a complete douche. Want another beer?" she asks once she's in the kitchen.

The swish of her hips as she saunters up to the fridge momentarily hypnotizes me. I slam my eyes shut and take a deep breath, turning my attention back to the show. One chef is yelling at her teammate about adding too many eggs to the batter, while another one just dropped a bag of flour. For a second, I flash back to my mom doing the same thing, then picture her staggering around to clean everything up.

Jax's phone dings, and this time I cave and reach over for it. Steven's name is on the screen, over the background photo of Jax and me that we took after a practice one night. In it, she's looking up at the camera, and I'm looking at her. My hair is flying over my face. We're laughing.

"Sorry, babe," Jax says, reappearing and grabbing the phone from my hand. "I'll tell him to stop." She hands me both of the beers and plunks down beside me. Then she types out a quick message and places the phone down emphatically on the side table. "There," she says.

"Thanks." I smile at her as she settles into the couch. Her playful gaze roves over me, making me blush. "What?" I say, fidgeting.

"You're just really hot." I laugh as she pushes herself up onto her knees. "You laugh because you know it's true," she purrs as she moves toward me. I put the beers on the floor next to the couch and lean back, letting myself slide under her as she tugs at my hips, straddling me in one quick move.

"Well, you're not so bad yourself," I say. She leans down and kisses me, the bitter taste of beer on her tongue. I kiss her back, and she moves against me. Her hands start to move down my waist. But I pull back and catch my breath. She just smiles and kisses down my jawline, then my neck. Her fingers dance along my stomach as she inches up my shirt. My hands wrap around her back, and my hips thrust upward to meet hers. She kisses me again.

Ding!

I tear my lips from hers. “Really?”

“No, babe,” Jax says, rearranging herself so that one of her legs is between both of mine. Her index finger finds my chin, and she turns my head so that I have to look at her. She presses her thigh against my center. “It’s just me,” she says, her voice low. “Just you and me.”

Her eyes are locked on mine: cagey pools of blue in their sea of black. Her lips are parted, the bottom one swollen from kissing me. I bite my lip, my mind swimming with both lust and irritation. I want to forget about him. I want to forget about New Year’s. I want to forget about what we’ve become.

Jax’s leg begins a rhythm against me, and I close my eyes, forcing myself to fall into her. Just this time, I tell myself, I’ll let her. I’ll let her help me to forget.

CHAPTER FORTY

"Jax, have you seen my phone?"

"No," she hollers back from the kitchen.

"Maybe I left it in the locker room?"

"I have no idea. But hurry up, will you? The pasta's almost done."

Frowning, I shovel through the bottom of my closet, raking through pairs of running shoes and old soccer socks. I grab my workout bag and turn to empty its contents onto the floor. Several rolls of athletic tape spill out, along with a water bottle, my geology textbook, and my phone.

"Aha!" I toss the bag aside and crouch down to sift through everything. "Found it!" I shout, untangling the headphone cords. I move to stand back up when a small pouch underneath my water bottle catches my eye. I lean one knee to rest against the floor and reach down to pick it up.

"That's great," Jax shouts. "Time for dinner!"

"Coming!" I glance at the doorway but don't get up. Instead, I hold the pouch in my hand, memories rushing back to me. I can't help but smile when I tug open the top of the pouch and drop the necklace into my open hand. I turn the stone over. And even though I know it's not possible, it still feels cold, just like the night Joey left it on my windshield.

"Kyle?"

I quickly shove the necklace back inside the pouch, tucking it into the top drawer of my bedside table. Out in the living room, Jax is dishing spaghetti onto plates at my tiny kitchen table that doubles as my homework desk. She scurries back to the counter and grabs a bottle of wine as I sit down. Reaching over me to pour a glass, her other arm stretches around and sets a blank envelope next to my plate.

I look up at her. "What's this?" She smirks and shrugs. I turn it over and pull out two tickets. "Oh, wow. Tickets to see *Rocky Horror* live?" Jax looks satisfied, placing the wine bottle in the middle of the table and scooting her chair closer to sit next to me. "But what's the occasion?"

"Well," she says, taking a sip of her wine. "It's March. Our nine months is coming up. Plus," she looks down, toeing at the carpet, "I still feel bad about New Year's and everything. I wanted to get you something." Her eyes flicker up to mine. "Besides, I know you've mentioned wanting to see this."

I stare at the tickets. "April twenty-second, that's in three weeks."

Jax nods. "I figure a weekend trip right before the last few weeks of school will be good for us. What do you say to a road trip to the city?"

I look at Jax. Her eyes dance between my own. As I watch them, I can't help wishing they'd stand still for just a moment. I wish I could read what always seemed to be just behind them. And I wish I was ecstatic about her gift. The last few months haven't been easy. When I open my mouth to speak, Jax stops me, her hands landing on my knees.

"Hey. Kyle, look. I know things haven't been great between us lately. I know that. But let me make it up to you. Please?"

I place the tickets down next to my fork, the food steaming on our plates when I place my hands down on top of Jax's.

"All right," I say. "Let's do it."

Her smile spreads and she kisses me. Then she reaches for our glasses, handing me mine. "I think this calls for a little toast."

I eye the white wine shimmering back at me. "Just one, right? You know I have that test in Spanish tomorrow. My grades have been slipping enough as it is."

She winks. "Relax, babe." After another swallow of her drink she replaces our glasses on the table and tugs me closer to her.

"Jax," I say when she stands up and over me, settling herself down on top of my thighs. "What about dinner?"

She runs her hands through my hair, leaning my head back so I have to look up at her. "We'll get to it," she says before pulling me into a kiss. "But for now," she whispers next to my ear, "let me make things up to you again."

CHAPTER FORTY-ONE

I stand behind Jax with one of my arms curled around her waist, sipping from my vodka cranberry with my other hand. My eyes close as the burn of the liquor hits the back of my throat. Jax presses into me, and I open my eyes to her head bobbing along to the eighties cover band currently playing. It's a modest but energetic crowd inside the small bar we'd wandered into about an hour ago, courtesy of the fake IDs Jax borrowed from Haley.

After *The Rocky Horror Show*—which had been amazing on all sorts of levels—we had walked down Sixth Street hand in hand to check out the famed Austin nightlife. We strolled along the sidewalks taking everything in: the burger patties sizzling on their corner grills, the gold-painted bodies glittering under the dancing streetlights, and the muscle-shirted men hollering outside of bars. "Ladies' Night! First one's on us!"

Eventually we had been drawn into this bar, pulled like a ship toward the howling of a siren.

"I love this song," Jax breathes into me, turning her face to whisper in my ear. Then she plants a quick kiss on my cheek. I look down at her and feel like we're almost back to where we began last summer. Jax looks stunning in a simple black tank and her signature ripped jeans over a pair of dark Converse. As she turns back to the band, raspberry perfume and Dove shampoo invade my senses.

"Thank you for tonight, Jax."

She squeezes my hand that I have wrapped around her waist. The drummer bangs out the final notes and the crowd cheers. Jax takes a sip of my drink, licking her lips as she eyes me.

"Anytime, hot stuff," she says, then nudges the drink up to my mouth. "Drink up." She winks and turns back to the band. Then the bartender, who had been hovering nearby for the last three songs, slams two shots down on the bar behind us.

"Two Vegas bombs," he says before tossing a rag over his muscular right shoulder. "Courtesy of the gentleman at the end of the bar."

We both turn to look down the bar; a tattooed guy smirks and glances down at Jax's cleavage. Jax waves at him and grabs the two drinks. "Jax," I say, holding up a hand. "Come on, I thought we were going easy tonight."

Jax's eyes are like stars under the heavy eyeliner and mascara, and they have that familiar glint in them. "We can't be rude," she says, still smiling.

"I'm sure the nice tattooed man will live if we don't drink his shots."

Jax stares at me then downs the red liquid. "Kyle, come on," she says. "Let's have fun."

I shake my head. "I already have a drink."

She looks at me for a second then shrugs. "Fine. More for me."

"Jax, wait—"

But she's already pouring the second shot down her throat, then makes a show of wiping her mouth clean. The bartender takes the glasses away when I pull Jax closer to me. The crowd jostles around us in anticipation of the next song, and Jax squirms to break free from the grip I have on her arm.

"Come on, babe," she says, turning to the crowd. "Let's have fun! This is our night." She kisses me hard, then steps back, laughing.

"I thought we were already having fun," I tell her as the band starts up another song.

She bumps my hip with hers. "Kyle, it's okay. Loosen up."

Something over Jax's shoulder catches my eye before I can respond. A flash of red.

Jax stumbles and turns to look behind her. "What?"

I shake my head. "Nothing. I just thought I saw…"

"Who? Emily?"

"No." I stand on my toes to look over the crowd. It couldn't have been. I scan the faces in the bar. But nothing. "Sorry. I just…I thought I saw Joey."

Jax crosses her arms and leans against the bar. "Joey? Really?"

"Jax, I just thought I saw her. That's all."

"Sure, Kyle."

I sigh and finish off the rest of my drink. "What now, Jax?"

"Like you don't know?" She sneers, signaling for another drink from the bartender.

I watch her guzzle down half a beer, searching her face. "Jax, what are you talking about?"

"Kyle, everyone knows she was crazy about you last year. God, I remember her flirting with you at every practice, that tall freak."

I blink as her words hit me. "Don't talk about her like that."

"Whatever," Jax mutters, another gulp of her beer gone. "I'm the one who got you, so it's all good."

"What do you mean, 'the one who got me'?"

She swallows and sets her beer down. "You know what I mean, silly. Come on." She nudges me playfully. "Let's just watch the show."

I shove my hands into my jeans pockets. The room thumps as the music slinks between the crowd and up over the grungy walls. Frustration rises inside me, and I can't take it anymore. "I'll be right back."

"Where are you going?" Jax grabs my wrist as I start off toward the other side of the room.

"Bathroom," I tell her, swiping my arm away from her. "I'll be right back." I push through the crowd, Jax's calls disappearing behind me.

With my head down, I make my way through hordes of people, inching my way into a narrow hallway off the main room. Several leather couches line the walls and the two bathroom doors are on the left.

"Kyle, wait!" I hear Jax call behind me. She must have followed. I just push open the door into the bathroom.

"What did you mean, Jax?" I finally ask, spinning around at the sink counter. A woman who had been drying her hands turns to look at us as Jax rushes into the room. She's wide-eyed as she hurries out, leaving us alone. "What…was I some freshman game you were trying to win? A new trophy for your shelf, or notch in your belt?"

"Of course not," she says, stepping toward me. Her voice drops lower, and her false sincerity suddenly comes through loud and clear. "I mean, you have to admit," she grabs my hands, her face inches from my own, "you had no idea what you were doing until I stepped up to show you."

I yank my hands back from her grip. Before I can reply, she cuts me off.

"I'm sorry, okay?" Jax says. "Kyle, they're just words. You know I can get carried away. I'm sorry."

I shake my head. "I know, Jax." I look up at the ceiling. "But that's all I've been hearing for months now. 'I'm sorry. I'm sorry.' Honestly, I'm getting sick of it."

"Hey," Jax says, moving closer, her hands on my hips. "Kyle. Don't talk like that." Standing so close, I smell the liquor on her breath. She must have taken another shot before chasing after me. Her eyes are hazy, and she wobbles a little.

I look down and realize just how exhausted I am. My drink from earlier starts to churn in my stomach, and I hate how it feels. I hate the headache forming in the back of my head. I hate the false elation swimming in my gut that will desert me at the first signs of daylight. And I hate this never-ending cycle I'm stuck in with Jax. "I don't want to do this anymore."

"Kyle, baby, come on," Jax says. Finally, I bring myself to look at her. She's tugging at my shoulders. Now she's pulling me into a stall. I put my hands up as she locks the door.

"Jax. No, come on." But she doesn't listen. She continues to murmur into my ear. The smell of her suffocates me. Her kisses sting my neck. "Jax. I don't want this. Please."

"Kyle, just let me." She presses me against the wall and her fingers start to unbutton my jeans. I catch her hand.

"Jax, stop!"

She does stop and stares at me. Tears burn my eyes as she steps backward. "Fine," she finally says, pulling back her shoulders. "Whatever you want, Kyle." The room spins around me as she tears open the stall door and thunders out of the restroom.

I gather myself, my jaw clenched when I call after her. There's no telling what she'll do like this. "Jax, wait. Where are you going?"

I pause when I see myself in the mirror. My reflection is haggard. Lines are etched around my eyes; creases sit deep in my forehead. The bags under my eyes make me look twenty-nine, not nineteen. After a moment, I pull open the door to follow after Jax.

I freeze the second I see him standing in the hallway. I hardly recognize him and wonder briefly if he's from that same place on the other side of the mirror. The place where the person I've become looks nothing like who I thought I would be.

But when he speaks, there's no mistaking him.

"Dad?"

CHAPTER FORTY-TWO

Dad?" I blink twice, then three more times to make sure I'm seeing things right. My drink, it seems, has finally decided to kick in.

Jax turns back around at the end of the narrow hallway. I look from her to the man standing in front of me in the tight, poorly lit space. The man who is undeniably my father. And next to my father, a tall blonde wearing cat-eye makeup behind a pair of black glasses, clutching an alligator-skin wallet beneath her arm.

When I look back at Jax, her face is bewildered. She meets my gaze, then throws up her hands. "Jax," I call after her. But she turns and disappears into the crowd. My dad, who had been watching us, clears his throat and stands up taller. I swallow and blink again, straightening up to match him.

"Kyle," he says. He removes his hand from behind the blonde's back. My eyes go from him to her, trying to take in everything.

His hair is tousled and his face unshaven, making him look rugged and younger and not at all like his business, busybody self I was so accustomed to. His leather jacket—which, I didn't even know my dad *owned* a leather jacket—squeaks as he shoves one hand into his pocket. The woman has a similar jacket on over a purple blouse and a knee-length black skirt. With heels on, she's a good two inches taller than my dad.

Taking a deep breath, trying to gather my senses to achieve some sort of understanding as to what is in front of me, I finally manage to speak.

"Do you have gel in your hair?"

Good one, Kyle.

My dad clears his throat again and turns to the blonde whose attention has already wandered back to the band. "Kim, um, this is Kyle. My daughter."

The blonde turns her head and smiles widely at me. "Hey, honey," she says, her accent Texan but fairly neutral, making me think she's from the city.

I nod then focus on my dad. He's running his fingers through his chestnut hair, the same as my own, and clears his throat.

"Kim?" I ask, hoping he can feel the heat rising up in me but can't hear the way my voice cracks.

"Kyle," he says slowly, "we should talk."

The blonde—Kim, I guess—gives my dad's shoulder a pat, then says, "You know what? I'm going to grab a drink."

My knees feel like they're made of Jell-O as I watch her give my dad a quick kiss and stroll off toward the bar. I lean to my right, briefly searching down the hall for Jax. But I can't find her in the growing crowd.

My eyes move back to my dad. My head is spinning. The liquor in my stomach spoils, and I fight the urge to heave.

"Kyle," my dad says. "Please, let me just explain some things."

Yes, please, I think, staring daggers at him, explain to me what exactly is going on here. What are you doing here? Where is Mom? What are you wearing? Please, explain to me what you're doing with beautiful blond Kim in a bar on Sixth Street with goddamn gel in your hair? I would love answers to these questions. My mind reels. I straighten myself up as best I can despite the fact that the lights around me are swirling in nauseating circles. I pull my shoulders back, ready to fire off all of these questions at him, my face flushed with fury.

However, when I open my mouth to speak, all I manage to do is puke.

CHAPTER FORTY-THREE

"Kyle, are you okay, sweetheart?"

I stumble against the wall behind me, bracing myself and trying not to step into the puddle of fresh vomit at my feet. I look up and hope the glare in my dad's direction is one of infuriating disgust, though I'm pretty sure it's more "sad drunk college student who can't hold her liquor."

"Don't call me sweetheart," I mutter through gritting teeth.

"Come on, let me help you clean up," he says, stepping toward me.

I swat his arm away, using all my willpower to stand up straight. The room is still spinning. I look around, hoping desperately for Jax to come back, but she's nowhere to be seen. I fall against the wall, my hand slipping so that I land with a thud against the bricks. I realize I'm still outside the restroom when I hear a toilet flush.

Then, before I can stop him, my dad is pulling me away from the wall and over to one of the tattered leather couches toward the end of the hallway, farther from the music and the crowded bar. My feet trip over themselves as we walk and I try to maneuver through the people on my own. Eventually we make it to the couch, and I pull my hand away from him, falling onto the worn, brown cushions. I cover my eyes, rubbing my forehead when my dad takes a seat next to me.

"Kyle, what are you doing?"

I scoff, glancing at him through my fingers covering my eyes. "What am I doing? Seriously? I can ask you the same question."

My eyes manage to focus on my dad long enough to see him

run his hands through his hair—his goddamn gelled hair—then clear his throat. "You're nineteen, Kyle."

"I'll be twenty in two months."

"That doesn't give you an excuse to be at a bar drinking. You're underage. How did you even get like this?"

"How do you think, Dad? A bottle of wine back in the hotel room. Another drink here." I wave my hand carelessly but gag before I can continue.

My dad places his hand on my knee. I want to shove it aside, but my head is pounding and despite myself, it comforts me to have him so close. "Dammit," I grumble, feeling myself fall back into memories, like him taking care of me after I broke my arm on my bike when I was nine years old. I pinch my eyes shut and force myself into the present.

I take a deep breath. "Do you want to tell me what the hell you're doing here? With Kim," I add, sneering as her name passes my lips.

He pulls his hand back, rubbing it along his own knee now. "Kyle, there are some things you have to understand..."

I stand up then. Those words and the solemn tone of his voice carry the weight of a two-story house, and my chest feels like it's going to cave in on itself. I lean against the opposite wall, one hand on the grimy bricks while the other rubs against my ribs as if I can force air into them with each painful push.

"Kyle." There's a shuffling sound, and my dad's hand falls on my shoulder. "Are you all right?"

His aftershave is the same: musty with a hint of something floral. It makes me cough. "I can't breathe," I finally choke out.

Then my dad is guiding me down the hallway again. My chin bobs against my chest, but I glance up through my eyelashes as we walk under the green exit sign, and he leads me out into a back alley. "Over here," he says, his voice gentle. We round the street corner, past the over-filled dumpster and several rusty fire escapes lining the back of the restaurants and bars. We end up near the front door, I realize, when I slump against a wall plastered with bright paper advertisements.

"Wait here," he tells me before going back inside.

My head throbs while throngs of people wander past. I'm

tempted to sit but force myself to hold on to my dignity—what's left of it—and use it to hold myself up. My black boots kick away an empty ketchup packet somebody dropped on the sidewalk. Eventually, my dad slips past the large doormen and grabs my elbow.

"Where's Kim?" I ask him.

"You're what's important right now, sweetheart."

I start to ask him to please stop calling me that, but when I open my mouth I nearly throw up again.

"Come on," he says, and when I look up, he's glancing down the street. "There's a little place on the corner we can go. Let's get you something to eat."

"I'm not hungry," I say, but a gentle nudge in my back puts my feet in motion. I'm surprised when they don't slow down but instead follow half a step behind, past several bars and a tattoo parlor until we're under the bright neon sign of a small diner. He holds the door open for me. My balance wavers when I look up at the storefront lights, but my dad braces me and helps me inside.

I collapse into a red booth just inside the door. My dad settles in across from me when a waitress appears.

"Something to drink?"

My head hangs heavy in my right hand, pressed up against the large window facing outside, and I force myself to look at the elderly woman with crinkled eyes narrowed at her notepad and gray hair pulled back in a loose bun.

"Two waters, please," my dad says.

After she turns to go, I excuse myself to the bathroom.

My dad reaches up when I walk past him. "Kyle, we need to talk."

I move my arm away. "I just need to pee. Please."

He nods and lets me go. I stumble into the tiny bathroom, just large enough for me to stand in. I lean over and hang on to the sink. Looking at my reflection in the mirror is unbearable, so I turn on both faucets and let the water pool into my cupped hands. Splashing my face, I let my fingers linger against my cheeks. They're hot. Then my fingers find my tired eyes and scrub off the little makeup I had on, and I watch it run down the drain.

Back out at the booth, there's a tall cup of ice water and a plate of grilled cheese waiting.

"I figured you could use something in your stomach."

I grab the cup and chug half of it right there. My dad sips his through a straw, eyeing me warily.

"I'm all right," I explain to his concerned look. Grabbing my sandwich, I mutter tiredly, "Go on, tell me," and take a bite.

My dad drums his fingers along the metallic edge of the table. "Well, you probably know I have several new clients here in Austin."

"Is Kim one of them?" I ask, sarcasm dripping from my voice.

"Actually, I've known Kim for quite some time. And she was just hired on as our location's new manager for the IT department."

"How fortunate for you." I swallow a thick piece of bread, grateful it helped to slow the world's spinning.

My dad is quiet for a moment. "She's a very smart woman. We, um, we attended several technology seminars together. She's spoken at many of them."

"Is she smarter than Mom?" I fire back before taking another gulp from my water and slamming the cup down just a little too hard. "So smart and spectacular that you feel like you have to dress like this?" I gesture to his jacket. "Or has this always been your weekend getaway attire to win over the ladies?"

"I could ask you the same thing, honey." He reaches across the table to grab one sleeve of my button-down, then nods toward my leather pants. "This doesn't look like you."

I shake my head, ignoring his comments. "How long has this been going on?"

His eyes flicker down to his hands then back up to mine. A bike-taxi pedals by the window. We both turn to watch as the happy couple in the back sits closely, oblivious to anyone else on the road. After they pass us, my dad runs a hand through his hair. "I don't expect you to fully understand, Kyle."

"Enlighten me."

"Your mother and I…you know…you know your mom and I love you. And we love each other."

"No," I say, cutting him off. "If you loved her, you wouldn't have Kim wrapped around you like a shiny office trophy."

My dad watches me, and I take another drink until all that's left are the ice cubes. They clank against the plastic when I set the cup down.

"I do love your mother, Kyle," he tells me, holding up his hand when I open my mouth to protest. "I love her. I always have. But I'm not in love with her. Not anymore. And neither is she, with me."

The words hit me like a cleat to the gut. My eyes water and the acid in my stomach boils over. I lean back, my hands pushing against my thighs, willing my grilled cheese to stay down.

"Kyle," my dad says, but I hold a finger up.

"Please, Dad, just…wait." There it is. There are those words. Those words that we had been so afraid to say for so long. And despite the fact that I knew they existed, that I knew those words were lurking in the corners of our home, scurrying through the darkness, I had never been ready to hear them.

Until now.

I close my eyes, forcing myself to breathe.

"So," I say, pushing my now empty plate forward and lifting my head, "the seven-day workweek, the business trips you two go on, the office expansions—those were all part of the plan to, what, give yourselves more room apart? To find somebody else? To find Kim?"

My dad rests an arm on the table as he explains. "It didn't start like that. You know your mom and I have worked hard your entire life. We wanted to work hard for you and Kevin. But, yes, work did take over. Your mom and I saw less of each other. Saw less of you and your brother." His eyes shine with tears. "We tried, Kyle. We did. But people change. And as much as your mother and I love each other, we just aren't right for one another. Not anymore."

With another deep breath, I run a hand over the back of my neck. I can't find the words for a response, so my dad takes this as a cue to continue.

"When your mom and I got married, she was this wonderful, beautiful, breathtaking goddess that I would do anything for. And don't get me wrong, she is still all of those things. And for her, I was some goofy guy who she, for some reason, fell in love with," he says, allowing himself half a smile. "And more than anything, I wanted to be the one to bring her happiness in everything that we did. I wanted to be the one to make her smile and live to the fullest. But at some point, I stopped being that for her. And she for me. And that's not something you can force. It's just not. It becomes too hard." He glances outside, back toward the bar. "And eventually, you have to realize that, if it's not right and things have come to a standstill, then it's time to move on."

I exhale. At the start of his speech, I had truly feared that each sentence would cluster around us and squeeze the life out of me until I couldn't breathe anymore. But instead, the exact opposite happened. It was as if each confession pulled a lightness from me that I hadn't felt in years, not since before my parents' arguing began. Not since before I started feeling things for Beth.

I reach for his hand. He wraps both of his around mine. "I'm sorry, Kyle."

I shake my head, tears streaming down my face. "I'm not saying that this doesn't suck." I sniffle. "But I will say that I kind of had an idea something was going on. And thank you for telling me."

He blinks back tears. "You know I love you."

The dam breaks. Tears rush from my eyes, and I hunch over, falling into my hands. There's a squeak of old leather, and then an *oomph* on my side of the booth when my dad sits next to me. He pulls me close. I reach for his chest and he wraps me tighter in his arms.

I'm not sure how long I let him hold me. But I don't want to leave his arms, the arms that feel like a shield, keeping away the rambunctious customers, the bright lights, and the awful memories from tonight.

It's not until I lean back to wipe my nose on the palm of my hand that I remember Jax.

"Oh God," I mumble, glancing around, surprised she hasn't torn through the door or gone parading down the streets.

My dad grabs a napkin, blows his nose, then returns to his side of the booth. His eyes are still wet when he asks, "What is it, honey?"

My hand rubs against my temple. "It's my…it's Jax. I completely forgot about her."

Removing his jacket, my dad's brow furrows. "Jax. That girl I saw you with in the bar?"

"Yeah. She's my…she's really drunk. I should…I need to go find her. Get her back to our hotel."

My dad's eyes narrow and he licks his thin lips. "Well, you're in no state." He holds up a finger then. "I have an idea." He reaches into his jacket pocket and pulls out his cell phone.

I grumble, annoyed at myself for not spitting the truth out, and lean my forehead into both of my hands. My elbows stick to the crumbs scattered around my plate. When my dad greets Kim on the other end of the phone, I look around the crowded diner. The lights have quelled their stinging against my skin, and the air finally reaches my lungs. Then it hits me: *this is your chance.* I shake my head, muttering under my breath while my dad speaks with Kim. I hear him ask her for a favor. Again, that voice calls out. I bunch my eyes closed, but it only grows louder.

"Thank you," he says. "Yes, she's about Kyle's height, blond. Her name is Jax. She's Kyle's—"

"Girlfriend."

It's quiet. So quiet that I momentarily think my dad pulled a vanishing act. But when I lift my head, there he is. His mouth is open, midsentence. After what seems like an hour, he clears his throat before continuing. "Girlfriend," he says slowly. I watch him nod. "Yes, that's right." I give him our hotel address, which he passes on to Kim. Then he thanks her again, and hangs up.

My dad's gaze is lasered in on his cup of water, which drips condensation onto the table. I realize I'm shaking and briefly wonder if I can flatten myself against the seat so much that I just disappear into it and am able to run from what will inevitably be the most awkward conversation of my life. But before I can, my dad speaks.

"Kim will get your…she'll get Jax a safe ride back to your hotel. She said she found her near the pool tables."

I nod, grateful. "Thank you. And, um, tell Kim thank you, too."

"I will." He pauses. "Sounds like your friend was pretty drunk."

I take a deep breath, wondering at the look in my dad's eyes. For a moment, I think the fear I see in them must be my own, reflected back at me across this cluttered table. But it dawns on me that now, it's not me who's scared. It's not me who is afraid to hear the truth.

"She's not my friend," I say slowly. "Jax is my girlfriend." My dad licks his lips again, then pushes himself back against the booth. His unease, for whatever reason, gives me the courage to continue. "And not, like, *girlfriend* the way Mom talks about her college roommates. Jax is my…" I exhale through the word again. "Girlfriend."

My dad's eyebrows knit closer together, and I practically hear the wheels turning in his head. He takes a slow, deep breath.

"I see. She did look familiar," he says thoughtfully like he's choosing his words with the utmost care. "She's on your team, isn't she?"

"She is."

He ponders this a moment. "How long have you two been seeing each other?"

Somehow, my response comes quickly, as if the words have been waiting just below my tongue for ages and can't wait to be shared. "We've been dating for about nine months." The scene in the bathroom tonight comes back to me, and I shake my head. "Well, we were dating. I don't think we will be for much longer."

I look sideways at my dad. His mouth is stretched in a small, knowing smile.

His eyes flicker uncertainly to his hands but manage to meet mine when he says, "I'm sorry for making you feel like you couldn't tell me."

My eyes well up and I wipe quickly at them. Biting the inside of my cheek, I take a breath and release the rest of my secrets.

"It's been so crazy, Dad." My voice shakes. "Everything since school started. Since high school, really. With soccer and the Tornadoes." I dance around the words, trying to find the right combination to explain everything I've been feeling for the last few years. "I had this crush on Beth, my Tornadoes teammate. And that just started this whole thing." I speak quickly, breathlessly, but can't slow down for fear of not being able to start again. "I liked her so much, Dad. And she helped me realized I was…I was gay. And I thought I'd have things worked out by now, but it's just been so complicated."

"Complicated?"

"Unbelievably. I, um…do you remember Joey?"

His eyes take in the fluorescent lights buzzing above us. "She's the one who tagged along to our dinners after your games sometimes last year. The goalie?"

"That's the one."

"She's a very nice young lady."

I can't help but laugh at his dad-like comment. "She is. She's wonderful, actually."

"Where is she tonight?"

I shrug. "I'm with Jax. And I screwed everything up with Joey." I squeeze my fists tight and rest my forehead against them. "I don't know what I'm doing, Dad."

We sit in silence for a little while. People shuffle in and out the front door. Two women walk by, arm in arm, and I envy the way one of them says something to make the other laugh.

My dad's voice breaks me from my thoughts. "Do you remember, in the eighth grade, when soccer season coincided with basketball?"

Holding myself after a sudden chill makes me shiver, I fix my gaze on him, uncertain where he's going with this. "I do."

"Up until that point, everyone in athletics played multiple sports, including yourself. You got those genes from your mother, by the way." His eyes crinkle and he continues. "Playing everything was easy to do because the seasons were spread throughout the entire school year. Besides, you were good at them all, so why not?"

I pick at the edges of a sugar packet plucked from behind the salt shaker as he continues. "But then, when basketball and soccer were both happening simultaneously, the coaches encouraged everyone to choose between the two. Except you—"

"Tried to play both."

He nods. "I remember your excitement in the beginning. You came home, practically bouncing off the walls announcing that you'd made both teams. You were so thrilled, and your mom and I were very proud." He smiles, his eyes distant. "But after about two weeks, you started missing basketball practices because of soccer games. You would come home exhausted. And your grades took a dive."

I dip my head, my eyes concentrating on the granules packed inside the pink wrapper. "How come you and Mom let me do that?"

He chuckles. "You were so headstrong! You still are," he adds with a nudge of my hand. "Besides, we figured you wouldn't make it the entire three months. And we were right. After about five weeks, you finally quit the basketball team."

I remember that day. I hadn't been so physically exhausted until then; as tired, I realize, as I feel now. "I thought I could manage it all."

"We all want to believe that we can please everybody, Kyle. I think some part of you felt like you'd be disappointing everyone if you didn't try to do both. Like if you had just picked one team right off the bat, you would be letting the other one down."

His words are like a bandage being slowly pulled from an old wound. My skin feels raw, exposed, and I wrap my arms around myself like they might cover the vulnerability seeping from my bones.

After a minute, I lean back and rest my palms on the red pleather of our booth. My dad does the same.

"Your mom and I have always loved you, Kyle. And we always will. No matter what."

My eyes brim with tears again, and I blink them back, turning toward the window. The weight of what felt like eight different worlds steps off my shoulders, and at that moment, I forget the bar. I forget the puke stuck to the bottom of my shoes. I even forget Kim. And I forget Jax.

For the first time in our lives, we have spoken the truth. It's out. Our perfect family image that took years of effort to build is finally beginning to wear at the edges.

And God, does it feel good.

Chapter Forty-Four

"And then what happened?"

I cough more sobs into the phone. Emily waits patiently while I blow my nose. "Well, after telling my dad all about the last two years, about everything really, he helped me find Jax. It was Kim, actually, who managed to corral her and get her out of the bar. She was drunk out of her mind, otherwise…otherwise, I would have done it then and there."

"Broken up with her?"

I nod. "But I knew if I did it then, she wouldn't even remember."

"Probably accurate."

I wipe my nose and toss the Kleenex into the already full trash can next to my bed. "Yeah. Not sure how that's going to go when the time comes."

"Where is she now?"

"At home," I say, leaning back against the wall behind my bed. "I canceled our reservation last night, I was so angry. Packed us up and drove us back here. Put her to bed and came home."

"Well, hey," Emily says, her voice soft. "I just got out of a Sunday study session at the library. How about I come over for a bit? We can talk about all of this. I'll bring donuts!"

I smile. "That sounds good, Em. Thanks."

❖

"I brought glazed, cinnamon twists, and bear claws!" Emily says excitedly as I let her into my apartment. She stands smiling proudly in front of my door, then looks around, her face falling. "Oh my God, Kyle."

"I know," I say, leaning down to scoop up three sweatshirts that have wrapped themselves around the base of my couch. "I've been a little preoccupied lately."

Emily walks over to the table piled with geology books and Spanish practice quizzes. She does a 180 turn, her eyes wide and worried, until she finally sets the box of donuts down on the counter by the sink. "Well," she says, "nothing a little spring cleaning can't fix." She pulls two plates out from my cabinet and hands me one with two bear claws on it.

We wander through my cluttered apartment, Emily hurriedly picking up clothing and tossing it onto my couch on the way to my bedroom, where I return to my desolate pile of pillows and tear-soaked sheets. Emily takes a seat at the edge of my bed, folding her skirt under her knees and taking a bite of a cinnamon twist.

"So," she says after a few chews, while I pick up more blobs of tissue from under my pillow and dump them into the trash. "Your dad spilled the beans."

"He did. It's all out there."

"And you're…okay about everything?"

I pick at the donut on my plate. "Honestly, Em? I kind of am. I mean, you know how we are." She gives me a sympathetic smile. "My family always had to put on a show. It didn't matter if we were throwing a party or just sitting around the dinner table. We never talked about what mattered. Ever. So, yeah, it felt really good to finally hear somebody telling the truth for once. Including myself."

"You told your dad?"

"I did. About Jax. About Beth. About myself. Everything." When I look up at her again, Emily has tears in her eyes. She sets her plate down and leans over to hug me. She lets out a string of Spanish, her voice filled with relief.

"You either said you're extremely proud of me, or there's a bear in the kitchen."

Laughing, she sits back and wipes at her eyes. "What do you know? Your Spanish is improving."

I blink back tears and wipe my dripping nose. "It did feel pretty incredible to finally tell him." Emily watches me. "Part of me still can't believe I did it."

"I always knew you could," she tells me.

I lean back against my bed frame, a new lightness overcoming me.

After a minute, Emily rearranges herself on the bed. "So, what now?"

I shrug. "Well, remember that big fight my parents had on New Year's, the one I told you Kevin called me about? I guess they had been talking about separating. My dad wants to move to Austin. My mom was still holding out, to keep face, I guess. But I think maybe now they'll be able to make progress on that."

Emily picks at my comforter. "And Kevin? How is he?"

"Dad told me he's going to talk to him. But I have a feeling he'll be okay."

"Your brother's more mature than half the team," Emily says, then bites into her cinnamon twist. "His range for dealing with emotions has always been impressive."

I laugh. "I know. I think he should've been born first."

Emily chuckles. Just then, there's a knock at my apartment door. I glance at Emily, who shrugs and says, "Don't look at me."

"I thought you were kidding when you said you were going to order a pizza," I tell her, playfully nudging her leg as I get up.

"I *was* kidding!" she shouts through a mouthful of donut as I make my way through the living room.

I laugh and open the door. "Pepperoni or pineapple?" I ask to who I realize is not a delivery person but instead a very confused-looking Joey.

"Um, pineapple?" she says as the branches sway behind her outside.

"Joey?" I ask. "What…um…what are you doing here?"

"Not delivering pizza, I'm afraid to say."

"Joey!" Emily scurries up to stand next to me at the door. "Hi!"

"Oh, hey, Emily," she says, brushing a hand through her hair. "I just wanted to drop these off." She holds up a folder. "Coach's summer workout. You missed the meeting last week."

It takes me a few seconds to remember what she's talking

about. My brain seems to only register the tint of her hair in the afternoon sun. Emily nudges me when I don't respond. "Oh, right. Last week." I clear my throat and step aside so Joey can come in. "I had that geology lab."

"That's so nice of you to drop those off," Emily says, skipping over to the table to clear a spot for Joey to place the folder. I notice her scanning the room, but she doesn't say anything. Her eyes are curious but kind when she eventually asks, "Are you two having one of your Sunday movie days or something?"

"Actually…" Emily says, and I can tell she's about to launch into another made-up excuse. Reluctantly, I take a deep breath. At this point, there's no room for excuses anymore.

"Actually, Emily came over because I'm a mess. If you can't tell," I say, gesturing to the room. Joey raises an eyebrow. I glance at Emily, whose eyebrows are shooting up over her glasses. "The truth is, yesterday was one of the worst and best nights of my life. My dad told me that he and my mom are going to separate. I met his new girlfriend, and she's actually not that bad. She helped me chase down my drunk girlfriend. Who, by the way, will no longer be my girlfriend once she wakes up from her hangover. Oh, and I saw *Rocky Horror* live."

Emily's mouth hangs open, and she stares at me and Joey, who slowly nods. After a few moments, Joey says, "Well, I hear that's a great show."

"It was."

Joey's gaze holds mine, and Emily eventually clears her throat. "You know what, I'm…um…I just remembered Alex wanted my opinion on this piece he's working on." She runs into my room and hurries back out with a bear claw. "To go," she says before grabbing her purse off the counter and heading for the door. "Sorry to rush out." She turns to me. "Kyle, call me later, okay?" I nod and she glances at Joey. "Help yourself to the donuts."

"Thanks. I'll make sure Kyle doesn't eat them all." The three of us grin. I move to open the door for Emily, who waves before dashing to her car in the parking lot. I stand for a moment, leaning against the open doorway. The spring breeze feels nice on my face. I take a deep breath when Joey says, "Do you want to talk about it?"

I close my eyes. I can't remember the last time Joey and I even had a conversation. Or the last time she and I were alone. Her being here now, standing across the room, makes every part of me feel calm. But I shake my head and open my eyes to the clear sky. "It's beautiful out there."

Joey fiddles with the papers on my table. "Springtime in Texas," she says. "If there's not a tornado or a freak hail storm, it's pretty gorgeous." She reaches out to lean against one of the chairs. "My parents have these magnolia trees back home." Her voice is distant, and I see her eyes shift, conjuring the memory from the back of her mind. "I always loved lying underneath them this time of year. Their scent would cling to my T-shirts, and I'd refuse to let my mom wash them. I wanted to smell like those trees all the way into summer." She stands upright, as if sharing such a thing surprised her back to the present. "Bluebonnets are nice, too, I guess."

It hits me how much I missed her. When she moves to join me in the doorway, I cross my arms and look up at her. "Thanks for coming by. And thanks for not judging me," I add, gesturing to my baggy sweatpants and messy ponytail.

Joey shrugs. "We're friends, right? That's what friends do."

When I look into her eyes, they're unbelievably clear. Like the sharp edge of a quartz crystal. The blue in them matches her shirt that she wears under a brown jacket. "Well, thanks again," I tell her. "And tell Andrea hi for me. She and I had Spanish together last semester."

This time Joey crosses her arms and leans against the open doorjamb. "Andrea?"

"Yeah, you know. You two have been going out."

Joey cocks her head. "Where did you hear that from?"

My face grows warm. "Well, Elaine mentioned that…"

Joey laughs. "Oh yes. The team gossip train. I should have known." I grimace and shrug. Joey stands up. "That ship sailed a couple months ago. But if I see her, I'll tell her you say hello," Joey says with a grin.

"Oh." I look down, hoping the blush in my cheeks fades quickly. "Well, thanks again anyway, for swinging by."

"Sure, short stack."

A strong gust of wind suddenly blows through. The door flies against me, pushing me forward, then it bangs into the wall with a sharp thud.

"Whoa," Joey says, helping me grab hold of it. Together we push against the howling tunnel of wind and manage to close the door. I'm laughing when she says, "You were saying about the weather?" Still smiling, I turn so that my back rests against the now closed door. Joey's palms are flat against it, her arms up over me where she had pressed the door shut. I swallow and she does the same, her gaze floating down from my eyes to my lips.

She lowers one of her arms and her fingers carefully dance along my hairline, then trace the side of my face. My eyes don't leave hers, but that pit in my stomach from the last twenty-four hours is gone. In its place is that feeling. That feeling I'd had that night at Alex's party. The feeling I was sure both of us felt in that silly shower stall over a year ago. It's the feeling I was convinced I could hide underneath drunken nights with Jax. That feeling I'd told myself I was better off running from.

But what if I didn't this time?

I lift myself up off the door, tilting my chin up. Joey smiles and her palm cups my face gently.

"Kyle?" she says, her voice soft.

"Yeah?"

"I really should be going."

I nod and breathe for the first time in what feels like days. But Joey's hand doesn't move from my face. We're closer now. Her warm breath caresses my cheek and before I can help myself, I close the gap between us. My lips brush hers lightly at first, but that's all it takes for that feeling to spread like wildfire. Her hand pulls my face closer, and she's returning my kiss. Our lips move together, just like they did the first time. Except this is different. That night in Alex's apartment, I was scared and excited and wondering what everything meant under those dancing blue lights. I had no idea what I really wanted. I didn't know what to think. But now I know I have been lying to myself, ever since that moment, about what I was truly feeling.

My lips press harder against Joey's, kissing her deeply. And I understand now: *she* is exactly what I need.

"Wait," she says breathlessly, gently nudging my shoulder back so that we pull apart. Our foreheads lean into one another, our breath coming in staggered bursts.

"What?"

She takes a deep breath, then leans back to really look at me. "I can't. No, not like this."

Still breathing hard, I work to collect my thoughts. She's right, of course. Technically, I'm still with Jax. Even though the last couple of days sealed our fate as a doomed couple. Joey and I shouldn't do this. No matter how right it feels.

"God," she breathes, looking around my apartment like an easier way around all of this is written somewhere on the walls. "Kyle." She reaches up and runs a hand over my cheek.

I take a deep breath. Then, somehow, the words stumble out of my mouth, though I can feel them fighting against every fiber in my body. "You're right. We shouldn't."

Joey nods and runs a hand through her hair. "Right. So…I'm going to…I'm gonna go."

"Okay," I say, moving so that I can open the door for her.

Once she's out on the porch, hands adorably shoved back into her pockets, she says, "I'll, um, I'll see you around."

I smile and will myself to close the door as she turns to go. Once it's shut, I fall against it, my back hitting with a dull thump. My eyes close, and I let myself live again in the feeling of Joey's body against mine, in the taste of her lips. Finally, I allow myself the thought I'd pushed so far down into me, I didn't think it existed any longer.

I am absolutely, head-over-heels in love with Joey.

CHAPTER FORTY-FIVE

"I must say, Kyle, you two seemed perfectly civil last week at the end-of-season party."

I sit near one of the large front windows in the ice cream shop across from campus with Emily and bite into my Neapolitan double scoop. "Hmm," I say, wiping my mouth, "if you call acting like I didn't exist civil, then yes, Jax and I were perfectly civil."

"I'm just trying to say that I'm impressed," Emily says between licks. "Not by you, obviously, because you know how to act like a human being. But I am happy that nobody threw lawn furniture into the pool or started a catfight. Although I was certain the entire night that the glares from T. would bore holes into the back of your head. Thought I needed to follow you around with a fire extinguisher."

I laugh. "Honestly, Em, she has a right to feel the way she feels. Jax is her best friend."

"I know," Emily says with a wave of her hand. "I just wonder how next year will go now that you two are no longer together. At least T. will be gone, and Jax will be a senior."

"As will you, my friend." I nudge her shin with the toe of my running shoe. "Can you believe it?"

Emily's eyes are wide when she shakes her head, making her dark curls bounce. "Not at all. Just like I can't believe it's already May." She takes another bite from her chocolate chip scoop, then asks, "What do you think you'll do over the break?"

"I'm going home."

Emily smiles at me.

"I missed a lot last year. I want to go home and hang out with Kevin. Help with whatever my parents decide to do."

Emily reaches out her hand, placing it on top of mine on the table. "I'll be around if you need me, okay?"

"Thanks." She pulls her hand back and fiddles with the fringe on her skirt for a second. "Go ahead," I finally say. "I know you want to ask."

She bites her lip, then leans forward. "I'm sorry, Kyle. It's just…you and Joey kissed. *Otra vez!* That's so exciting! It feels like Christmas!"

My cheeks warm, and I dip my head to hide my smile. "It was pretty amazing."

"So," Emily says, "any plans to get together over the next few months?"

"No, not really. I said good-bye to her at the party. I don't…I don't want to rush anything." I take another bite of my ice cream. "Besides, after everything I did, everything I put her through, I don't blame her for wanting space. I'm just glad that Joey and I are friends again." This comment warrants the most incredulous look from Emily, and I can't help but laugh. "All right, well, she and I are… getting back on track again. Which makes me happy."

Emily nods approvingly. We sit quietly for a few minutes, enjoying our respite in the cool blast of air-conditioning from the warm spring day outside. Then the door to the ice cream shop opens, and a burst of conversation comes, the scraping of shoes scurrying over the checkered floor. The crowd strides boisterously to the counter. Jax doesn't see me. She chats with Elaine as they wait behind the rest of their group in line. Her hair is up in a ponytail, and her hands move erratically as she talks. Emily follows my gaze, then whips back around.

"Oh my God." Her voice is just above a whisper. "Kyle, I'm sorry. I didn't know she'd show up here."

"Emily, relax." I reach out and pat her hand. "It's really okay."

At the sound of my voice, Jax glances back. When her eyes meet mine, for a moment, I think I see a small glimmer, a miniscule part of her that I was never able to see before. The place inside that she would always hide from me. From everyone. For a moment, I am moved by the flash of vulnerability, the thing I had always hoped to touch. Then it vanishes and leaves me wondering if it was ever really there at all.

She turns back to her conversation with Elaine.

"Are you okay?" Emily asks me, her voice still low.

"Do you remember when I told you about the first time she took me here?"

"Oh my God, that's right. Kyle, I completely forgot. We could have gone somewhere else. Anywhere else."

I lean back and sigh. "No, Em. It's just memories. You don't have to worry anymore. It's over."

"I know, Kyle. I just worry, what if she, you know, tries to stick her sharp claws back into your heart. She had you in so deep."

"I understand." My eyes flicker to Jax, then land on the table in the back corner. The table for two, dimly lit, hidden away. "She doesn't control me," I say, then look back at Emily. "Not anymore."

Epilogue

"If this is the last box for now, do you mind if I head over to the park? I'm behind on Coach's workouts. I'll be back once it's dark."

Mom sets a box filled with old pots and pans on top of the kitchen counter and wipes her brow. "Of course, honey. Go ahead."

"Don't be too long. Remember we've got your latest *Call of Duty* tutorial tonight," Kevin reminds me excitedly.

"How could I forget?" I reply, punching his arm as I walk past him and hurry down a hallway to my room. While I toss my phone into my workout bag, Dad pops his head in. "Kyle, do you know where I put that toolkit you guys got me for Christmas a couple years ago?"

"Under the sink?"

He grins. "The one place I haven't looked. Thank you." He disappears, and I tug my running shoes on and grab my soccer ball out from under my bed. The tattered shoe box stares back at me from the dark. I pull it out, brushing my fingers along the dusty top as I stand. Then I walk over to my desk and pull out each of the books, stacking them next to my laptop.

My eyes land on the small pouch nestled against my Spanish dictionary. After cleaning off the last book, I pull the pouch open and reach in for the necklace. I quickly put it on, then tuck the stone beneath my T-shirt.

Back in the kitchen, I fill up my water bottle, then say bye to my family before heading outside. The heat is just beginning to subside as the sun starts its descent in the open Texas sky. I let the heavy air settle over me, breathing in the bustling city while I cross the street and walk past the old playground, over to my wall.

As I set down my workout bag, I notice that today the playground is vacant. I drop the ball, catch it in the crook of my foot, then lower it gently onto the pavement. Over lunch last week, Emily told me that two of the incoming freshmen are midfielders, so I shouldn't let the summer get by me again. Starting positions can disappear as quickly as they come. So I waste no time and start in on my routine.

It's hard to believe two years have passed since I was out here that summer, concerned much less with my soccer game and much more with my nonexistent yet all-consuming personal life. As the ball bounces back at me, kick after kick, I sweat under the fading sunlight while the last twenty-four months roll over me along with the warm breeze. Some memories flutter inside my heart. Others still cause me to cringe, which makes me fumble the ball. I stand with my hands on my hips, breathing hard. I use the base of my T-shirt to wipe my brow and go fetch the ball that's rolled a few feet away onto the grass.

"Looking decent, short stack."

I freeze at the sound of her voice. When I turn to look over at the school, she's walking toward me between a grove of ash trees. Joey's in bluejean cutoffs and a dark blue camp T-shirt. Her hair is down, the shade of red beginning to match the evening sky. Her long legs make short work of the distance between us, and I nudge the ball along to meet her at the edge of the pavement.

"What are you doing here?" I ask, placing the ball under one of my feet to keep it in place.

"Well, turns out I have an aunt who lives in Emily's neighborhood. I was outside her house helping her with some groceries when Emily came by, walking a dog with Alex. We got to talking, and you know how Emily is."

I chuckle. "How long did you get stuck there?"

"Only an hour," Joey replies. "Not too bad." We both laugh before she says, "And, well, I figured since I ran into her, I'd ask her where you live. I know you mentioned you'd be home all summer." She digs her hands into her pockets. "I just thought I'd come by and say hi."

My stomach has been doing somersaults since she walked up. "How did you know to find me here?"

She hitches a thumb over her shoulder. "Well, when I went by your house, I ran into your dad first, who, by the way, greeted me as the 'Amazon girl with the ferret.'"

I grimace. "God, sorry about him."

Joey just laughs. "It was fine. And then your mom came out to the garage where I was talking to your dad. She told me you came over here to practice." As she speaks, I can see the spark of curiosity regarding the scene at my house.

"Notice all the boxes?" I set my foot down so that I'm planted on either side of the ball. Joey nods. "Yeah. So, my dad's moving out in September."

She looks concerned, then reaches out her Converse-clad foot, inching the ball away from me. "How's all of that going?"

"Surprisingly well, actually. I mean, it's not easy or wonderful by any means. But it's like this immense, weighted blanket has finally been lifted off every room in our house. We're actually talking as a family now, which is nice. My parents have stopped keeping so much from Kevin and me. It's weird but in a good way."

"That makes sense," Joey says, flicking the ball up with her toe to catch it. "It's a big change, though."

"It is." I take a dive for the ball, but she flips it up and out of my reach, extending her arm up to catch it above my head. "But change can be good. Even if it seems like the most painful thing in the world at the time."

"I see we have a new, wise Kyle on our hands now." Then she holds the ball out. I go to grab it, but she pulls it back. I lunge forward, so Joey switches the ball to sit between her hip and her elbow. I manage to knock it loose, and it goes rolling toward my workout bag. After a quick glance at Joey, I race over to it and get there a few steps ahead of her.

"I went easy on you," Joey says through a grin.

"Sure." I lean against the wall, leaving the ball next to my bag as the sun dips behind the towering ash trees. "Thanks for coming by, Joey."

"No problem." Her eyes follow a crack in the pavement, then

look up to meet mine. "It's good to see you trying to keep your skills up to par." Her foot fiddles with the soccer ball.

"We can't all have your natural talent."

"Very true." Joey ignores the look I shoot her and adds, "You're even out getting some fresh air. I was prepared to find you locked inside, video game control firmly in hand."

I tap the ball away from her. "Why do you always think I live under an Xbox rock when I'm not playing soccer?"

"Oh, an Xbox rock. You'll have to show me what that one looks like." Then she half disguises, "Nerd," under her breath with a fake cough, and I give her a shove.

"Hey now." She throws up her hands. "That was a compliment." I'm still laughing when she reaches over and tugs on the chain around my neck. My hand finds hers and helps to pull the stone from under my T-shirt.

"You're wearing it again." She's so close that I can see the different shades of red running through her hair.

I swallow. "Of course I'm wearing it. I love it."

Her gaze meets mine, and it flashes with something I haven't seen before.

The feeling that erupts in my stomach is like a thousand caged butterflies trying to be free. I clear my throat to keep my composure, step back, reach down to grab my bag, and throw it over my shoulder. "Well, I should be getting back."

Joey bends to pick up the ball. She tucks it under one arm, then reaches her other one out to me. "Walk you back?"

The butterflies explode from their cage when I take her hand, lacing my fingers between hers. She smiles, and a grin fills every inch of my face. Together, we wander home side by side as the first pair of stars appears in the warm summer sky.

About the Author

Sam Ledel is originally from Dallas but recently relocated to San Diego with her girlfriend, whom she met while working abroad in Peru. She has a BA in creative writing and is currently working on a young adult fantasy novel.

Books Available From Bold Strokes Books

A Call Away by KC Richardson. Can a businesswoman from a big city find the answers she's looking for, and possibly love, on a small-town farm? (978-1-63555-025-2)

Berlin Hungers by Justine Saracen. Can the love between an RAF woman and the wife of a Luftwaffe pilot, former enemies, survive in besieged Berlin during the aftermath of World War II? (978-1-63555-116-7)

Blend by Georgia Beers. Lindsay and Piper are like night and day. Working together won't be easy, but not falling in love might prove the hardest job of all. (978-1-63555-189-1)

Hunger for You by Jenny Frame. Principe of an ancient vampire clan Byron Debrek must save her one true love from falling into the hands of her enemies and into the middle of a vampire war. (978-1-63555-168-6)

Mercy by Michelle Larkin. FBI Special Agent Mercy Parker and psychic ex-profiler Piper Vasey learn to love again as they race to stop a man with supernatural gifts who's bent on annihilating humankind. (978-1-63555-202-7)

Pride and Porters by Charlotte Greene. Will pride and prejudice prevent these modern-day lovers from living happily ever after? (978-1-63555-158-7)

Rocks and Stars by Sam Ledel. Kyle's struggle to own who she is and what she really wants may end up landing her on the bench and without the woman of her dreams. (978-1-63555-156-3)

The Boss of Her: Office Romance Novellas by Julie Cannon, Aurora Rey, and M. Ullrich. Going to work never felt so good. Three office romance novellas from talented writers Julie Cannon, Aurora Rey, and M. Ullrich. (978-1-63555-145-7)

The Deep End by Ellie Hart. When family ties become entangled in murder and deception, it's time to find a way out… (978-1-63555-288-1)

A Country Girl's Heart by Dena Blake. When Kat Jackson gets a second chance at love, following her heart will prove the hardest decision of all. (978-1-63555-134-1)

Dangerous Waters by Radclyffe. Life, death, and war on the home front. Two women join forces against a powerful opponent, nature itself. (978-1-63555-233-1)

Fury's Death by Brey Willows. When all we hold sacred fails, who will be there to save us? (978-1-63555-063-4)

It's Not a Date by Heather Blackmore. Kade's desire to keep things with Jen on a professional level is in Jen's best interest. Yet what's in Kade's best interest…is Jen. (978-1-63555-149-5)

Killer Winter by Kay Bigelow. Just when she thought things could get no worse, homicide Lieutenant Leah Samuels learns the woman she loves has betrayed her in devastating ways. (978-1-63555-177-8)

Score by MJ Williamz. Will an addiction to pain pills destroy Ronda's chance with the woman she loves, or will she come out on top and score a happily ever after? (978-1-62639-807-8)

Spring's Wake by Aurora Rey. When wanderer Willa Lange falls for Provincetown B&B owner Nora Calhoun, will past hurts and a fifteen-year age gap keep them from finding love? (978-1-63555-035-1)

The Northwoods by Jane Hoppen. When Evelyn Bauer, disguised as her dead husband, George, travels to a Northwoods logging camp to work, she and the camp cook Sarah Bell forge a friendship fraught with both tenderness and turmoil. (978-1-63555-143-3)

Truth or Dare by C. Spencer. For a group of six lesbian friends, life changes course after one long snow-filled weekend. (978-1-63555-148-8)

Children of the Healer by Barbara Ann Wright. Life becomes desperate for ex-soldier Cordelia Ross when the indigenous aliens of her planet are drawn into a civil war and old enemies linger in the shadows. Book Three of the Godfall Series. (978-1-63555-031-3)

A Heart to Call Home by Jeannie Levig. When Jessie Weldon returns to her hometown after thirty years, can she and her childhood crush Dakota Scott heal the tragic past that links them? (978-1-63555-059-7)

Hearts Like Hers by Melissa Brayden. Coffee shop owner Autumn Primm is ready to cut loose and live a little, but is the baggage that comes with out-of-towner Kate Carpenter too heavy for anything long term? (978-1-63555-014-6)

Love at Cooper's Creek by Missouri Vaun. Shaw Daily flees corporate life to find solace in the rural Blue Ridge Mountains, but escapism eludes her when her attentions are captured by small town beauty Kate Elkins. (978-1-62639-960-0)

Twice in a Lifetime by PJ Trebelhorn. Detective Callie Burke can't deny the growing attraction to her late friend's widow, Taylor Fletcher, who also happens to own the bar where Callie's sister works. (978-1-63555-033-7)

Undiscovered Affinity by Jane Hardee. Will a no-strings-attached affair be enough to break Olivia's control and convince Cardic that love does exist? (978-1-63555-061-0)

Between Sand and Stardust by Tina Michele. Are the lifelong bonds of love strong enough to conquer time, distance, and heartache when Haven Thorne and Willa Bennette are given another chance at forever? (978-1-62639-940-2)

Charming the Vicar by Jenny Frame. When magician and atheist Finn Kane seeks refuge in an English village after a spiritual crisis, can local vicar Bridget Claremont restore her faith in life and love? (978-1-63555-029-0)

Data Capture by Jesse J. Thoma. Lola Walker is undercover on the hunt for cybercriminals while trying not to notice the woman who might be perfectly wrong for her for all the right reasons. (978-1-62639-985-3)

Epicurean Delights by Renee Roman. Ariana Marks had no idea a leisure swim would lead to being rescued, in more ways than one, by the charismatic Hudson Frost. (978-1-63555-100-6)

Heart of the Devil by Ali Vali. We know most of Cain and Emma Casey's story, but Heart of the Devil will take you back to where it began one fateful night with a tray loaded with beer. (978-1-63555-045-0)

Known Threat by Kara A. McLeod. When Special Agent Ryan O'Connor reluctantly questions who protects the Secret Service, she learns courage truly is found in unlikely places. Agent O'Connor Series #3 (978-1-63555-132-7)

Seer and the Shield by D. Jackson Leigh. Time is running out for the Dragon Horse Army while two unlikely heroines struggle to put aside their attraction and find a way to stop a deadly cult. Dragon Horse War, Book 3 (978-1-63555-170-9)

The Universe Between Us by Jane C. Esther. Ana Mitchell must make the hardest choice of her life: the promise of new love Jolie Dann on Earth, or a humanity-saving mission to colonize Mars. (978-1-63555-106-8)

Touch by Kris Bryant. Can one touch heal a heart? (978-1-63555-084-9)

A More Perfect Union by Carsen Taite. Major Zoey Granger and DC fixer Rook Daniels risk their reputations for a chance at true love while dealing with a scandal that threatens to rock the military. (978-1-62639-754-5)

Arrival by Gun Brooke. The spaceship *Pathfinder* reaches its passengers' new homeworld where danger lurks in the shadows while Pamas Seclan disembarks and finds unexpected love in young science genius Darmiya Do Voy. (978-1-62639-859-7)

Captain's Choice by VK Powell. Architect Kerstin Anthony's life is going to plan until Bennett Carlyle, the first girl she ever kissed, is assigned to her latest and most important project, a police district substation. (978-1-62639-997-6)

BOLDSTROKESBOOKS.COM

Looking for your next great read?

Visit BOLDSTROKESBOOKS.COM
to browse our entire catalog of paperbacks, ebooks,
and audiobooks.

Want the first word on what's new?
Visit our website for event info,
author interviews, and blogs.

Subscribe to our free newsletter for sneak peeks,
new releases, plus first notice of promos
and daily bargains.

SIGN UP AT
BOLDSTROKESBOOKS.COM/signup

Bold Strokes Books is an award-winning publisher committed to quality and diversity in LGBTQ fiction.